Welcome back to Memphis, where when the sun goes down, shit starts popping off. The three major female gangs ruling the gritty Mid-South are the **Queen Gs**—who keep it hood for the **Black Gangster Disciples**. The **Flowers**—who rule with the **Vice Lords**. And the **Crippettes**—mistresses of the **Grape Street Crips**.

Rules are: There are no damn rules. Survive the game the best way you know how. If you want to be king, show no remorse. Memphis's divas are as hard and ruthless as the men they hold down. Your biggest mistake is to get in their way.

Also by De'nesha Diamond

The Diva Series
Hustlin' Divas
Street Divas
Gangsta Divas
Boss Divas

Anthologies
Heartbreaker (with Erick S. Gray and Nichelle Walker)
Heist (with Kiki Swinson)
A Gangster and a Gentleman (with Kiki Swinson)
Fistful of Benjamins (with Kiki Swinson)
The Ultimate Heist (with Kiki Swinson)

Published by Kensington Publishing Corp.

King Divas

DE'NESHA DIAMOND

KENSINGTON PUBLISHING CORP.
www.kensingtonbooks.com

DAFINA BOOKS are published by

Kensington Publishing Corp.
119 West 40th Street
New York, NY 10018

All Kensington titles, imprints, and distributed lines are available at special quantity discounts for bulk purchases for sales promotion, premiums, fund-raising, and educational or institutional use.

Special book excerpts or customized printings can also be created to fit specific needs. For details, write or phone the office of the Kensington Special Sales Manager: Kensington Publishing Corp., 119 West 40th Street, New York, NY 10018. Attn. Special Sales Department. Phone: 1-800-221-2647.

DAFINA and the Dafina logo Reg. U.S. Pat. & TM Off.

ISBN-13: 978-0-7582-9255-1
ISBN-10: 0-7582-9255-4
First Kensington Trade Paperback Printing: April 2015

eISBN-13: 978-0-7582-9256-8
eISBN-10: 0-7582-9256-2
First Kensington Electronic Edition: April 2015

10 9 8 7 6 5 4 3 2 1

Printed in the United States of America

The Memphis struggle continues . . .

Acknowledgments

Special thanks to our heavenly Father, who blessed me long before I had the common sense to realize it. To Granny, who continues to inspire me, though it's from up above now. My sister Channon "Chocolate Drop" Kennedy—you're still the best. My beautiful niece, Courtney—I love you.

To Selena James and Marc Gerald, many thanks for being by my side through troubled times.

And of course the fans, who have been loving the series from day one. You don't know how much your love and support have sustained me.

Best of Love,
De'nesha

Cast of Characters

Ta'Shara Murphy was once a straight-A student with dreams of getting the hell out of Memphis, but she took a detour from her dreams when she fell in love with Raymond "Profit" Lewis, the younger brother of Fat Ace. The war between the Vice Lords and her sister LeShelle's set, the Gangster Disciples, puts her between a rock and a hard place. When she failed to take her sister LeShelle's warning to heart, she was unprepared for the consequences.

LeShelle Murphy is Queen G for the Memphis Gangster Disciples. Not only does she love her man, Python, but she also loves the power her position affords her, and there is nothing that she won't do to ensure that she never loses any of it, which includes doing whatever it takes to keep her younger sister in line and handling the many chicken heads pecking at her heels.

Willow "Lucifer" Washington is Fat Ace's right hand and as deadly as they come. A true ride-or-die chick to her core. The latest explosion between the sets will have her true feelings bubbling to the top, and when she's forced to step up and lead, she proves that you don't need a set of balls to wash the streets with blood.

Maybelline "Momma Peaches" Carver, Python's beloved aunt, believes and acts as if she's still wildin' out in her twenties. With an arrest record a mile long, Peaches is right in the thick of things, but when old family secrets start coming home to roost, her partying days may be far behind her.

X   CAST OF CHARACTERS

Shariffa Rodgers is the ex-wifey of Gangster Disciple Python. She was kicked off her throne and nearly beaten to death after getting caught creeping. Now married to Grape Street Crip leader Lynch, Shariffa not only wants payback, she wants her new crew to take over the entire street game.

Qiana "Scar" Barrett is a Vice Lord Flower and the younger sister of Vice Lord soldier Tombstone. She's long been in love with Profit and will do anything to see Ta'Shara removed from his arm. She crossed enemy lines to forge a deal with Queen G LeShelle. When she didn't complete her end of the bargain, her chickens came home to roost.

Captain Hydeya Hawkins is the new Memphis police captain unraveling the secrets and corruption of her predecessor. But the straight-arrow cop has a few secrets of her own.

Consequences

1

Momma Peaches

The Power of Prayer Baptist Church is filled with the sounds of gunfire. Bullets splinter the wooden pews and shatter a few stained-glass windows. Between the steady firing, my nephews Terrell and Mason sling the word *muthafucka* back and forth. Dribbles's loud ass screams like the crazy white woman she is and Terrell's dangerous cousin, Diesel, is blasting by his side. What Dribbles and I had hoped to be a joyous reunion between the two estranged brothers who have for decades been rival gang chiefs with the Vice Lords and Gangster Disciples has now descended into total chaos.

And I'm lying here with a damn bullet in my side.

Stop. Please. My desperation only rings inside my head because it takes too much damn energy to get my mouth to work. *Am I dying?* While I wait for God to answer, I realize that the possibility doesn't scare me. Not like the last time, when I was cold and sick in my nana's old house, where I waited for Alice, my baby sister, to finish me off after she kidnapped me. If anything, I'm disappointed. I had hoped that this family could finally heal its deep wounds.

Mason a.k.a. Fat Ace, who up until a few months ago we'd believed to be long dead—sold when he was a baby to some trifling drug dealer by Alice, for a couple of crack rocks—had been, all this time, growing up across town under the Vice Lords' protection. The Vice Lords—our street family's mortal enemy. And Mason isn't just any Vice Lord soldier, he is the damn chief. Mason's older brother, Terrell, known on the street as Python, is the Gangster Disciples' head chief and has been mourning his brother's absence all these years.

When I learned the truth that Mason had actually been kidnapped by Alice's white crackhead best friend, Dribbles, it was too late. All of Memphis had seen him and Terrell killed in a fiery crash off Memphis's Old Bridge on every local news channel. But like two phoenixes, the brothers had somehow survived the crash—only to now be trying to kill each other over a horrible misunderstanding. After I'd entered this church and prayed for guidance to get through this meeting, I'd been shot—not by Mason who'd showed up minutes later, but by my old frenemy and neighbor, Josephine Holmes. That old fat bitch believed I was moving in on her imaginary man, Pastor Rowlin Hayes.

After Josie wobbled her big ass out of here, Mason and Dribbles showed up and tried to help, but when Python came in and saw Mason covered in my blood, all hell broke loose.

Rat-at-tat-tat-tat.

Rat-at-tat-tat-tat.

It's like watching a war of giants. The three men, all six-four to six-five, are stacked with muscles and littered with tattoos. Diesel stands out because of his light honey-brown complexion, pale eyes, and *GQ* looks. But he's as deadly as the brothers Mason and Terrell when it comes to power.

The two brothers are harder on the eyes. Both are dark black with scars and purpling second and third degree burns all over their bodies from that fiery car crash. The one thing that stands out about Mason is his one brown eye and his one milky-white-colored eye.

A bullet zings across my cheek, splitting it open. *Get behind a pew.* But that takes energy. Energy that I don't have. I'm stuck lying here in a pool of my own blood in the Power of Prayer Baptist Church.

Pow! Pow! Pow!

"Please. Stop," I croak.

"You're a dead nigga," Terrell roars, his face a demonic mask as he fires off more shots.

Diesel sprays bullets in Mason's general direction.

Dribbles screams—but the men show no mercy.

Mason slings Dribbles behind a stone partition on the church's stage before turning and firing back.

I work my mouth to say something, but I can't get the words out.

Two bullets slam into Terrell's muscular thighs. He tumbles and bends a knee, but his finger never eases off the damn trigger.

Diesel is nailed in his left shoulder, but it may as well have been Nerf ball bullets. He continues firing and advancing forward as though he didn't feel a thing.

I have to do something—anything to stop this potential carnage. I'm too weak to do anything other than pray. *Please. Lord, please.*

Click. Click.

Terrell and Diesel's clips are empty. The cousins go for their backup clips, and Mason chooses that moment to fire shots while he drags Dribbles toward the back of the church.

"Get that muthafucka," Terrell barks.

"I'm on it, cuz." Diesel slaps in another clip and races after Mason.

"Nooo," I croak, choking on my own blood. The devil keeps messing with me, threatening to take my nearly seventy-year-old ass out. But I didn't survive one hell with Alice only to be taken out, right here in the Lord's own house. No. I refuse to go out like this. I search within my soul for strength.

Terrell kneels besides me. "Aunt Peaches, can you hear

me?" He rolls me over onto my back. Pain rips through my entire body. It's all I can do to hang on to consciousness. "We're going to get him. Don't you worry," he promises. His large black eyes glisten. "There's no fucking way that I'm going to let him get away with shooting you. You hear me?"

I smack my dry lips, but my tongue feels as if it's too large for my mouth and my words get buried in my throat. It breaks my heart. I reach up and touch his scarred and burned face. It's important that he calms down and listens to what I have to say, but all I manage to do is paint his cheek with my blood.

"Don't die on me, Peaches. You're all I have left."

"That's not true," I choke out, thinking of his new wife, LeShelle. She wasn't who I wanted for him, but at least from time to time she acts as though she truly cares for him. "I'm not going anywhere," I whisper, trying to convince him as well as myself.

"Please. I don't know what I'd do without you." He leans over until our foreheads touch and his hot tears splash onto my face.

Terrell, a mountain of a man, pulls me into his lap and rocks me.

In the distance, tires squeal and shots are fired. This whole meeting couldn't have gone any worse. *Tell him. Tell him before it's too late.* I suck in a breath, but my body rejects it as I choke.

"Easy. Easy. Take it easy," Terrell says. "I'm not going anywhere," he promises.

He thinks I'm going to die. It's written on his face.

"Lis—listen," I croak. "He didn't do it."

"Shh. Shhh. Don't try and talk right now. I got you. Rest."

Rest. I close my eyes. My soul longs to rest, but I can't. I have to get the truth out. "Mason."

"Shh. Shh. It'll keep," he tells me.

"But—"

"Help is on the way," he promises. "I'm sure someone has reported the gunfire."

Frustrated, I slide my bloody hand from his face over to his lips to get him to hush. "Please. Let me get this out," I say, panting and choking over what air I manage to inhale.

The floor trembles as Diesel rushes back into the church.

"Did you get him?" Terrell asks.

I roll my head toward Diesel.

He shakes his head. "Sorry, cuz. They got away."

Relieved, I slump in Terrell's arms. What strength I have evaporates to the point that I can barely keep my eyes open.

At long last, the familiar wail of the police sirens catches my ear.

Diesel taps Terrell's shoulder. "Look, cuz. We have to get you out of here."

"I'm not going any damn where," Terrell barks. "I'm not leaving her here like this."

"There's nothing we can do for her," Diesel says, like my ass has already transitioned.

Terrell stiffens his jaw and shakes his cousin's hand off of his shoulder. "I said that I'm not leaving her."

I'm touched by his loyalty—and as much as I want him to stay, he can't. "Terrell, baby," I whisper. "G'on now. I'm going to be fine."

He shakes his head. "No. I can't do that."

"It's okay." I pause, swallow, but end up choking again.

Terrell beats himself up. "Damn. Damn. We should've gotten here sooner."

"Don't do that. I'm going to be all right. You'll see."

Terrell searches my face.

I'm an excellent poker player and put on my best, most earnest face, and even flutter on a smile that I don't feel. "I promise. I'm going to be all right. I'm going to pull through this. But if you stick around all you're going to accomplish is going to jail." He knows it's true. He's the most wanted man in Memphis for not only killing the daughter of the late captain of police, but for kidnapping the son that he had with the girl. If he's caught, they'll give him the needle.

The sirens grow louder.

Diesel touches his arm again. "You go, cuz. I'll stay with her."

Terrell glances over his shoulder and up at him. "Yeah? You'd do that for me?"

"Of course, cuz. We're family."

Terrell nods, but he doesn't move to get up.

"Go," I tell him.

He's torn. It's written in every inch of his body language.

"Go," Diesel urges. "I got this." He kneels down beside Terrell. "Get out of here, man."

Terrell hesitates. My hand falls from his face. "Go."

Misty-eyed, Terrell's gaze shifts between me and his cousin. At long last, he climbs to his feet. "I'm counting on you, cuz."

"I won't let you down."

"I won't let you down, either," I say. "I promise."

Terrell nods and slowly backs out of the church.

Relieved, I exhale and close my eyes. I need to rest for a minute. As darkness descends, I remember that I didn't tell Terrell about the shooting. "Diesel," I say, licking my lips and forcing my eyes open again.

"Yeah, Aunt Peaches?"

"You have to tell Terrell something for me." I grip his arm. "Promise me."

"What's that?"

"Mason didn't do this," I pant. "He didn't shoot me. That damn Josie that lives across the street from me did this shit. Mason showed up afterwards. You gotta tell Terrell."

Diesel's eyes turn green. His eyes have always been like a mood ring: at times they appear blue and other times green. "What?"

"You have to tell him. I don't want him going after his brother over this. You tell him, all right? Stop the war between those two. They're brothers. We have to heal this family."

My surge of strength ebbs away while the sirens grow louder. Diesel shakes his head. "No. I don't think I'll tell him that."

Confused, I peel my eyes open again.

"You see, I need for old cuz to take out Fat Ace. Kind of clear the field, if you know what I mean. If I tell him that Fat Ace had nothing to do with your shooting, he'll go back to wanting to meet and bond with that nigga for old times' sake. Nah. I need this new cuz out of the picture before I lose even more of my investments."

"But . . ."

"And I can't have you ruining my plans either." His beautiful eyes go ice-cold. "I'm really sorry about this, Auntie. It's not personal."

Before I can ask him what the hell he's talking about, there's a loud *POW!*

I jump as hot lead slices through the center of my body—and before the next wave of pain hits, everything goes dark.

2
Ta'Shara

Profit and Lucifer . . . kissing.

I stand outside Lucifer's house, gawking at them through the open window and feeling like a fool. *This is not happening. It can't be.* No matter how many times I blink or how hard my heart hammers against my chest, Profit and Lucifer remain lip-locked in the middle of that living room, *kissing.*

Finally, I stumble backwards with my eyes burning. Not until the tears blur my vision do I spin away and race back to Profit's crib. Hyperventilating, I rush into the house and slam the door.

"T, are you all right?" Mack asks, her brows high on her forehead.

Fuck. Why are these bitches still here? Last night, Mack and Romil, who I met in jail, threw me an impromptu party to officially welcome me into the Vice Lords' Flowers. Now it's late into the next morning and these chicks still don't know how to go home.

"T?"

"Get out," I tell them. "The fucking party is over."

Romil twists up her face. "What? But we were about to—"

"GET OUT!"

They jump, but then only stare at me.

"OUT! GET THE FUCK OUT OF MY GODDAMN HOUSE!"

Eyes big as fuck, everyone scrambles.

"All right. All right. You don't have to shout. We're going," Romil says.

Mack, moving slowly, eyeballs me like she's trying to read my mind. It takes everything I have not to throw shit at her hard-of-hearing ass. "What's wrong? What happened?"

"Goddamn it." I take off to the master bedroom, where I slam the door and fall back against it. When I look at the bed that I've been sharing with Profit for months now, my blood boils. Pushing away from the door, I head straight for the closet, snatch out my clothes, and toss them onto the bed. Next, I rush over to the chest of drawers to grab my things.

Hurry up. I move faster, but my hands and arms tremble. Then my legs and knees go weak. I'm barely able to get them to support my weight. I get one armload of clothes over to the bed before I collapse into a heap on the floor. Fuck my tears. I'm struggling to breathe. No matter what I do, I can't get enough oxygen in my lungs.

"How could he do this to me? He said that he loved me. He said that he would always take care of me. I risked and lost everything to be with him. I was a good girl. I made straight As and was listed on the honor roll. I had wonderful foster parents and lived in a nice midtown home, with a bright future ahead of me. Once upon a time, I had a best friend, Essence, and I even had a fucked-up sister in LeShelle. I threw all of it away to be with *Profit*—and that muthafucka does *this* to me? How could he?" I rake my hands through my hair a few times before I tug and pull chunks of it out.

"No, God. Noooo! Please don't let this be happening. Please." More hair slides through my fingertips. Somewhere in the back of my mind, I know I need to stop, but I can't. "It's not fair. None of this shit is fair."

"Girl, you're playing with fire." Essence's voice floats to me

from an old memory. She told me from the giddy-up not to go down this path, but my hardheaded ass did it anyway. I listened to my heart, not my head. I knew the street politics of hooking up with Profit from the moment he told me his name at the Germantown mall. Despite my sister, LeShelle, being in the street game with the Gangster Disciples, I had stayed out of the bullshit, but then Profit—with those big, brown eyes, deep-pitted dimples, and soft-looking lips—had me believing the impossible. I was book smart but street dumb, and now look where it's landed me.

I've been raped, branded—committed to a mental institution. I attempted to kill my sister. I was doped up and slammed into a padded room. Even then, I was given a second chance to go back to my nice, safe, suburban home, only to have LeShelle burn it down *with* Tracee and Reggie, my foster parents, inside. Also inside was LeShelle's girl, Kookie. The police think that I had something to do with it and I'm currently out on bail. I'm innocent on that charge, but last night I really did kill someone: a clerk at Hemp's Liquor Store. It was self-defense, but who in the fuck is going to believe that?

Homeless, I moved here with Profit—believing in his fucking lies that we belonged together. Now he's kissing Lucifer?

Lucifer.

She's not *any* woman. She's Mason's girlfriend *and* the meanest and most dangerous bitch in the street game. What am I going to do—fight her for him? Shit. I might as well slice my own neck. Hell, she even looks like a mean Laila Ali. Every enforcer in the game is scared of that bitch. Who the hell am I to step to her? I'm just some stupid seventeen-year-old girl who thought that she was in love. Profit has made a fool out of me.

I glance over into the bedroom mirror and stare horrified at my thinner than normal frame. My brown face, pale. My long hair, stringy. Hell, I'm a teenager and I'm already developing huge bags under my eyes. *No wonder he's attracted to Lucifer. I'm a mess.*

Crying so hard that my face aches, I don't know what else to do. I have nowhere else to go.

Think. Think. Think.

Not a damn thing comes to mind. I'm fucking useless. I don't have a goddamn thing to live for. When I open my eyes, my gaze lands on the gun on the nightstand.

You could end it all. Right here. Right now.

I pause for a moment, waiting for another voice to step in and talk some sense into me.

Silence.

My breathing slows and a strange calm descends over me. I stop pulling out my hair. Suddenly, the gun is the only thing that exists in the world.

You can do it. You can end all of the pain for once and for all.

It sounds so nice—and final.

I climb up onto my knees and inch toward the nightstand as if under a spell. I pick up the gun. It's heavier than I remember. I hold it like it's the most precious thing in the world. The answer to *all* of my problems. Tears stream down my face as I place the barrel into my mouth and click off the safety.

3

Lucifer

Snapping out of my shock, I step back from Profit's wet kiss and slap the fuck out of him. "What the hell?"

Profit staggers his six-foot-three body back and blinks his large brown eyes at me. "I'm sorry. I don't know what got into me."

That pretty boy, puppy-dog look may work on his girlfriend, Ta'Shara, but not me. "I'm engaged to your brother," I roar. "Have you lost your mind?" I place my hand on my *very* pregnant belly to remind him that I'm also carrying his brother's child.

He shakes his head, his caramel-colored skin now blotchy with embarrassment. For the first time he doesn't seem to know how to work his tongue.

"Say something, goddamn it. Before I shoot you or something." I'm not being flippant. I am that angry.

"I don't know. I wasn't thinking."

"You damn right you weren't thinking." I process this shit again. "I thought you hated my ass."

"I do. I mean, I don't. I mean—fuck, I don't know what the fuck." He storms over to the couch and plops down.

"Oh hell, no. You can't stay here." I shake my head. His ass might be confused, but I sure the hell am not. I have a man.

Mason is my man and I love him very much. I always have, ever since we were kids. Profit, on the other hand, has done nothing but given me grief.

During the months that Vice Lords thought we had lost Mason, Profit and my brother Bishop caused all kinds of waves within the set. They conspired behind my back to knock me off my throne. If he had been any other nigga I would've murked his ass for even thinking that shit. Now Mason is back, I'm pregnant with his kid and even have his rock on my finger, and suddenly his little brother makes *this* move? Where the fuck they do that shit at? Not to mention, Profit's girl is two doors down. He's been through hell for that bitch—and now he's throwing his tongue down my throat? It doesn't make sense.

"I'm sorry," he says, looking confused. "I don't know what came over me."

"I don't know either, but this shit better not happen again."

"It won't," he swears, climbing back up to his feet. "Can we keep this shit between us?"

"Who the fuck am I going to tell? Mason? As far as I'm concerned, the shit never happened." I cross my arms, mainly for his fucking protection. "You need to get your shit and get the fuck outta here." Now I'm uncomfortable with him in my house.

He nods and turns to grab his shit from off the floor. He avoids making eye contact as he scrambles for the door. Once it slams shut behind him, I'm left staring at the damn thing.

"What the fuck?" I swipe my arm across my lips to remove the taste of him. It's not that Profit isn't a good-looking boy—or man; he is. There's not a bitch on Ruby Cove that wouldn't snatch his fine ass up if he batted his brown eyes at them—but I'm not one of them. Profit's like a little brother to me, an annoying teenage brother—but still a little brother. Jesus. If I wasn't pregnant right now, I'd pour myself a stiff drink to help me get over this shock. How in the hell did I miss the signs that Profit had a thing for me? As far as I can remember he's acted as though he couldn't stand the sight of me. When we thought Mason was dead, he blamed me—guilt-tripped me into feeling like a piece of shit for not protecting his older brother. He insinuated and whispered to everyone who would listen that I couldn't or didn't have what it took to run the Vice Lords. Now he wants to pull some bullshit like this? Is he testing me? Is he going to wait and see what I'll do next? I pause on that shit. Now *that* sounds like some shit Profit would pull. My shock now has transformed into suspicion.

That sneaky muthafucka. Was he really trying to entrap me? Now what am I supposed to do—tell Mason before he does? Then again, if I talk and Profit doesn't, then I'll be the cause of a rift between them.

This is some fucked-up shit—and I don't appreciate being put in this position. I'm damned if I do and damned if I don't. I slide my hand across my growing belly. One thing for sure, I need to think this shit through. I sense a trap in here somewhere.

Turning away from the door, I climb the stairs. All the while, I curse Profit's ass out. I have way too much shit on my plate to now add this heap of bullshit. I have two Crippettes to kill: Shariffa and Trigger for their part in my brother Bishop's murder. Plus, I have to be on the lookout for the heat I'm gonna get from other biker gangs for wiping out the Angels of Mercy bikers.

The Vice Lords have three wars in the streets, I'm pregnant, and now I'm caught up in this shit where my loyalty may be questioned because Profit kissed me. I don't know. It's days like this that make a bitch start dumping lead in every damn body she sees. I don't need this shit. I don't appreciate this shit. The more I think about it, I should've put a cap in Profit's ass when I had the muthafucking chance.

Discarding my robe, I climb into the shower, but the pelting heat does nothing to settle my nerves. I play that damn kiss over and over in my head and each time the shit's pissing me off more.

To tell or not to tell? Fuck. I don't know the answer.

While standing beneath the spray, I keep hearing my phone ringing from the adjoining bedroom. For a fleeting moment, I'm tempted to ignore the damn thing, but in my position, you never know when you'll need to take care of an emergency. Finally, I shut off the water and grab a towel to go answer the phone.

Mason's burner number flashes on the screen and my heart thuds. *Did Profit already blab this shit to his brother?* Fuck. I'm surrounded by pussy-fuck muthafuckas. I answer the call, prepared for any damn thing. "Yeah?"

"Willow," Mason barks. "I need you!"

4

Ta'Shara

With the gun barrel still in my mouth, the bedroom door explodes open. Profit sees me and freezes in his tracks. A look of horror etches his features. "What the fuck are you doing?" Profit roars.

Tears streaming, I shift my gaze toward him.

He throws up his hands and then creeps farther into the room. "Okay. Okay. Be cool, baby. I don't know what this is about, but everything is going to be all right."

Baby? *Baby?* How in the hell does he have the nerve to call me baby? After what I saw?

"Don't do this. Please, T." He inches closer. "Give me the gun. C'mon." He reaches out to compel me to hand over the weapon. "Give it to me."

My trigger finger trembles. I can end it all right here. Right now. My brain splattering across this room will haunt him for the rest of his life. I could destroy him. If only I could pull the fucking trigger.

"T, please, sweetheart. Don't do it."

My resolve snaps. I ease the barrel from my mouth.

"That's my girl. There you go," Profit says, his body coiled tight with tension.

"How could you do this to me?" I ask.

His brows dip in confusion. "Do what?"

"How could you do it to us—after all we've been through? After all we meant to each other? How could you betray me like that?"

Profit lowers his hands to stand upright.

"I *saw* you," I inform him. "You and Lucifer."

All expression falls from Profit's face. "How long?" I ask. "How long? Hmm? How long have you two been sneaking behind my back? Are you and Mason sharing her now? Is that it? Is she pregnant with your baby—or his?" I ask, growing angrier from his silence. "Say something, dammit! I deserve that fucking much."

"It's . . . I'm sorry."

"You're sorry?" I ask, incredulous. "Is that it? That's all you got to say? You're sorry? Look what I gave up for you. Look what I lost! My life! My family!"

"T, calm down."

"Calm down? Don't fucking tell me to calm down!" I jump to my feet with the gun clutched in my hand.

"All right. All right. You're right," he says, contrite. "I owe you an explanation."

"You're damn right you do." Hysteria borders my sanity.

"T, it's not what you think."

"I know what I saw," I shout, waving the gun in his direction. "Do you think I'm stupid?"

"What you saw," he says, "was me making a stupid, stupid mistake. Fuck!" He runs his hands over his short-cropped hair. "I wasn't even fucking thinking straight. There's nothing going on between me and Lucifer."

"I *saw* you kissing her!"

"Yes! I kissed her—and it was the first and only time that it has ever happened. I swear. I don't know what made me do it. But after she slapped the shit out of me I fucking woke up."

I stare him down, weighing whether I believe his bullshit.

"T, I'm not in love with her. There's nothing going on. I . . ."

I wait, but he doesn't seem to be able to complete his sentence.

"I fucked up. I don't know how else to explain it. A'ight? I fucked up—for a split second. It was just a kiss. It didn't go any further than that. Can you forgive me?" He steps forward.

I step back.

"Baby. T, I promise you that it will never, *ever* happen again. Please. You *have* to believe me."

"I don't *have* to do a damn thing," I snap. "You're a liar—and a cheat. I regret the day that I ever laid eyes on you. From the moment I met you, my life has turned into a living hell. And there's nothing that I can do to change it back."

Profit keeps moving forward. "T, give me the gun. We'll talk it out."

"Why? Am I supposed to believe that you suddenly give a damn about us—that you give a damn about me?"

"Ta'Shara, baby. I swear nothing has changed about the way I feel for you."

"What are you talking about? *Everything* has changed. You can't be that stupid not to realize that. *Nothing* is going to be the same again. That's my fucking point!"

"Baby, I'm sorry. Please. You have to forgive me. It was a momentary . . . I don't know what it was."

I glare and shake my head. "So I'm supposed to believe that you were momentarily confused—that you forgot that you already had a girl riding and dying with you. Is that it? You're a confused, forgetful muthafucka?"

He huffs in exasperation.

"After all that we—no. Scratch that. After all *I've* been through."

"C'mon, T. I get that you're upset, but we've been in this together. *I* laid shot up in that hospital on prom night."

"Boo-fucking-hoo. In the grand scheme of things that shit is *nothing* compared to what LeShelle and her thugs did to me that night. I was the one who was fucking gang-raped and branded like a fucking animal. *I* was the one in a goddamn mental institution. I was the one who had to take on that bitch

LeShelle, one-on-one, only to be doped up and placed in a padded room. Then when I get out, she burns down my home with my foster parents inside. Now I'm stuck here—dependent on your cheating ass."

"All right. All right. This isn't a fucking contest," he says.

"No. Because you'd lose."

The bedroom roars with silence as we glare at each other. We're seconds from saying some shit that we can't take back.

"You're right," he says, his body slumping in defeat. "I have no excuse. None. I wish that I could take back those few insane seconds—but I can't. I'm sorry I hurt you. You're my heart. You know that. If I have to spend the rest of my life making up for those few seconds, I will. If you give me the chance. I don't want to live without you by my side. I need for you to believe that."

I laugh. "I don't know what to believe." My tears fatten.

Profit takes the opportunity to close the rest of the distance between us, and then reaches for the gun. "Please. Give it to me."

I draw a breath and then release the gun.

Profit clicks on the safety.

Immediately, I unleash a torrent of punches, clocking him in the head, chest, face. Any and every damn where. At first he ducks and dodges, but then he caves and takes the blows, wrestles for dominance, and then pulls me into his arms. When he's had enough, he tosses the gun onto the bed.

"I hate you! I hate you! I hate you!" I fight until exhaustion.

"Shh, baby. It's all right. I got you."

"I hate you," I wail.

"I know, but I'm going to fix this. I promise."

He *still* doesn't get it. The Bonnie and Clyde fantasy is over.

Profit's cell phone chirps. He scoops his android out of his pocket and frowns at the screen.

I can't help but ask, "What is it?"

He looks up. "It's 9-1-1. Mason is in trouble."

5

Lucifer

I disconnect the call with Mason, text 9-1-1 to the top team, and then throw on some clothes. By the time I exit the house, Charlie a.k.a. Tombstone is in the whip, ready to roll.

"Where are we headed?" he asks.

I jump into the backseat, rocking an AR-15. "Hit I-55." I get Mason back on the phone.

"Where you at?" he barks.

"Need your coordinates," I say and then relay them to Tombstone and text Profit again.

"I'm headed to Dr. Cleveland's. Meet me there."

"I'm on it," Tombstone says, overhearing the call.

The questionably ethical doctor has long looked the other way when treating life-saving emergencies for the Vice Lords—mainly because we pay with stacks of cash and bricks of cocaine. Anxious, I fidget in the backseat. My man has recently returned from the dead. I won't be able to handle it if I lose him again. *What the fuck happened? Why in the hell did I even encourage him to meet up with his older brother?* Blood don't make you family. After learning that the two rival chiefs are brothers and seeing the anguish on Python's face when he realized who Mason was, I went against my own street code and encouraged Mason to heal old wounds. I should've known better. Some of the most evil shit out here in the streets comes from muthafuckas that look like you.

There'll never be a truce between the Gangster Disciples and Vice Lords. How fucking naïve can a bitch get?

"Stupid. Stupid. Stupid."

"What was that?" Tombstone asks, looking up into the rearview mirror.

"Drive," I bark.

"You got it."

Dismissing Tombstone's nosiness, my mind scrolls through a series of bad scenarios that could've gone down at that church. The shit that happened between our people and the Angels of Mercy biker club pops into mind. *Could this have been another damn setup?*

Ever since Uncle Skeet, the former captain of police, was killed by Mason's real mother, Alice, a couple of months back, the Vice Lords needed a new arms dealer. I fucked up and struck a deal with the notorious biker gang. Those muthafuckas double-crossed me with the Gangster Disciples and nearly took a chunk of us out. I still don't know how that shit went down. But there was no mistaking that it was Python shouting for his brother on the top of the roof that night. He couldn't have known that Mason would be at that delivery. At the time, everyone thought that Mason was dead. I still recall the raw emotion in Python's voice. It was full of pain and anguish, but looking back on it now, maybe it was hatred. Had I gotten it wrong again and Python wasn't longing to reunite with his brother—but instead was still determined to kill him? Street beef dies hard out here. More often than not, blood doesn't trump gang affiliation.

In record time, Tombstone whips into Dr. Cleveland's driveway out in Tunica, Mississippi—a town right over the state line.

I hop out of the ride before Tombstone stops. After scanning the perimeter, I bust through the front door without knocking. "Where is he?"

A nervous Dr. Cleveland points. "He's upstairs."

"Is he all right? What the fuck?" I don't wait for an answer, but I take the stairs two at a time. "Mason!" I draw my gun. "Mason!"

"In here."

I follow the sound of his voice to a bedroom—and get another shock. There lying in a bed on bloody white sheets is Dribbles. I lower my gun. "What the hell happened?"

Mason, sitting in a chair, blood drenching his shirt, looks up at me with his one brown eye and one milk-white eye. "She's not going to make it."

I rush over and press his burned and scarred head up against my chest. "Don't say that. I'm sure that she's . . ." My gaze falls on Dribbles's ghost-white face. In fact, she's one shade from blue. *She's not going to make it.*

I look down at Mason's hard but sad eyes with no words to comfort him. "I'm sorry."

He lowers his head. He loves this woman—like a real mother. He never cared that she snatched him from his *biological.* He'd made it clear that as far as he was concerned, she'd *saved* him from a crackhead who'd put him in her kitchen oven. It didn't matter that Dribbles, who earned her nickname because as kids we'd always see slob dribbling from her mouth whenever she was high as a kite on the street, was no angel and struggled for years with crack too. She'd married her pimp, Smokestack, and together they raised Mason and had their own kid, Profit, together. Once Smokestack got locked down, she found the strength to clean up her life. After that, she got the fuck out of Memphis. The only reason she'd returned was for the funeral we'd prematurely had for Mason a few months back. Since then, she got caught up again, trying to fix this or that before getting snatched by Mason's real mother, Alice Carver.

Alice had escaped from the mental institution, kidnapped

her sister, murdered Uncle Skeet and his wife, and was seconds from putting Dribbles into the ground before Maybelline Carver, Momma Peaches, escaped from the house's basement and rammed her sister into an oak tree—saving both of them.

Duty bound, Dribbles wanted to right an old wrong. I got swept up too. Now look what has happened.

I fight the urge to interrogate Mason. He'll tell me the details in his own time, in his own way.

Mason's grip on his mother's hand tightens. He's trying to force life back into her frail body.

"What can I do?" I ask.

"There's nothing that can be done." He pauses. "Is Profit with you?"

I tense up. "He should be here any minute."

"Good."

I nod.

The silence grows as the seconds tick by. I'm going to stand here for as long as he wants me. He needs all the comfort that he can get. As sorry as I am for Dribbles's possible transition from this world, I'm relieved that my man is in one piece.

"I'm still trying to play that over and over in my mind," Mason says, shaking his head. "But I can't get the pieces of the puzzle to fit."

I squeeze his shoulder, encouraging him to take his time.

"We went to this church where she and . . . my aunt had agreed to meet. The whole ride over, I had this bad feeling. But Mom was so excited that I pushed that shit to the side and went anyway."

And I pushed you, too. Guilt skips down my spine.

"When we entered the building, there she was . . . lying on the floor with blood all around her."

I frown, thinking that the CD scratched or something. "What?"

He nods as if he's making perfect sense. "Maybelline . . . she'd been shot."

"By who?"

He shrugs. "I don't know. We raced over to her and when she looked up at me, it was with so much . . . *love*. It blew me away because I wasn't prepared for that."

The room goes silent again while he relives the moment.

"Then all hell broke loose. Python stormed into the church. He took one look at Maybelline and then me—and drew the wrong damn conclusion."

"So he thinks that you . . ." I grasp the situation and can't believe what I'm hearing.

Mason nods. "I tried to tell him, but that nigga wasn't hearing shit. Him and some other nigga went for their piece and I went for mine. I had to fuckin' shoot our way out of there."

"Oh shit."

"Exactly." Mason gets to his feet. "I caught two to the shoulder." He pulls his shirt down to show me.

"Mason—"

"They're clean. Went straight through—but Dribbles took four hits while trying to get back in the car. I don't know who that muthafucka was with Python, but his ass got added to my fucking shit list."

But it was all a misunderstanding.

"At first, I didn't know that she'd been hit. She didn't say anything when I jetted out of that muthafucka. I was all in my head space, pissed as shit and going the fuck off. Then a minute later, she slumped over in her seat like a rag doll." He moves closer to the bed, still holding Dribbles's hand. "She doesn't deserve this shit."

"I know, baby." I rub his back, wishing that I could take away his pain. "I'm so sorry." There are so many questions still lingering.

"Sorry isn't going to change a fuckin' thing, now is it?" His angry glare slices toward me.

I pull back, stunned. Is this when he starts blaming me? A

laundry list of emotions scroll over his face a few times before he shakes his head.

"I'm sorry," he says and then pulls me into his embrace. "This isn't your fault. It's those nasty Gangster Disciple roaches. They'll pay for this. I'll make sure of it, even if it's the last thing I do."

6

Hydeya

"Hello, Isaac," I greet him through my half-rolled-down car window outside the Federal Correctional Institute.

My father's smile falters. "I was hoping that you'd call me daddy."

"And people in hell pray for ice water," I counter. "Are you going to get in or are we going to go over our Christmas list too?"

Isaac's smile broadens again. "Still the tough cookie, huh— like your mom." His hand pounds the top of the car. "All right. I could use a ride." He straightens up and then strolls around the car to the passenger's side.

As he moves, my eyes narrow. For a man in his sixties, he doesn't look a day over forty. He's six feet, chocolate brown, with impressive prison muscles. Effortlessly, he oozes power and strength. Once upon a time, I admired that about him—if not envied. Now, as captain of the police gang unit, I'm worried.

Isaac pops open the passenger-side door and settles into the seat with an easy smile.

"Buckle up," I tell him before starting the car.

He looks at me. "Why? Who is going to give *you* a ticket?"

"Do it."

"Will do, Lieutenant Hawkins." He reaches for the seat belt.

"It's captain," I inform him, but there's no surprise in his face. "You already knew that."

His smile stretches wider. "Congratulations, princess. I'm proud of you."

I laugh before thinking.

"That's funny?"

"Actually, it's hilarious." I pull away from the curb and get us back on the main road.

"Look. I know we've worked from opposite ends of the law, but I shouldn't have to remind you that hasn't *always* been the case."

I clench my jaw and cut him a sharp side-eye.

"I recall picking *you* up from jail a couple of times when you were younger, back when you had your nose all up that one li'l nigga's ass. What was his name again?"

I grind my jaw until it feels like it's starting to lock.

"Casey—Carson—C—"

"Cash," I snap. "His name was Cash." I know damn well that Isaac hasn't forgotten my ex's name. When you dangle a boy over a balcony by his foot, I'm pretty fucking sure that the name sticks.

"Cash." He nods, smiling. "That's right. I kept thinking that his momma should've named him Chump Change."

"You're not funny."

He shrugs. "Wasn't trying to be."

Tension thickens the air between us. I don't know why Isaac insists on ripping off scabs and exposing old wounds. The thousands of letters that he's sent me during his ten-year stint—each one more desperate than the last—lead me to believe that he wants to turn over a new leaf. For the longest time, I didn't understand him. He disappeared from my and my mother's life without so much as a "fuck you."

For most of my life I hated him, which caused me to act

out. I joined the Folks Nation and helped turn South Chicago into Chiraq. Looking back on it now, I'm pained to admit that I did it all to get his attention. After countless crimes, heartache, and numerous overdoses, it was my stepfather, Dyson, who pulled me out of the abyss and straightened me out. I owe everything to that man.

So why am I here?

The man next to me is a stranger—I need to remember that.

Isaac cracks under the car's silent pressure. "Look. I'm sorry. I got us off on the wrong foot."

I cut him another side-eye.

"Okay. I always start us off on the wrong foot," he amends, placing a hand over his heart. "I'm truly sorry. Can we start over?"

I meet his stare and see his sincerity. Grudgingly, I cave. "All right."

His lips split into a wide smile. "Good. You'll see that things will be different between you and me, going forward. I'm a new man."

"So you kept telling me in your letters."

"It's true. A man does a lot of soul searching when he's locked down in a six-by-eight jail cell doing a dime bid. It's plenty of time to think over your life and review all the mistakes you've made." The car falls silent once again as he gazes out of the passenger's-side window. "The streets are hard on a black man, but at the same time, it's all most of us have. These concrete jungles are where a man learns how to be a real man. The slightest show of weakness and your family is putting you into the ground."

"There's more out here than the streets, Dad." I wince the second the word *dad* flows out of my mouth.

His smile stretches from ear to ear as his eyes warm. "I know that now. Plus, I'm getting too old for this shit. I mean what the fuck do I even have to show for any of it?"

It's not easy, but I hold my tongue. I learned a long time ago not to believe a damn thing that comes out of his mouth. Isaac is a smooth liar. According to my mother, he always has been.

"I'm out, Hydeya," he says. "I hope you believe that." He waits for me to say something, but everything I want to say will hurt his damn feelings.

Isaac continues. "Who knows? Maybe one day soon you'll invite me and Peaches over for dinner so I can meet this *white* boy you married."

"Let's not get ahead of ourselves," I counter and then soften the blow by adding, "Let's take things one day at a time."

He nods with a confident smile. Clearly, he believes that he can win me over. I'm not so sure and I don't want to make it easy for him.

Then again, here I am.

Isaac adds, "None of this will be easy. I'm going to have a hard enough job getting my home in order. Peaches and I . . . aren't exactly on the best of terms. After all she's been through with Alice, it's probably going to take a miracle to save our marriage, but I'm prepared to do all I can to set things right."

What in the hell makes him think that I want to hear about his marital problems, especially to a woman he deserted me and my mother for? Years of resentment curdles my blood. I don't hate Maybelline Carver—*hate* is a strong word—but I don't care for the woman—or her family.

When I finally get him over to Shotgun Row, Isaac sighs. "Hmph. The place looks exactly the same."

I pull to a stop in front of Peaches's house. Isaac's heavy gaze returns to me when I don't shut off the car.

"Aren't you coming in?" he asks.

"No. I have a lot of work to get to."

He nods. "Another time?"

I take a deep breath and then lay into him. "Look, Isaac. I don't know whether you're pulling my chain or not with all your talk of turning over a new leaf, but I do want to make one thing clear: Memphis is my city now. I'm responsible for keeping the citizens safe from thugs like you—and I take my job seriously. As you've seen, the streets are really crazy right now. So until I'm convinced that you're an average Joe Citizen, I'll be watching you."

Our eyes lock during a mini-battle while we size each other up for the battle ahead. After a minute, his lips slide into one more smile. "So that's a rain check then?"

"Sure. Whatever."

He unhooks his seat belt and then climbs out of the car, but before he shuts the door, he leans down. "Thanks for the ride. I'll call you."

I give him a flat smile, certain that I look like an idiot.

"Bye, princess." He shuts the door. Instead of watching him walk into the house, I pull away from the curb. In my rearview, I see him standing there, watching me go.

Good. I want to make sure that he takes me seriously. As bad as the gang wars are now, they could get seriously worse if King Isaac gets back into the mix.

Suddenly, there's a loud screech and a horn blares.

Cutting a look to my right, an SUV barrels toward me. "SHIT!" I slam on my brakes, narrowly missing being T-boned at an intersection.

Horns blare and tires screech as cars slam on their brakes to avoid colliding. A few were unsuccessful, causing pileups.

I shift into cop mode, hit my flashing lights, hang an illegal U-turn, and take off after the fleeing SUV.

I whip from lane to lane, trying to catch up to the black Escalade. At the same time, I reach for my phone and call into dispatch. "This is Captain Hydeya Hawkins. I'm in pursuit of a black Escalade, speeding west on McLemore. I'm requesting backup."

At the intersection of Florida Street, an 18-wheeler Walmart delivery truck pulls out.

"Shit," I exclaim again.

I drop the phone and swerve into oncoming traffic.

"Fuck!"

A hard yank on the wheel and I swing in the opposite direction, sideswiping a minivan but saving my life.

The Escalade takes the cloverleaf on two wheels onto I-55, and then takes off like he's on a NASCAR track.

I lean over and fish for the phone. When I get dispatch back on the line, I rattle off the SUV's license number. A couple of seconds later, I'm told the car is registered to Barack Obama. "Well, someone has a sense of humor."

Two cop cars join the chase. I lock on to this sonofabitch, determined to take this crazy driver down.

7
Cleo

Diesel Carver. I can't figure that man out. My performance at Club Diesel last night was a smash success. I had the crowd in the palm of my hand—and even grabbed the attention of the club's owner. That was the point. Diesel Carver is a man with a lot of power, inside the industry and out.

My fiancé/manager, Kalief, swears Diesel is the man who's going to take my career to the next level. But Kalief swears by a lot of shit. After meeting Diesel, I have my doubts. Diesel Carver has a thuggish handsomeness about him with his name tatted around his neck, but he's a little too pretty-boy for my taste with those light colored eyes that seem to change with his mood—and I don't like how he came at me, skinning and grinning about my ass being a star. But he looked more like he wanted me to be the star in his bedroom and not the stage. The scarred-up bitch sitting next to him didn't look like she appreciated his roaming eye either.

I brushed off his whack game and told him that I already have a man, but the new boss on the block appeared unfazed.

Kalief and I have been together since high school. He had all the girls sweating him. He was Morris Chestnut-like fine and knew it. It didn't hurt that he also knew how to stack paper.

When he stepped to me, I smacked him down. But he dusted himself off and tried again.

We soon found out that we both have a love for music. We spent hours at his crib, listening to the oldies. Looking back, those were the best days of our lives. Back then, it was easy to love him. He was kind, warm, and funny. He had so many big dreams. He saw our asses going straight to the top. He believed in it so much that I got caught up as well. After high school, Kalief proposed and pressed me to make him my manager. My singing was supposed to save him from the streets too. I said yes, but we never did make it down the aisle. Since high school, Kalief and I have been grinding to make shit happen. Now here we are, years later, and Kalief and I are exactly where we started. Still engaged and hustling in this fucked-up industry. Only now he is a drug addict with a gambling problem, a lying problem, and a cheating problem.

My ass should have been ghost a long time ago—but there is something that's keeping me glued to Kalief. I wish I knew what it was so that I could cut the strings and fly on my own. My thoughts are interrupted by Kalief's cell phone buzzing and vibrating on the nightstand.

I glance over at Kalief to see if he's going to wake up and answer it, but he's sprawled out and lying so still that I wonder if his ass is even breathing. I squint down at his chest and then sigh—whether in relief or disappointment, I don't know.

Immediately, I feel guilty. Kalief and I have problems, but I shouldn't be wishing death on his ass.

Buzz. Buzz. Buzz.

My gaze shoots back over to his cell phone, my curiosity piqued. I throw another cautious look at him before slowly reaching over his body to grab the phone. He thinks his ass is slick by putting a pass code on here, but Kalief isn't that damn deep or complicated. I punch in his birth date and unlock his phone.

Two missed calls.

I press the phone icon and then check recent calls.

"Mom?" *What the fuck? This nigga's mom is dead.*

Heat rushes into my face as I climb out of bed and creep to the bathroom. Once I'm in there, I lock the door and then I click over to his instant messages and read the conversations this nigga has been having with his dead mother. The second I click on "Mom," a scroll of dick pics and pussy shots fill the screen.

This muthafucka. I click on other names in his contact list. Thot after thot smiles up at me. *I knew it. This nigga ain't never going to change.*

I bolt out of the bathroom and make a beeline for the bed. With everything I have, I throw his phone dead in his face.

The muthafucka finally jumps up, screaming, "WHAT THE FUCK?"

"I fuckin' hate you, you lying, cheating piece of shit."

"Whoa. Whoa. Whoa." He climbs out of bed. "What the fuck are you bitching about?"

"You, nigga! Your goddamn *mom* called while you were sleeping."

"My mom?" Then the light clicks on in his eyes.

"Yeah. Uh-huh. Fuck you! I'm out of this bitch!" I turn around and start snatching up clothes.

"Baby. Baby. Baby. Wait." He tries to snatch my clothes out of my hands.

"Let go!"

"It's not what you think, baby. I swear."

I stop struggling. "Oh? Then why don't you explain it to me? Why are you exchanging dick and pussy pics with a bitch labeled *mom* on your phone?"

He blinks. Clearly his brain ain't thought that far ahead yet.

"Yeah. Yeah. Busted, muthafucka!" I snatch my clothes back and hop into them in record time. "I'm so sick of this shit."

"C'mon, Cleo. They're pictures. It's not like I fuck the bitch."

"Really? That's the shit that you're going to roll with?"

"What? I'm being honest. That trick ain't nobody."

"*Every* time I catch you, you crow about bitches not being nobody—until they pop up with babies that look just like you."

"Aww, man. Not that shit again."

"Yeah, nigga. *That* shit again. You're always up in my face about how much you love me, but you done put three babies on three different bitches since I've been with you. Random bitches—that you don't *ever* remember fucking. I'm sick of this shit."

He sighs like I'm the one being unreasonable. "How many times do I have to apologize for that shit? Huh? I fucked up, but that shit is in the past. You gotta let that shit go."

"No. I need to let you go. I need to let this fuckin' situation go." Spinning, I head for the door.

Kalief snatches me by the arm. "C'mon, baby. You don't mean that shit."

"The fuck I don't. I'm *tired*." He wrestles to wrap his arms around me—but I keep blocking him.

"You know that you're not going to go anywhere, baby." He hits me with his soft brown eyes. "You know that there ain't no other nigga who can love you the way I do."

"*This* is love? All this fucking bullshit? Let's be real, I'm the only muthafucka in this who's being faithful. And for *what*? I ain't getting shit out of this relationship."

"How can you say that after last night?"

"Last night?"

"I got you at the right place—at the right time. I'm telling you that Diesel is going to put us on. He got the connects to make it happen."

"Fuck that green-eyed nigga. He ain't no different than the last nigga you said was going to put us on—or the nigga before that. The only thing that I could tell during that meeting with him and his niggas is how much he wanted to *fuck* me."

That wipes the smile off Kalief's face. "He said that?"

"Pretty fucking much. He didn't say shit about going into the studio, or working with any of his hot connects, or even contracts. He looks at me like a piece of meat. Oh. I'm sorry. He did say that I needed to get a new manager—and you know what? He's right. You're fired!"

I'm out of here.

"C'mon, Cleo. Don't be like that," Kalief yells after me. "You know that we've come too fucking far for this shit. You know those bitches don't mean shit to me. They're a . . . friendly distraction. You're the only girl I want. Hell. We can go down to the courthouse right now!"

"Kalief, please. I wouldn't marry your ass if you were the *last* muthafucka breathing." I wiggle my feet into my sneakers and rush out of the bedroom.

He catches up to me.

"Get out of my way."

"No. Not until we talk this shit out."

"C'mon, Kalief. We keep playing this same muthafuckin' game and nothing *ever* changes!"

"It will. I promise. I won't look at any other bitch—*ever!* A'ight? Happy?"

"Does it look like I'm fuckin' happy to you?"

He sighs as if I'm being unreasonable. "I said I was sorry. Damn."

SLAP!

My hand stings from slapping the shit out of him. "Asshole!" I march around him, grab my purse, and snatch open the front door.

Not suprisingly, Kalief follows me out in his fucking boxers. "Baby, baby. Please. Wait up!"

Ignoring his ass, I open the car door and hop inside. When I try to slam the door shut, Kalief wrestles me for it.

"Cleo, stop being a fucking bitch."

"Kiss my ass!" I throw my entire weight back with the door and end up catching his fingers as it slams.

"GODDAMN IT!" Kalief swings around, shaking his hand in the air to ease the pain.

I lock the door, jam my key in the ignition, and start the car.

Kalief goes for the door again, but after discovering that it's locked he starts tapping the window and then pounding the roof. "Cleo, open the damn door! Enough of this shit!"

"Watch your feet," I shout through the window before stomping on the accelerator. The car jets backward out of the driveway. When I peel away from the house, I flash him a bird.

As I ride home, I'm all up in my feelings, but in the back of my mind I ask myself: *Is this really the end of our relationship?*

My cell phone rings. I scoop it out of my purse while keeping one hand on the wheel. Seeing Kalief's name on the screen, I toss the phone aside and roll my eyes.

The sudden wail of police sirens snaps me out of my rambling thoughts. I glance around to see what the hell is up. It could be anything around here. The war of the streets has gotten to the point that gunshots and police sirens have become the city's never-ending soundtrack.

I don't see anything in my rearview, but the sirens are definitely getting louder. Since I'm already in the area, I may as well swing over by the church and pick up my new robe before tomorrow morning's service. I have another solo this week. The moment I go to make a right off McLemore, a black SUV jets out from nowhere and nearly sideswipes me. "Muthafucka!" I lay on my horn. *Python?*

Everyone slams on their brakes. One car that was almost T-boned hits its police lights and takes off after the fleeing vehicle.

I chuckle at the driver's bad luck and continue on to the church. As I pull into the parking lot, I see another car jetting away. "What the fuck is going on?" I catch the driver's profile. *Diesel?* Nah. It couldn't be.

I roll up on a curb, trying to twist around in my seat for a second look. "Oh my God. It *is* that nigga." I spin back around in my seat and wonder what the hell is going on.

Seeing Python makes me think of his wife, LeShelle—and LeShelle reminds me of my deceased little sister, Essence. There isn't a day that goes by that I don't blame myself for her death. I knew that shit was suspect when LeShelle's girls Kookie and Pit Bull stepped to Essence in Fabdivas Hair Salon to do some bullshit errand. I tried to stop it, but the girls pulled rank. LeShelle was the leader of the Queen Gs—so I had to fall back.

Months later, my little sister was dead. She was doused in gasoline and set on fire at a gas station.

LeShelle's lying ass told everyone that Lucifer, with the Vice Lords, was behind it—and everyone believed her. Myself included. I swore that I would get back at the bitch even though she is the most feared woman in the game. I didn't care. But when my path crossed the infamous Vice Lord, Lucifer, in the middle of a cemetery, I was told the truth. She'd gotten the drop on me while I was visiting Essence's grave.

By the time I thought to go for my weapon, Lucifer had made it clear that such a move would be suicide. So there was no reason for her to lie. LeShelle, on the other hand, doesn't have an honest bone in her body. Fuck. She had her own sister raped and then dumped a full clip into the girl's boyfriend right in front of her. And if the latest rumors are to be believed, the bitch also murdered her sister's foster parents. What kind of evil bitch does that kind of shit?

I haven't told the rest of the family. My brothers, Kobe and Freddy, would lose their shit and probably do something stupid—and probably get themselves killed.

My solution was to go against the grain and snitch LeShelle out to Lucifer. I told her where the bitch was about to marry her nigga, Python. I figured she could do us both a favor and take the bitch out.

' Turns out LeShelle and Python have nine lives because they survived the Vice Lord drive-by as they were exiting the church. But one day the bitch will get what's coming to her. After all, karma is a bitch.

Shaking my head, I realize that the shit is not my business. I whip into the church's parking lot and then quickly jog inside.

The scene before me stops me in my tracks.

"Momma Peaches?"

8

Hydeya

"Goddamn it! Get out of the way!" I lay on the horn to get these slow-ass drivers to move, but everybody jams on their brakes and threatens to give me a heart attack.

It's ten blocks before another cop car joins the action.

The fleeing driver is stealthy and adroit as he weaves in and out of traffic. This muthafucka should've gotten a career with NASCAR. When he hangs a sharp right, I'm certain that the heavy utility vehicle is seconds from rolling.

Miraculously, it stays up on two wheels and leaves its tread marks on the asphalt. When it bounces back down onto all four tires, it takes off like a fighter jet. My only recourse is to let loose another string of profanities.

CRASH!

Behind me, a patrol car doesn't make the turn. I look up into my rearview to see the car has slammed into a white F-150.

"Fuck." I tighten my hands on the steering wheel and jam the accelerator to the floorboard. A dozen blocks later, I have six police cars flying behind me. With each red light we jet through, my heart climbs higher into my throat. These dangerous police chases can go wrong in a split second. Times like these, a cop questions whether the job is worth it.

CONSTRUCTION AHEAD.

I fight the instinct to ease off the accelerator while the reckless demon ahead of me taps his brakes. His speed reduces a good ten miles an hour. I'm confident that I'm going to get this muthafucka as I close the distance between us. When I realize that there's a chance of slamming into him, the subject makes a hard right.

I hit my brakes and release the wheel.

Construction workers in orange vests drop their shit and scramble out of the way.

I overshoot the turn and slam into a huge metal traffic sign.

Bam!

My head bounces off the side window and rattles a few marbles loose. I shake the shit off while the workers stare, wide-eyed. I get back in pursuit as the other police cars reach the turn.

The SUV has pulled farther ahead.

"C'mon. C'mon. C'mon." My hands lock back onto the steering wheel as I regain lost ground. The next several intersections prove to be more difficult for all, but I'm able to catch up with the subject.

The SUV brakes—hard.

He wants me to slam into him.

"Shit!"

My foot rams the brake and I brace for impact. At the last moment, the SUV hangs a left, stops, and then to my surprise, opens fire.

A second before the bullets fly, I see the driver. Recognition bolts through me. *Python.*

Rat-ta-tat-tat-tat.

Rat-ta-tat-tat-tat.

I duck as my windows explode. The assault is quick, but feels like it goes on forever.

Python peels off.

I clench my teeth and unsnap my service weapon. If I catch up with this muthafucka, there's no way I'm taking his ass in alive. Despite my bullet-riddled car, I launch back in pursuit. Less than a minute later, a tire explodes with a bang.

I spin out of control and scream as I flip completely off the road and down a hill.

9

LeShelle

West Memphis, Arkansas

SHELLE—D AND I GONE TO MEET MY BROTHER. BE BACK LATER.

"This muthafucka has lost his damn mind!" I rage at the text
message Python sent my ass an hour ago. I done wore a fucking hole into the carpet in the master bedroom in the small ass
hideout while calling and texting his ass back, but the muthafucka won't answer his fuckin' phone. How many times has
this nigga jumped all over my ass about not answering when
his ass calls? Too many goddamn times to count. "Aaagh!"
Spinning around, I throw the phone as hard as I can at the
wall.

Bam!

A hole opens up in the wall but my anger has me turnt all
the way up and I reach for any and every goddamn thing to
throw at the muthafucka.

Lamps. *Bam!*

Clock radio. *Bam!*

I swipe shit off the damn dresser and then take our clothes
out of the closet and fling them everywhere. "I'm so sick of his

shit! Shit! Shit! Muthafucka got my ass stuck out here in bumble-fuck Egypt while boss bitch Lucifer and silly bitch Shariffa with the Grape Street Crippettes run the streets in Memphis." This ain't what the fuck I signed up for when I married the chief of the Gangster Disciples. I signed up to be the head bitch of the Queen Gs. I signed up for power, money . . . and even to be a part of a real family—since my backstabbing sister, Ta'Shara, ain't about shit.

Exhausted, I drop to my knees and battle back my hot, angry tears. Why can't Python let go of this obsession about Fat Ace being his brother? They have been battling in the streets for supremacy for more than a decade. I don't know if that nigga is his long lost brother or not—and frankly, I don't give a shit. It won't change a fuckin' thing. Too much time and blood have been invested in this war.

The war we're fucking losing.

We haven't been on our throne on Shotgun Row since Python murked his pig baby momma, Melanie, and landed his ass on the federal Most Wanted list. Python hid our ass out here in West Memphis, Arkansas, and then called up his shady-ass cousin Diesel from Atlanta to handle *our* fucking shit. What muthafuckin' gangster does that shit? Diesel already got Atlanta on lock. It's clear that nigga raced his pretty-boy ass up here to expand his empire—not to fucking babysit. Python don't see that shit. My man trusts that nigga. Bottom line: Shit is spiraling out of control. I got to figure out how to fix this shit with a quickness. I been through and sacrificed too damn much to let Python lose his goddamn mind.

I'm all in my feelings when I hear the front door slam.

My heart skips as I jump to my feet and race out of the bedroom. "It's about muthafuckin' time," I shout. "Do you know how long I've been calling your ass?" I race down the hallway and around the corner to confront Python in the living room, but I take one look at my man's face and pull up short. "What happened?"

Huffing and puffing, his face twisted in rage, Python ignores my question and unleashes a series of hard punches into the wall.

I watch him as chunks of plaster explode and spray everywhere.

I step back. After all the shit that we've been through—and we've been through some unimaginable shit—I've never seen Python *this* angry. His rage has rendered his ass fucking unrecognizable.

My heart skips a beat. Have my skeletons fallen out of the closet? Did I fuck up by giving that teenage bitch Qiana a window of opportunity to bury my ass? Her stupid ass has been sleeping with Diesel, a VL enemy, and didn't know it. The question is, has Diesel blabbed everything to Python about the hit job?

A strong part of me refuses to feel guilty about the shit. What's one less baby momma and jizz-baby running around? The way Yolanda's retarded ass kept refusing to stay in her lane and disrespecting my crown, I had to take care of that bitch. Shit. I thought I'd taught her a lesson when I pistol-whipped her ass up in Fabdivas Hair Salon in front of the other Queen Gs—but basic bitches can't learn. She called herself getting back at me by doing a shitty drive-by when I was exiting a club one night, but that non-aiming bitch signed her death certificate with that punk-bitch move. I did what I had to do. I didn't give a fuck about her carrying one of my nigga's seeds. He got plenty of those ugly niggas running around Memphis. The bitch deserved every damn thing she got. My only regret is not handling the damn job myself. I enlisted a kiddie banger who can't follow fucking directions. I blazed up Essence, one of my own girls with the Queen Gs, because she was on that bitch's shit list in exchange for her to murk my headache and the blood clot growing inside of her. Now the situation is a full-on migraine. Yo-Yo is gone, but Qiana snatched the baby

Yo-Yo was carrying. *Why?* The only answer I can come up with is the li'l bitch planned to play me.

I suck in a breath and prepare my ass for anything. Ain't shit I can do about it now.

Python stops punching the wall—only to release a lionlike roar from the depths of his soul.

The hairs on my body stand at attention while every muscle coils in preparation to be his next target.

"You were right," he growls.

I hear the words, but I'm confused. "What?"

He pants and paces, opening and clenching his fists.

I stay back in case he does punch something else: me. "What the fuck are you talking about, Python? What happened?"

"That muthafucka shot Momma Peaches."

Those are more words that don't make sense to me. *Momma Peaches? What the fuck does she have to do with any of this?* "I thought your text said that you were going to go talk with—"

"Fuck that nigga," Python roars again. "The next time I'm gonna smoke his ass on sight."

"Okay."

"I mean it. The next fucking time, we're going to end this shit for once and for all. It's settled. The two of us can't be on this muthafuckin' planet. Blood or no fuckin' blood. That nigga is dead."

My heart leaps with excitement. *Finally!* "But wait. You said Momma Peaches has been shot? What are you talking about?"

He huffs. "Aunt Peaches arranged the meet-up. She said the woman who'd raised Mason wanted to make shit right. When Diesel and I got there . . . Aunt Peaches was laid out . . ."

I blink. "Laid out? She's dead?"

He swings his fist around and punches the air. "I don't

fucking know. Diesel made me get out of there before the police showed up."

Damn. The old bitch ain't been out of the hospital a hot minute and she's already taken some heat? "All right. Start from the beginning."

Python ignores me and keeps pacing around.

Frustrated, I snap, "Python! Fuckin' talk to me! What in the hell happened?"

He spins around and kicks an end table. The lamp goes crashing to the floor—but that shit ain't enough. He advances farther into the living room and kicks the coffee table. Bricks of coke and stacks of rubber-banded cash fly everywhere.

There ain't shit for me to do but wait for him to finish with his temper tantrum. A few minutes later, the entire living room is a wreck. Knickknacks, chairs, and electronics are tossed around the room by the human hurricane.

"Are you done?" I ask.

For the third time, Python ignores me. He drops to his knees and the sound that rumbles from his chest is like a wounded animal on its last legs. The shit touches and even scares me. My man is beyond hurt. I recognize that pain. Ungluing my feet, I walk over to him. Despite the glass and broken furniture, I kneel next to him and pull his trembling body over so that he can lay his head on my shoulder. His warm, fat tears drip onto my collarbone. Never in a million years would I have thought this moment could happen. Real niggas don't cry. How many times has he told me that? How many times have I drilled it into my own head? Then again, this is his aunt Peaches. He already thought he'd lost her once, but to lose her again? I don't know whether he'll be able to handle it.

I let the minutes tick by while Python rages, cries, and then tries to pull himself together. I get it, but at the same time, I'm feeling some kind of way about the double standards in our situation. It was on his orders that I chopped and burned my relationship with my own sister, to prove that I was his ride-or-die and to get my wedding ring. Now I've been watching him pine and risk everything we have left to raise his brother's dead memory from the grave. At least he seems to be over that bullshit.

Now Momma Peaches is another story. She raised Python—saved him from having to grow up with a crackhead mother who, in the end, lost all her goddamn marbles. Growing up on Shotgun Row was no picnic, but it's where Python learned to be a man—and a leader. "Everything is going to be all right," I tell him. Mainly because Peaches can take a licking and keep on ticking. "I'm sure she is going to be fine."

"There was so much blood." Python shakes his head. "When I walked into that muthafucka and saw . . . him hovered over Aunt Peaches like that . . ." Rage ripples across his face.

"Start from the beginning," I say again. "I need a clear picture of what the fuck went down."

He nods, but takes in several deep breaths before he gets started. "Aunt Peaches got word to Diesel that Mason and his other *mother* wanted to meet."

Clamping my jaw tight, I keep my commentary to myself.

He glances up at me. "I didn't tell you because I know how you feel about the situation. I thought that it was the peace offering that I was looking for. I mean, now that I know who he is and shit—and what I did to him, putting him in that oven. I thought it was the opportunity I wanted and needed to make shit right. Blood is thicker than water, right?"

But not thicker than bullshit.

"My damn family is fucked up," he rants. "Muthafucka made a damn fool outta us." Python sniffs, but there are no tears in his eyes now—only rage. "The meeting was set up at a church—not too far from Shotgun Row. It's a good damn thing that I asked Diesel to come with—or my ass would've been caught wide open."

Diesel. Diesel. Diesel. I'm so sick of that muthafucka I don't know what to do.

"The second we walked in and saw him over Peaches—blood everywhere—it was a wrap. I wish that we'd got there a little sooner, you know? Maybe I could've stopped that shit from going down."

"Don't start that," I tell him. "Fat Ace is a fuckin' low-life thug. That shit ain't news."

Python nods, listening to reason. "You right. You right. I lost sight of that shit for a minute. Blood don't make niggas family. Loyalty does." His rage softens a bit. "That's why I wifed you. You've always been loyal to a nigga—even when he's being stupid and acting all brand-new."

I don't know what to do with that backhanded compliment. "Finish the story."

"I snatched out my piece. What the fuck you think? Fat Ace said some shit, but I wasn't hearing it. I wanted that muthafucka toe-tagged right then and there. Aunt Peaches is my heart." He glances back up at me and adds, "Next to you. You know that."

I let the shit slide. This is no time to be nitpicking his ass.

"At least Diesel is a stand-up nigga. He had my back as we turned that muthafucka into the goddamn Alamo up in that bitch, but the fucker and his white momma got away. Diesel gave chase while I checked on Aunt Peaches."

The way he stops the story makes my heart pound. I'd assumed that she was still alive. "She's not . . . dead, is she?"

Python shakes his head. "No. But she was weak as fuck. I didn't want to leave her—but I heard the police sirens and Diesel insisted that I go. I left once he promised to stay with her."

Diesel. Diesel. Diesel.

Python looks around like he's searching for something else to throw, but there's not a damn thing in this room that's standing.

"I'm glad that you've finally come around to seeing shit my way," I tell him.

He says nothing so I reach over and cup his chin and force him to look at me. "Forget about that muthafucka. Mason Carver is dead. He died years ago. You got that? That nigga that shot your aunt is our enemy. He's the fuckin' leader of the goddamn Vice Lords. He's not your brother. He ain't shit to you. You got that?" I lean forward and place my forehead against his while our eyes lock. "*I'm* your family. Me and Momma Peaches. And we're in this shit until the world fuckin' blows. You got that?"

He nods. "Until the world blows."

10

Cleo

"Momma Peaches!" I drop everything and race over to her. "Oh my God. What happened?" There's no movement. *Is she dead?*

I race to find a pulse, but I've never done this shit before and I can't tell one way or another because of my heartbeat hammering in my ears. I lean all the way over and place my ear up against her chest. "I don't hear anything," I declare in shock. "No! No! No! You can't die."

Momma Peaches is a legend on Shotgun Row. Years ago, Essence and I got busted by the cops while working in her shoplifting ring. There were never any harsh feelings; she bailed us out and took good care of us when our mom died. Momma Peaches took care of everybody at some point or another. Everybody in the neighborhood loves Momma Peaches.

"I have to get you to the hospital," I declare, realizing that the sirens are getting closer. "Hang on, Momma Peaches. Help is on the way." Not taking the chance that the sirens are for someone else, I scramble back to where I'd dropped my purse to dig for my cell.

"This is 9-1-1. What's your emergency?"

"Yes! I'm calling from the Power of Prayer Baptist Church over on Florida Street. A woman has been shot."

"Is the woman breathing?"

I wrench my neck back around to Momma Peaches's still body and practically will her chest to move. In my anxiousness, I really can't tell. "I . . . I don't know."

The operator asks me another question, but at that moment, tires screech outside.

"Wait. I think—"

"Freeze! Hands up!" The police charge inside.

I drop the phone. "Please. Hurry. She needs help. She needs a paramedic. She's hurt."

"Hands up!"

"But—"

"Hands up!"

Swallowing my anger, I lift my hands. The next thing I know, I'm planted facedown on the carpet. *What the fuck?* A three-hundred-pound pig bitch jams her knee in my back and then pats me down.

"Is anyone else here in the church with you?" she barks in my ear.

"I don't know," I snap. "I got here and found her like that."

Once the cops are satisfied that I've been neutralized, another officer shouts, "All clear," and they finally attend to Momma Peaches's still body. I note now that she's a dull grayish blue. *She's dead.*

Tears blur my vision. I don't understand. What the hell happened in here? Why was Diesel speeding away? Was he involved in this shit? Only then do I gaze around and take in more of my surroundings. Splintered wood, shattered glass, and blood spread throughout, it's clear that the place had been turned into a war zone.

At a church?

Without warning, I'm unceremoniously hauled to my feet and shoved toward the front door. "Wait. Wait. I had nothing to do with this," I say, panicked that they are taking my ass to jail.

"We'll take your statement downtown."

"Downtown? But why?" A cop opens a car door and tells me to sit.

"This is bullshit. You don't have any grounds to arrest me. I already told you that I wasn't even here when this went down."

"Calm down, ma'am. No one said anything about you being under arrest, ma'am. We're securing the area." She gestures for me to have a seat in the back of the squad car.

"No, thanks. I'll stand," I say.

The asshole looks as though she wants to slap the cuffs on me.

"Since I'm not under arrest, I prefer not to be treated like a fucking criminal, if you don't mind."

"Suit yourself." The cop sighs again. "You want to tell me what happened here?"

A migraine creeps up on me. "I told you. I don't know. I came here to pick up my new church robe before heading home. I . . ." I stop myself from mentioning seeing Diesel blaze out of the parking lot. Snitches don't get stitches in Memphis. They get body-bagged.

"You what?" the officer prompts.

"I . . . was so shocked to find Momma Peaches lying on the floor like that. I've known her my whole life."

For the first time, the cop's face softens with compassion.

Despite my concern for Momma Peaches, my mind keeps roaming back to Diesel and his possible involvement in this shooting. Given the amount of damage inside, surely he wasn't banging against his own aunt. Did she get caught up in the crossfire?

Kalief hasn't missed an opportunity to tell me about Diesel's long reach of power. Though it's a little disturbing if he's still out here gangbanging like a low-level foot soldier. *Maybe he was the intended victim?* That makes more sense. Then again, I don't know why I'm trying to come up with an excuse for the guy. The muthafucka doesn't mean anything but a check to me.

"Excuse me," a man says.

I turn toward him as he's extending his hand.

"Hello. I'm Lieutenant John Fowler. I'm the lead detective for this investigation. How are you? Can I get you anything?"

Finally. Somebody with manners. "No. I'm fine. Thank you."

"Do you mind if I ask you a few questions?"

More questions. "No. Not at all."

"First: Can I get your name?"

"Cleo. Cleo Blackmon."

The paramedics finally arrive. I swing my attention away from the lieutenant and watch the emergency responders scramble out of the van. Dread crashes over me in waves.

"You'll be missed, Momma Peaches," I whisper, shaking my head. "You will be missed."

"They're upstairs," she tells us.

Profit nods and takes off, leaving my ass downstairs with *her*.

Simmering, I close the door behind me. Despite her pregnancy, Lucifer still carries a dangerous aura. The large baby bump doesn't change a damn thing.

My admiration has turned to hatred. I glare at her, trying to see what attracted Profit. She's beautiful, powerful, confident, *and* dangerous. The Flowers look up to her and the soldiers fear her. How can I compete with that? She's everything I'm not and everything I wish I was. Being in the same room with her stirs up all my insecurities. Maybe at the end of the day, Profit is like the other Vice Lord soldiers. He wants a real boss bitch to ride and die in the streets with him, not some clingy, bougie bitch with a psycho sister who pumped a full clip into him. Keeping shit real, I'm only here because I got caught up. I didn't chose this life . . . it chose me.

Lucifer stops pacing. "Is there a problem, petal?"

Unlike the times before, I glare right back. "Yeah. There's a problem."

"Oh?" She steps forward. "And what's that?"

I cock my head. "You."

Alarm bells sound off in my head as she moves closer.

"Is that right?" Her dark eyes trap mine.

"Seeing how you like *kissing* other women's men," I add, refusing to back down. If I can go toe-to-toe with LeShelle then I can do the same with the bitch who's a threat to my relationship with my man.

"What?"

"Cut the act. I saw you two this morning. *Kissing.*"

Her face hardens and goes cold.

The warning bell rings again.

"Look, petal. I can see that you're all in your feelings right now and you're two seconds away from letting your mouth write a check that your ass can't cash. So let me clue you in on what you really saw: your man kissing *me*. Apparently, what

11
Ta'Shara

"**W**hat do you mean that Dribbles has been shot?" My anger zaps out of me as Profit's face drains of color.

"I don't know. Get dressed," he orders, and then spins around and races out of the bedroom. "I'll be out in the car. Please hurry."

This morning has been crazy as I leapfrog from one emotion to another in a span of an hour. I'm still angry, but I can't forget how Profit was there for me when I lost my foster parents. It would be wrong to turn my back on him now.

When I finish getting dressed, I rush out to the car. Profit is reading something from his phone.

"Do you know what happened?" I ask.

"No. Lucifer only texted me an address."

I wince at the mention of her name and my emotions make another leap. We ride from Ruby Cove in a coffin of silence. The awkwardness makes the whole scene more depressing.

Twenty minutes later, we arrive at a two-story, brick home in Tunica. I push back my confusion and questions and climb out of the car.

Profit rushes ahead of me and pounds on the door. Within seconds, it swings open. Once inside, I come face-to-face with the last person I want to see right now. *Lucifer.*

you didn't see was my ass shutting that shit down. If you want to keep him at home, maybe you should get a shorter leash."

"Maybe Mason needs to put *you* on a leash," I counter. "You do everything else like a man, do you *fuck* like them too?"

A muscle twitches along her temple. It's a miracle that my ass isn't laid out on the floor right now.

"Are you challenging me, petal?"

I lift my chin. "I'm not scared of you."

"Then you're dumber than you look."

"Fuck you," I snap.

I don't even see her go for her knife, but I feel its sharp tip pressed against my throat. I don't have my razor blade, but I remain calm. "What? Are you going to kill me now?"

"The thought has crossed my mind," she says coolly. "But Profit is about to lose one woman in his life; he *might* get a little salty if he lost another—but there's always tomorrow."

I roll my eyes, tempting fate again.

"I'm going to say this shit one last time: I. Don't. Want. Your. Man. Understand?"

We engage in a stare-off.

"Is there a problem down here?" Mason's voice booms from the staircase.

Now what are you going to do? I turn a smug smile up at Lucifer.

"Maybe. I don't know," I tell Mason, but then direct a question to Lucifer. "Do you want to tell him or should I?"

Lucifer's eyes harden into black diamonds. "No. There's no problem," she says in a voice that dares me to contradict her. "We're all good. Aren't we, petal?"

Instead of answering, I push away from her. Both her and Mason's eyes follow me as I stomp up the staircase to find Profit.

At the top of the stairs, I peek into different rooms until I find the one where Profit kneels by a bed.

I don't recognize Dribbles. She's pale and already has one

foot in the grave. My emotions leap again. I walk up behind Profit and place a hand on his shoulder.

"Momma, you don't talk like this. You're going to get better," he tells her.

"We both know that's not true," she whispers. "But it's all right. I want you to know that I love you very much—and that I'm going to need you to be there for Mason. He's already blaming himself for this. It's not his fault. It's nobody's fault."

I'm lost in the conversation. I don't understand what's happening.

Profit shakes his head, not wanting to accept what she's saying. "Nah. That slithering nigga got to pay for this shit. An eye for an eye. That's the rules of the street."

Dribbles's pale face wrinkles with disappointment. "You sound like your brother. I was afraid that would happen when you moved back up here."

"Mom—"

"No. Listen to me for a moment. Don't make the same mistakes that I made. Get out of the street game. It'll destroy whatever happiness you manage to find. Trust me. Get out while you still can. It's too late for Mason. I know that. The streets are in his blood. Both him and Willow. But you two . . . There's still hope for both of you. I can see it."

Her words tug at me because they remind me of the warnings from Reggie.

"Promise me," Dribbles says, her voice fading. "Promise me that you won't follow the same path as your brother. You're eighteen. You're still young. You can go back to school, and then make something of your life. Become *somebody*. Make me proud."

The more she talks, the lower Profit's head hangs. In that moment we all know that he can't promise her that. It's a shame because seconds later, she stops breathing.

12

Hydeya

I'm alive.

Even though every part of my body aches, I've survived. A miracle. Clouds of smoke billow through the car vents, choking me. I cover my nose and mouth with one hand and use the other to push on the door. It's stuck. Frustrated, I drag my five-foot-eight body out of the window.

A few cuts later, I escape the car and then rake my thick hair back from my eyes. In the distance, police sirens and news helicopters fill the sky.

"Captain! Captain! Are you all right?" An officer arrives at the top of the hill and glances down at me. He looks pretty shook up.

"Yeah. I'm fine," I mumble, proceeding to climb up out of the ditch. "Did we get him?"

"They're still searching," he says.

"Goddamn it," I mutter.

The officer offers me a hand on the last leg of the climb. I ignore it to catch my breath. "It was fuckin' Terrell Carver," I tell him. "I recognized his face."

"Holy shit. For real?" he asks, shocked. "I thought he was dead."

"You need a priest, holy water, and a crucifix to kill the

devil," I say, my head clearing. I look down at my fucked-up car. "I need a ride back to the department."

"You got it, Captain."

The whole department is abuzz about the wild police chase where the subject eluded the police. It comes as a major blow against the department at a time when we can't afford to look bad in the press.

Back at the department, I head straight to the break room for a much needed cup of coffee. When I'm sure that no one is looking, I reach for the hidden bottle of bourbon in the back of the cabinet and then top off my drink. I'll need the kick before Chief Brown rips me a new asshole. She'll order another press conference to calm the media; not like those are working too damn well. In an election year, the bigwigs need to appear to be doing something about the violence.

The street wars have accelerated in recent years. Day and night, bodies drop like flies. Only Chiraq and Detroit stack higher body counts than Memphis. The city is under siege. So far, no one has been able to figure out the genesis of the wars. My money is on the department's former superhero, Captain Johnson, and possibly his daughter, Detective Melanie Johnson.

During the investigation of his *and his daughter's* murder, Lieutenant Fowler and I discovered that Melvin Johnson was Terrell Carver's biological father. His daughter couldn't have known about this because she was engaged in an affair with the notorious gangster. They even had a child together, Christopher, who is currently a ward of the state.

We also uncovered a surveillance video of Detective Melanie Johnson murdering her partner, Detective Keegan O'Malley. Weeks later, Detective Johnson herself was murdered, and strong evidence pointed to her lover slash half brother. Then Christopher went missing. Johnson's murder and Christopher's kidnapping landed Terrell "Python" Carver on the FBI's Most Wanted list.

Christopher was rescued months later from an abandoned

house out in West Memphis, but weeks after the child was re-turned to Captain Johnson and his wife, they were found slaughtered inside their home, by the child's *other* grandmother, Alice Carver. Now *she's* dead—killed by her older sister, my step-mother, Maybelline Carver, who she'd also kidnapped. Pretty soon I'll need a family tree diagrammed to keep up with this crazy-ass shit.

"Captain Hawkins, you're here," Detective Hendrix shouts, rushing over.

"Where else would I be?" I ask her.

"Lieutenant Fowler is looking for you."

"Why? What's up?" I gulp down my coffee.

"Another homicide. This one at the Power of Prayer Baptist Church."

My head snaps up. "Isn't that off Florida and McLemore?"

"Yeah. I think so."

Python. That thug is still in the game, dropping bodies—but at a church?

Hendrix rattles on. "I would help, but my partner and I caught three bodies last night at Hemp's liquor store over off Orange Mound."

"Okay. I'm on it." I drain the rest of my coffee, and then jet off to find Fowler. I spot him coming out of my office.

"Hey! You're looking for me?"

My ex-partner, Lieutenant John Fowler, shoots me a grim look. "A little tardy to the party, aren't you?"

"If I'd known that you'd be helpless without me, I would've showed up earlier to hold your hand."

"Cute."

"Besides, I ran into a little problem of my own this morning."

"Don't tell me that you were involved in the police car chase that's splattered all over the news."

"Okay. I won't tell you, but I'll be riding with you until I can get another vehicle assigned to me. Mine is totaled."

"Damn. Why does all the exciting shit always happen with you?" he jokes.

"Oh. That's not all. I got a look at the driver fleeing from that church you were called out to. Care to guess who it was?"

Fowler sighs. "Dale Earnhardt Junior?"

"Funny. No. Who's number one on our Most Wanted list?"

His face loses its amused look. "No."

"Yes."

"So you were right. Terrell Carver is still alive," he says, impressed.

"Don't sound so shocked. I'm *always* right. Now we have to figure how to find him and bring him in."

Fowler laughs. "Piece of cake."

I flash a smile as I walk with him in the direction of the interrogation rooms. "Who we got?"

"Have a look for yourself." Fowler opens the door to the observation room, where a two-way mirror reveals a blood-splattered woman who looks familiar.

"Where do I know her from?" I ask.

"Her name is Cleo Blackmon," Fowler says. "She's a member of the church."

"What's her story?"

"She claims that she discovered our victim when she stopped by to pick up her new choir robe for an upcoming revival."

"Choir . . . She's a singer." I nod, placing the face. "I saw her performing last night at Club Diesel."

"Ahh? You and the hubby finally getting some R & R time, huh?" Fowler grins. "I thought I detected a certain glow about you. Did you get you some?"

"None of your damn business," I sass back, chuckling.

"One day, I'm going to get back into the game. Find a hot girl with freak tendencies."

"What? You're already bored with the blow-up doll I got you last Christmas?"

"On the contrary. I plan to keep her as a chick on the side—or invite her in for a threesome."

We laugh at our foolishness.

My attention returns to the woman on the other side of the mirror. She's struggling to remain calm. "Did she see anything or anyone?" *I hope for the name Python.*

"Of course not," Fowler says. "You know the drill. No one ever sees anything."

Sighing, I ask, "Who's our victim?"

Fowler's deep breath warns me to prepare myself.

"Who?"

"Maybelline Carver."

13

Qiana

Sitting on the edge of my bed, doubled over in pain, I come to the realization that I'm a dead bitch walking. There's no ifs, ands, or buts about it. I have no one to blame but myself. I fucked over the wrong bitch. Now it's time to pay the piper.

Diesel kicked and stomped my ass into the floor last night after drugging and fucking me and . . . I don't even want to think about what may have happened with that damn Doberman pinscher, Solomon.

I shiver in disgust and then block the hazy memory from resurfacing. After I got my ass kicked, LeShelle ran my taxi off the road, killed the driver, and was seconds from murking my ass. Fortunately, she needs something: the baby. The baby I sliced out of one of LeShelle's enemies. I named him Jayson when I brought him here to live for a few months. I cut him out of his momma because LeShelle had failed to tell me that her man's side piece was due to deliver that child at any moment.

My clique, Li'l Bit, Tyneshia, and Adaryl, weren't down with killing a bitch who was nine months pregnant. So I solved the problem. Tyneshia still balked so I got heated and blasted a bullet straight through her dome. Fuck. I never liked the bitch any damn way. Plus, it got the other bitches to fall back in line so we could do the damn job. A deal was a deal, even when you make it with the devil. Recently, I had to secretly move Jayson because the cops came snooping around here. I'm just a half-step ahead of Captain Hydeya Hawkins and now a half-step behind LeShelle Murphy.

The deal: LeShelle murked one of her own bitches, Essence, who I felt had violated the laws of the street by hanging around Profit. In return, I got rid of one of her man's baby mommas. Still, I didn't trust the bitch and thought that keeping Jayson could serve as insurance. The plan backfired. Once LeShelle learned the baby was alive, she came after my ass. I'm alarmed at how easy it was for her to reach out and touch me. And I wasn't prepared for the bombshell that Diesel, my new nigga, was Python's damn cousin. I'm such a fool. Here I thought Diesel was this cool muthafucka with a mean dick game. Turns out, that nigga just gassed me up for information.

The birthmark.

Diesel and Jayson had the same horseshoe birthmark in the same damn place. Li'l Bit told me that shit didn't seem right—but did I listen? The birthmark must be a family trait. No. In fact, I never fuckin' listen. I've been through so much shit, and for what? Profit? Hell. That nigga was one of the reasons I went toe-to-toe with Ta'Shara—when she sliced up my face. The whole sweet, innocent shit is a damn act. The bitch's blade game ain't no joke.

Looking back, I never had a chance. Profit's nose has been shoved so far up Ta'Shara's ass, her farts must smell like potpourri. Shit has changed in the past year. Ta'Shara is a Vice Lord Flower bossed up with the prince of the Vice Lords. The bitch lives right across the street from me. The other girls in the set have welcomed her with open arms.

She won.

And now I'm stuck with her psycho-bitch sister. The shit ain't right.

My stomach pitches again. I race to the bathroom and

empty my guts. I have less than forty-eight hours to turn Jayson over, but I know if and when I do, LeShelle is going to kill both of us.

"Fuck!" I'm hit with another wave of bile and upchuck the rest of my Hot Pockets breakfast. After that, I dry-heave until my stomach locks up.

Knock. Knock. Knock.

"Qiana, are you all right?"

I groan, unable to pick my head up long enough to tell GG to go away.

She knocks harder. "Qiana?"

I still can't do it.

"I'm coming in." GG opens the door and pokes her head in. At seeing me hugged against the toilet, she freaks. "Are you all right?"

Do I look fuckin' all right?

GG rushes over to help. Next thing I know, she's grabbing face towels out of the linen closet and running them under cold water.

My annoyance fades when one towel touches the back of my neck. The shit feels so good that I sigh in relief.

"It's going to be all right," she says. "I know these hangovers aren't much fun."

I wish it was a hangover. This is a purging. Diesel gave me some potent nose candy last night that's still circulating in my system. While I was drugged up, Diesel easily got all the information he wanted. I gag and my stomach muscles turn into a solid knot. She places another towel around my forehead.

I sigh.

"There. You feel better now?"

At long last, I pull my head out of the toilet. "Yeah. Yeah. I'm fine," I lie.

"I'm surprised. You usually handle your liquor better than this."

I grunt, still not ready for a conversation. Maybe it's the way that I dodge her eyes that gets her to cock her head.

"Are you sure you're okay?"

"Goddamn it. I said that I'm fine!"

"All right. No need to snap." She stands up. "I was trying to help."

"I know—but I'm past that now," I tell her cryptically.

"What is that supposed to mean?"

Shit. Now I can't control my mouth. If I'm going to keep it real with myself, I'm backed into a corner. I don't know what to do. If I tell Li'l Bit and Adaryl about LeShelle's pop up last night, they'll lose their damn minds.

I need a fucking plan—quick.

"Qiana, what the hell is going on with you?" GG asks, eyeballing me hard.

I open my mouth to tell her to leave me the fuck alone, but to my horror, I burst out crying.

GG is stunned. "Whatever it is, everything is going to be all right." She settles on the floor next to me and then draws me into her arms. "I'm here."

Unbelievably, I cry harder.

GG's arms tighten. I want to push her away *and* pull her closer. *What the fuck is wrong with me?* My emotions are all over the place. I'm ashamed. This is not the way for a true Vice Lord Flower to behave. We roll and bang as hard as any muthafuckin' foot soldier in the game. I've worked hard to prove that I'm a boss bitch, but now I feel like a goddamn child on a playground, whose toy has been stolen. Pathetic.

"Shhhh. It's okay. It's okay," GG keeps saying. "You do what you need to do. I got you."

I hate to admit it, but I'm glad she's here. An hour goes by before I settle down.

I'm exhausted and my mind is fucking numb, but I push my way out of her embrace.

"Are you all right?" she asks tenderly.

"Yeah." I nod and wipe my eyes.

"Do you want to tell me what happened? Did something go down between you and your new boyfriend?"

"Boyfriend. Ha! Fuck that dirty nigga."

"Okay." She waits me out.

"Look. I appreciate your concern but—you can't help me."

"You don't know that. Why don't you give me a try?"

Tears flow down my face. I hate myself right now.

"C'mon. I've been in some shit before. And though me and Charlie aren't married, I hope you know that I do look at you like a sister. We're family—and I want to help."

"You can't help me. Nobody can."

"You're being dramatic."

"Fuck. If you only knew—"

"Then tell me! What am I missing? What happened between you and that nigga last night?"

Silence.

"Did something happen at the club? Is there another bitch—or are you still beefing with Profit's girl?"

"Fuck that bitch," I tell her.

"Then what?"

The silence grows to the point that my ears ring. The weight of GG's stare feels as if it's about to crush me.

She takes my hand. "Please. Let me help you."

What do I have to lose?

"I did something . . . bad." I finally meet her eyes. "I fucked up," I start, and then tell her the whole damn, pathetic story.

14

Hydeya

"Who?" I ask. I'm sure I didn't hear him right.

Fowler nods. "Can you believe it? The woman is a legend, even in these sacred halls."

The floor tilts beneath my feet—enough so that I reach for the nearest wall to steady myself. The vertigo only lasts for a few seconds, but in that time, my mind races with a million questions. The first one being: How in the hell am I going to tell Isaac?

"Are you all right?" Fowler asks.

"Yeah. Yeah. I'm fine." I shake off my shock, but it doesn't work. At most I buy time to recover. I struggle to pin down the exact emotion that I'm feeling. *Relief? Joy? Sadness? Confusion?* Hell. It's a mix of them. After all, I have a complicated relationship with the woman—even though she doesn't know me from Adam. Since she escaped from her troubled sister, Maybelline Carver has looked into my face several times and never once recognized me. I kept waiting, since I look a lot like my father, but it never happened.

Surely Python didn't shoot his own aunt. I'd heard for years from Isaac how close the two were. No. That puzzle piece doesn't fit.

"So . . . what's the theory? She walk in on something or was she the intended victim?"

"At this point, it's anyone's guess. The shooting was called in by several people in the neighborhood, but so far—"

"Nobody saw a damn thing," we chorus in sync.

"Of course," I add.

"Pastor Hayes is en route. I spoke to him over the phone and he said that he saw Maybelline before heading out to the hospital. We'll get a full statement when he gets here."

"All right." I glance over at Fowler. "Are you going in to talk to Ms. Blackmon?"

"Yep. It's how I make the big bucks." He winks and heads into the interrogation room. "Watch and learn."

"Will do, Obi-Wan Kenobi."

Fowler smirks as he opens the door.

I lean back against the wall and watch my former partner go to work.

"Sorry to have kept you waiting, Ms. Blackmon," Fowler says, handing the shaken woman a can of Diet Coke. "How are you doing?"

"Fine, I guess," Cleo says, shifting in her chair. "Do you know how much longer this is going to be?"

"Not much longer," Fowler reassures her. "I want to confirm that your statement is that when you arrived at the church you didn't see anyone else there and that you weren't witness to the actual shooting. Is that correct?"

There's a beat of hesitation. "That's correct."

She's fucking lying. I step closer to the two-way mirror and study her expression.

"You also said that you knew our victim," Fowler says. "Do you know if there's anyone who may have wanted to cause her harm?"

Another beat. "No. Everyone loved her—except maybe you guys. It's well-known that the po-po has been harassing her for decades."

"Maybelline Carver has quite a police record, but surely you're not insinuating that the Memphis Police Department had anything to do with her death?"

Cleo flashes a flat smile. "I'm answering your questions."

The observation door wrenches open. "Oh. Fowler is still interviewing?"

"Yeah. What's up?" I turn away from the mirror.

"Pastor Hayes is here."

"Ah. Okay. I'll talk to him." I march out of the room behind my colleague. It isn't too hard to spot the anxious pastor out in the hall.

"Pastor Hayes?" I offer him my hand. "I'm—"

"Captain Hawkins. Yes. I know. I've seen you plenty of times on TV. I, uh, came here as soon as I could. I can't believe that this has happened. Peaches, er, I mean, Maybelline—had recently joined the congregation."

Peaches. "Was she a personal friend of yours?"

"She was an *old* friend. She's lived in the neighborhood for at least fifty-odd years. Plus . . . I wasn't always a pastor," he says sheepishly.

I reach for my notepad again. "What time was it when you last saw her?"

"About two hours ago."

"And how was she?"

He hesitates. "To be honest with you she seemed . . . *troubled.*"

He has my full attention. "Troubled? What do you mean?"

"I don't know if you know, but Peaches had been through a horrific experience recently. She'd been kidnapped by her baby sister, Alice."

"Yes. I do know all about that."

"I had gotten the impression that Peaches was looking to turn her life around. It's not unusual after a traumatic experience. You understand?"

"Sure."

"Peaches attended a couple of services, but when I saw her this morning, I was surprised."

"Did she come to talk to you?"

"No. Actually, I found her in the sanctuary praying."

"Praying?" I repeat. The image is hard for me to get my brain around.

"Don't get me wrong—that's what the church is for. It was . . . out of the ordinary. I talked to her and told her that she was welcome to stay as long as she wanted. It's just that when I was talking to her . . . I don't know. She seemed to have a lot on her mind." He draws in another breath. "I don't understand who would do something like that—at the church of all places."

"Was she the only person there when you left?"

"Yes—wait—no," he waffles. "When I was leaving a church volunteer was arriving. She helps out in the office a couple of times a week."

"Oh? What's her name and how can I get in touch with her?"

"Josie. Josephine Holmes."

15

Shariffa

Tupelo, Mississippi

Everything has to be perfect.

I step back and survey my bloody handiwork. Trigger's chopped-up body has been strategically staged around the living room. It's important that I make sure this shit is a replica of Lucifer's handiwork when she killed Crunk at Crunk's Ink tattoo shop and my girls Bricka and Shacardi at Shacardi's crib. I have every detail, even down to Trigger's head spinning around from the ceiling fan. On the walls I write my name in blood with the ominous message:

You're next.

Next to that a five-pointed star and the single letter *L.*

"Perfect."

I have no guilt about this shit. The bitch got what she deserved. She didn't know that I'd learned the truth about her and my husband, Lynch. I made such a fool of myself for ever allowing that bitch into our bed. A harmless ménage à trois to keep the spice in our marriage. I thought that the bitch was my homegirl. She knew how to keep our fuckin' business out of the street. Both of those muthafuckas played my ass. Turns out, Lynch and Trigger went *waaay* back. Shady nigga Mc-Shady had even proposed to her before he met me. He'd even got her and her friends to befriend me in order to give me more street cred with the Grape Street Crips. None of those muthafuckas ever forgot that my ass used to flag for the Gangster Disciples as Python's main bitch *and* how I fell off my throne when Python learned my ass was creeping in the streets like he was. The shit almost cost me my life.

But it didn't. I crawled out of the gutter and climbed my ass up the Crips' ranks and landed the head nigga. When the war between the Gangster Disciples and the Vice Lords got wild, I seized the opportunity to bring Lynch's Kool-Aid gang into the mix. I found out the hard way that these niggas ain't got no heart to do no real battle. Me and my supposed crew—Brika, Shacardi, Jaqorya, and Trigger—took shit too far. A money hit at the Vice Lords' joint, Da Club, went seriously left and Lucifer's brother, Bishop, was gunned down. Now the most feared woman in the streets started tracking our asses down one by one, like Freddie Krueger.

Lynch couldn't even step up to protect us. When he tried to arrange a truce, Lucifer shot his ass in the foot and promised his ass that she'd finish me and Trigger off. Instead of going to war for his own wife, Lynch stashed me and his mistress out here in Tupelo to wait for the heat to die down. Only Trigger and I got into it and I killed the bitch myself. Now, I'm the last bitch in my crew standing. If I want to survive, I have to beat Lucifer at her own game.

Done, I strip out of the bloody clothes and rush to the bathroom in the master bedroom. The shower set to steaming hot, I plunge beneath the water and scrub myself raw. I have to get ready for the role of a lifetime if I'm going to pull this shit off. The first thing I have to do is get my damn story straight. I have to explain to Lynch how my ass is still alive.

A million and one scenarios speed through my head. All of them dumb as fuck.

Keep it simple. It's an important rule to remember. Muthafuckas always mess up by talking too damn much. Toweling off, I dress in record time, grab the yellow cleaning gloves and trash bags from the kitchen. Clothes in the bag, I head out the door and travel through the woods. Since I don't want to risk detection, it's best that I don't burn the clothes out here. With no shovel, I need to find a good hiding place to get rid of this shit. When I stumble across a narrow riverbank, I don't waste a beat, hurling the bloody evidence and gloves into the water below. As I rush back to the house, I hear tires crunching up the gravel road to the safe house.

Who the fuck is this? The terrifying thought that Lucifer really has found me crosses my mind. No shit. My heart stops as I crouch low and angle to see who has shown up unannounced. I instantly recognize the Range Rover when it comes into view.

Lynch. "What the fuck is he doing here?" My heartbeat kicks back into gear and then races like a muthafucka.

Lynch exits the vehicle and then, to my surprise, he opens one of the back doors for my twin four-year-old boys, Marcel and Julez, to hop out. "Are you ready to see Mommy?"

"Yeah," they shout, jumping up and down.

I slap a hand over my mouth while tears sting my eyes. This shit is about to go south in a real fuckin' way if I don't think of something quick—but I draw a blank.

Don't let them go in there. My feet refuse to move. The holes in my story suddenly seem big enough to drive a Mack truck through. Rooted to my spot by the tree, I watch Lynch and my kids enter the house. Seconds later, my babies scream at the top of their voices and then race back out. Lynch follows behind.

Get in there.

I climb to my feet and run from my hiding spot. "Lynch!" I shout, waving my hands in the air.

Everyone's head snaps in my direction.

"Mommy! Mommy!" My boys fly toward me.

I don't have to fake the joy of seeing them. Before now, Lynch has denied my request for them to visit. He claimed that it was too dangerous with Lucifer on a murderous prowl. I'm glad that he's changed his mind. I clear the last line of trees, drop and swing my arms open. Marcel and Julez rush into them so hard that I fall backwards onto the grass.

"Mommy, there's a dead body in there," Julez shouts, pointing back to the house. Tears stream down his face. I'm a piece of shit for letting them go in there.

"Shariffa, baby. Are you all right?" Lynch asks, catching up to me and the boys. "Are you hurt?"

"No. I'm all right," I say, giving my voice the right shaky inflection. "Did you see what happened to Trigger?"

"Of course I saw," he shouts. "What the fuck?"

"What does it look like? That bitch Lucifer killed her," I screech. "How did she find out where we are?" I stand and then flip the script. "*You* said that we'd be safe out here! How in the fuck did that bitch find us?"

The color drains from Lynch's confused face. "I . . . I don't know. Nobody knows about this place."

"That shit can't be true now, can it?"

He gives me the deer-caught-in-the-headlights stare while my sons crowd around my legs, crying. "Mommy there's so much blood."

I stare at Lynch like he's supposed to have the fuckin' answers.

Shaking his head, Lynch does the only thing he can do: apologize. "I'm sorry. I . . . I—"

"You're sorry? That's all you got? I could've been chopped

up and swinging around the ceiling fan too. *All* you can say is that you're sorry?"

"I'll fix this." He pulls me and the kids forward to wrap us in his arms. "I promise." He kisses me and pulls me back so that I can read the seriousness in his eyes. "I'm glad you're safe."

Are you? Even with his arms around me, I can't help but wonder if he would prefer that it was my head swinging around in the living room instead of his longtime secret girl-friend. If Lynch even suspected that I'm the one who chopped up and spread his snake-in-the-grass mistress's body parts around this shitty hideout, what would he do? The fact that my ass was number two to my own damn husband is beyond fucking sad. But I'm a survivor—and now it's time to become a conqueror. Time to kick the show into high gear. I lower my head and cry.

"Baby, it's okay. Calm down," Lynch soothes. "Tell me what happened—from the beginning."

He's more concerned about Trigger than these crying babies. I struggle to keep it together. "I got up this morning and needed to clear my head about this whole Lucifer situation, so I went for a walk. And when I came back . . ." I sniff. "Trigger was dead. I freaked out and ran back into the woods to hide. I didn't know what else to do."

Lynch's forehead creases at the tall tale.

Oh shit. Am I selling this shit right? I kick up the crying.

"Shh. Shh. I'm here now," he consoles, stroking the back of my head. "Nothing is going to happen to you. I'm here now." He kisses my forehead and then swears under his breath. "We'll move you somewhere else. Somewhere safer."

"We were supposed to be safe *here*," I snap.

"Mommy, I want to go home," Marcel wails.

"I do too," I say, staring up at Lynch. *Whatcha gonna do?*

He punts. "It's okay, baby. I know you're upset." Lynch takes me back into his arms. "Let me go in and take another look. You and the boys stay right here. Okay?"

I sigh and then release him to go back inside.

"No, Daddy, nooo," Julez cries when he realizes that his father is about to go back into the house.

"It's okay," Lynch reassures him. "You stay out here with Mommy. I'll be right back."

I nod pathetically and watch him go. Once he's inside, I grin from ear to ear.

16

Qiana

Tick. Tock.

After pouring my heart out to GG on my bathroom floor, I'm consumed by guilt. A long list of *could've* and *should've* strolls through my head.

"Calm down," GG says. "We just have to put our heads together and think."

"What is there to think about? I'm dead no matter what the fuck I decide to do."

"That's not true. You still have options. As long as you're here in Ruby Cove, you have a real layer of protection."

"So what? I'm under house arrest for the rest of my life—like that bitch Ta'Shara."

"Judging by that party the Flowers threw for her last night, Ta'Shara doesn't seem to be all that fucking concerned about her sister."

"Why would she? She has Profit, Fat Ace, and Lucifer protecting her like the Secret Service."

"And you have me and Charlie."

I cock my head. "No shade, but that's hardly the same thing."

"Then let's cash in your insurance card: Jayson."

"Fuck. My stupid ass told Diesel every fucking thing. What

makes you think that he hasn't gone and blabbed everything to Python?"

"Well, if he has, then it'll take care of your little problem, right?"

For the first time, a ray of sunlight parts the gray clouds of my depression. "You're right."

GG nods. "Python would probably place more stock in the word of his cousin than if the information had come from you."

"Yeah." The wheels start spinning in my head. "How do we find out?"

"We go and talk to Diesel," she says, shrugging.

"Talk?" I point to my busted face. "Does it look like that shady nigga is interested in talking with me? Hell, he'll probably kill me if he sees me again."

"Then I'll go talk to him."

"You? You'll do that for me?"

"Why not? You need help . . . and I consider you family."

I don't know what to say, but it strikes me as a *big* favor to ask. "I don't know. You don't know him . . . and what he's capable of." An image of Solomon flashes in my head again.

"I'll go with backup. Talk to him at his club. It should be safer. It's public."

"Public just means a higher body count. You know these niggas out here don't give a shit."

"Look. If he wanted to kill you, he would've done it last night. Don't you think?"

Maybe.

"Or . . . we can gather a posse. Your clique and my clique and we all go and meet LeShelle at Hack's Crossing Park. I can't imagine she's told too many people about y'all's arrangement. Maybe we can outgun the bitch."

I like that idea better, but, "Won't I have to tell your girls what I did to Tyneshia? How do you think that's going to go down, my killing another Flower? That shit could sentence me to a few bullets too." My anxiety triples. Death has me surrounded. I just don't know the method it's going to use to take me out.

She sighs as if she hasn't thought of that. The complexity of the situation has finally hit my girl. She looks as lost as I am. "Okay. Let's go over our options again. There's got to be an answer in here somewhere."

"The only answer is to get to that bitch before she gets to me! I don't know how I'll do that shit, since she seems to move through the streets like a goddamn ghost. I'd love it if that grimy Diesel does it, but I can't even risk you going to *ask* him."

"Then we do the posse thing."

"Yeah, and risk them killing me for treason. I killed Tyneshia, remember?" I've talked myself in a complete circle again.

"You know, my girls Mack and Romil are no angels. Maybe if you really humble yourself they'll overlook it."

That's a hard pill to swallow. "I don't know."

"Look, Qiana. I don't want to scare you or anything, but we really don't have a whole lot of options. There simply are no perfect answers to this. You got yourself into some serious shit and I'm *trying* to help."

She's right—and I know that she's right. It doesn't make making a decision any easier.

Tick. Tock.

I close my eyes and make a decision. "All right. Fine. Let's assemble a posse."

GG nods. "All right. Let's call your girls first."

I'm nervous as shit with my stomach twisted into knots. I'm not used to having to ask bitches for help, but here I am, standing before my girl's Li'l Bit and Adaryl and trying to act like my ass isn't in as much deep shit as it truly is. They could buck and show me their ass any damn minute. And then what in the fuck am I going to do—serve LeShelle my fucking head on a goddamn platter?

I glance over at GG and try to mimic her confidence, but fail miserably and start twitching in my seat like a crack addict on her first day of rehab.

Li'l Bit is the first to voice her concerns as her baby voice squeaks, "Is everything all right?" Her gaze swings from me to GG. "Has that cop been back?"

Captain Hawkins. Hmph. I wish shit was that simple. "Nah. I haven't seen her again."

Adaryl huffs. "So what the fuck are we meeting here about?"

Her fucking disrespectful tone marches all up and down my damn nerves. It takes everything in me not to snap back.

"We have ourselves a little situation," GG begins and then looks at me to bring the girls up to speed.

I take a deep breath, but have a hard time lifting my gaze from the floor. "LeShelle Murphy got the drop on me last night."

Li'l Bit gasps. "I fuckin' *knew* it. Shit. What happened? What did she say?"

"You mean after she capped a fuckin' cab driver and then put a loaded gun to my head?"

Li'l Bit gasps again and then bounces around in her seat. "Ohmigod! Wait. How in the fuck are you still breathing?"

I look over at Adaryl, who is shaking her head. "Let me guess. She wants the kid."

Clamping my jaw tight, I nod.

"Then give him to her," Adaryl snaps. "I don't see what the fuckin' problem is."

"She'll kill him," I say.

"And?" Adaryl shrugs.

"He's a fucking baby," I thunder back, incredulous. "I don't fucking kill or help kill children. Bitches got to have a code out here in the streets or we're no fuckin' better than animals."

"A code?" Adaryl laughs. "How does 'not killing your own' *not* make it into your damn code book? Huh?"

"Look. I get that you're still feeling salty about what went down with Tyneshia. I get that. You're free to feel some kind of way about that shit—but it doesn't change the problem we got."

"*We?*" Adaryl looks around to see if I'm talking to somebody else. "What's this *we* shit? The bitch shouldn't even know my—or Li'l Bit's—name. We didn't fucking strike a deal with the bitch. She shouldn't be coming after *us* for a muthafuckin' thing. This is *your* problem."

GG cuts in. "It's *all* of our problems. We're in this shit together."

"No. *We* ain't," Adaryl corrects her. "I don't know what the hell Qiana told you, but *we* told her not to kill that yellow bitch after we found out how fuckin' pregnant she was. Did she listen? No. In fact, she executed Tyneshia for speaking the damn truth. And then we left her ass there, which brings the fuckin' cops to our muthafuckin' door. Now she's telling us that the bitch that we did this shit for is gunning for *us*? The only way the bitch would know our names is if Qiana ratted us out."

I had noticed Adaryl trying to distance herself from me in the past month, but the bitch is really feeling herself right now.

"Did you?" Li'l Bit asks, looking at me with her eyes wide-open. "Did you rat us out to that crazy bitch?"

All eyes shift to me and I instantly start to sweat under the pressure. "No. I didn't tell the bitch nothing."

"Then she ain't looking for us and this whole thing is *your* problem," Adaryl insists. "I say you handle it and leave us the fuck out of it."

What the fuck am I supposed to say to that? I look over at GG and she seems stumped too. "I don't fuckin' believe this. You two are supposed to be my girls. We have each other's back."

"Nah. You severed that shit the second you put that cap in

Tyneshia. *You* made this damn deal with the devil. *You* killed that yellow bitch. *You* cut that baby out. And then you pretended to play momma to it. This is all on you, boo." She marches over and grabs Li'l Bit by the hand and forces her to stand up next to her. "As far as *we* are concerned, our asses wasn't even there. That's our story and if the shit gets out to the other Flowers, or the fuckin' cops, we're going to call you a fuckin' liar."

She fucking means that shit.

I stand up and stab Li'l Bit with a hard stare. "Is she speaking for you too?" I hold my breath. Li'l Bit and I have been tight since our asses were in diapers. We've shared every fucking thing. I know damn well that *she* isn't about to side with this bitch over me.

Li'l Bit's gaze drops to the floor.

My heart sinks to the pit of my gut.

"We *did* tell you not to kill that girl," she says softly.

My eyes burn as I nod my head. "All right. Fine. If this is how it's going to be, then so be it. I'll handle this shit on my own."

Adaryl grins and thrusts out her chin in satisfaction.

"And so we're clear: After tonight, I don't want to have shit else to do with you bitches. I don't know you and you don't know me. Cool?"

Li'l Bit's shoulders drop. "C'mon, Qiana. Don't be like that."

"Be like what? I have some crazy-ass psychopath bitch popping up like a fuckin' jack-in-the-box and you say that you are going to bail on me when I need you the most. You think I'm not going to feel some kind of way about that? Fuck. If y'all ain't going to be loyal, then maybe I shouldn't either."

The blood drains out of Li'l Bit's face. "What the fuck is that supposed to mean?"

"It means exactly what the fuck you think it means," GG interrupts. "Y'all are too deep in this shit now. And you can tell muthafuckas all you want that you weren't there, but I damn well will guarantee you that if Qiana goes down on this shit,

I'll make it damn clear to anyone that'll listen that y'all were involved too. Now who the fuck do you think that the other Flowers will listen to—me or you?"

The fucking room goes silent.

Feeling my swagger coming back, I fold my arms and smile snidely at them.

Adaryl rolls her eyes. "No. I'm sorry. But you can count me out. I don't want anything else to do with this shit."

She heads for the door.

"Adaryl!"

"Deuces."

17

Hydeya

I can't get Momma Peaches's death off of my mind. I want to head to the hospital to check on Isaac, but the chief and deputy chief are blowing up my cell. I don't have to answer to know that they want another press conference—*stat*. Surely the people in this city are already tired of seeing my face on TV every other day. Lord knows that I'm tired of being seen.

Captain Johnson made it look so easy. Of course, he was crooked as hell too.

"Oh. Good. You're here," Officer Foye says, poking his head through my door. "We got a hit on one of your cases." He plops a folder down on my desk.

"Which case?"

"The three bodies from Hemp's liquor store."

I blink up at him and finally swipe my mouth. "Hemp's? I don't know anything about that case."

"I dropped off a copy of the case file this morning." He gazes over my cluttered desk and then plucks out another folder. "Here it is."

I take the folder with sickening dread. The hits keep on coming.

"Officers Coleman and Hendrix are working it."

"All right. So what is it that you found?"

"Quick notes: There were three victims at the liquor store. One male, the owner; and two females. The two females have been fingerprinted and turn out to have records as long as the book *War and Peace*: an Emerald Jacobs and Nisha Randall. Body tats identify them as Vice Lord Flowers. They were killed by the owner, Muhammad Bassem."

"And who took him out?"

He gestures to the brown envelope he brought in. "According to that copy of the security surveillance, an unidentified woman who entered the store with the two victims and another female. Four women walked in but two women ran out."

"Burglary gone wrong?"

"Actually, no," he says, surprising me. "It actually looks like a clear-cut case of self-defense. The owner waged a personal jihad on the ladies for some reason, but hadn't counted on one of the women being an excellent shot."

I nod. "I'll take a look at the case a little later."

He gives me a sympathetic smile. "Been a little crazy around here lately, huh?"

"Something like that." The phone rings, but I can only manage to stare at it. *Please. Don't nobody bring me no more bad news.* The caller ID reads, "Chief Brown."

"Better answer it," Officer Foye warns. "She tends to go nuclear when she thinks she's being ignored." He backs out of the office with a wink.

He's right. I pick up the phone. "Captain Hawkins."

"In my office," Chief Brown barks and then slams the phone down.

Nuclear. I exhale and then drop the phone back into its cradle. "May as well go and get this over with," I mumble. Standing, I cram a cracker in my mouth and then rush to the chief's office. I don't know how much more of my ass she can chew, but it'll be interesting to find out.

However, the moment I step out of my office, I catch Diesel Carver breezing into the department. I stop walking mid-stride and stare as he sucks all the oxygen out of the room. Yes. He's handsome. My body's reaction is a testament to that. But he's something else too. He's dangerous. I've been unable to confirm it, but I'm from the streets. I know a dangerous man when I see one.

Fowler walks over and greets Carver and then leads him to a private room. He must've contacted Maybelline's nephew to deliver the bad news.

"Hawkins!"

I jerk at the sound of the chief shouting my name across the office like we're out in a field somewhere. Turning, I see her, grim-faced, waving me over.

"Coming." I resume my march to the chief's office. "You wanted to see me, Chief?"

"Have a seat," she tells me without looking up.

Chief Yvette Brown leans her petite frame all the way back in her squeaky leather seat. What the woman lacks in stature she makes up in power, which she wears well.

I cross her office to the empty chair across from her desk. Days ago she had me in here to order that I close my investigation into Captain Johnson's suspected illegal activities.

"I'm going to get down to the point," she says, lacing her fingers. "I know that your promotion was a few weeks back, but *some* are already expressing some concerns about whether you can handle the job."

My heart drops. "What kind of concerns?"

"Well, I don't know whether you've noticed, but the city does seem to be under siege. Dead bodies are popping up all over the place and that damn car chase this morning, where people are now shooting at news copters, has taken us to a new low. And where were you?"

"I was right in the thick of it," I tell her. "Spun off the road and was nearly wiped out."

"So are you taking responsibility for having lost this suspect? We look like amateurs out there! How are we supposed to have the city's confidence after that nonsense makes national news—again!"

"Chief Brown, I'm doing the best that I can."

"*That* is what concerns us."

I clamp my mouth shut in order to hold on to my temper. The last thing I need right now is to let my inner gangster come out.

"Look," the chief says. "You seem overwhelmed. Even the press has hinted as much."

Am I about to be fired? "I hear what you're saying—and I want to assure you that that's not the case. I can handle the job."

Doubt remains etched in her face. "I'll tell you what I want to do. I want to bring Lieutenant Fowler in. See how he works out."

"I don't understand."

"I'm putting you both under a trial period. See who really is the better fit for the job."

"A trial," I repeat like I'm stuck on stupid.

"Honestly, I think it's the best solution. You both work side by side a lot as it is, so what's a little friendly competition?"

She's fucking serious.

"Look. Don't take it personally. We can't have a citizenry living in fear. Fear leads to distrust. Distrust leads people to want change. People who want change march to the polls. Do I need to remind you that this is an election year? The mayor is feeling the heat. I can only carry the department so long, while case after case stacks up. Last year the clearance rate was forty percent. This year, we'll be lucky if we hit thirty-six percent."

"Chief—"

"No. No. I understand. Most of this mess happened on Captain Johnson's watch—and it's a little unfair for us to expect a huge turnaround in such a short time. But nothing in life is fair. We all play the hand that we're dealt. Am I making myself clear?"

"Yes. You're stabbing me in the back."

"I'm disappointed that you see it that way—but the bottom line is that we need to start putting some wins on the board."

"Understood." I stand. "Anything else?"

"Yes. You can sit back down. I'm not finished."

Our gazes crash. *This bitch is enjoying this shit.* Swallowing my pride, I lower myself back down into the chair.

"We're looking into maximizing our resources. The bigwigs have decided to form a multi-agency gang unit. It'll all be aimed at reducing gang activity in Memphis. It'll consist of six primary law enforcement agencies. We're going to streamline a lot of this shit so now the right hand will know what the left one is doing. We need to show the city that we're serious about winning the gang wars. You and Fowler will be the point of contact for our department. As a specialized unit, the MGU will use various techniques and methods to conduct long-term operations against gang leaders and hardcore members." She reaches for a folder.

I reach over to accept the folder.

"Everything you need to know about the new unit is right there. Acquaint yourself with the material." The chief flashes me her infamous plastic smile. "We're excited about this. I hope you are too."

"Absolutely," I lie.

The office fills with a thick, awkward silence.

"*Now* the meeting is over. You can leave."

"Yes, Chief." I climb to my feet and stroll to the door feeling humiliated.

When my hand closes around the doorknob, the chief adds one more thing. "By the way, I informed the media that you'll be conducting another press conference Monday morning."

"Yes, Chief." I exit the office, but I make damn sure that I slam the door behind me.

Complications

18

Cleo

After hours of questioning, I'm told that I'm free to go. Relieved and exhausted, I head out of the police department, still thinking about Momma Peaches. This news is going to come as a shock to the whole neighborhood. We'd all celebrated having her back after her horrendous kidnapping. I'm caught up thinking about how my own family is going to react, when I walk past an office window and spot Diesel Carver talking to Lieutenant Fowler.

My heart drops and I almost trip over air. *Why is he here? Has he come to confess?* The image of him jetting away from the church replays in my mind. I shake the question of a confession from my mind. I could be jumping to conclusions. Then I can't think of a logical reason why both him and Python were racing from the church within a couple of minutes of each other. If he wasn't involved somehow, why would he leave his poor aunt lying on the church floor.

My strides slow as I study the man's face. There's no emotion. He's sitting there as if he's in the middle of a championship poker game. I stop and wait. But as the minutes tick by, there's still nothing.

While the disturbing questions chase each other in my

head, Diesel turns his head and meets my gaze. At long last, emotions ripple across his face: surprise, and then pleasure.

My stomach knots as he flashes me a smile. I don't return the kind gesture. Instead, I spin around and march off. The moment I step out of the station and breathe in the cool air, my head clears. Still, I don't know what to make of my suspicions.

Don't get involved.

Sound advice when it comes to dealing with anything out here in the streets. I cared about and admired Momma Peaches, but Lord knows she and her family were always in the thick of some mess.

Essence was killed because she got in the middle of Ta'Shara's family issues. I'm not about to do the same thing with the Carvers. Whatever happened inside of that church ain't none of my damn business.

I rush across the parking lot to my car. The second I pop my butt into the seat, my cell phone rings.

Kalief.

I toss the phone aside. I'm *still* not in the mood to deal with his shit.

Tap! Tap! Tap!

Startled, I jump at the light tap on my car window. When I glance up, I'm surprised to see Diesel Carver. The front of his clothes are still covered in his aunt's blood. I hesitate, but then power down my window.

"Yes?"

The handsome devil flashes me a smile. "Trouble you for a ride?"

My hackles rise while the voice in the back of my head screams *No.* "Are you having car trouble?" I ask, glancing around the crowded police parking lot.

"Not exactly. I had an employee drop me off. I thought the interview would last longer than it did—but I don't want to be too much trouble if it's going to be out of your way."

He's offering me an out, but instead of taking it, I say, "No, it's not too much trouble."

"Great. I appreciate that." He winks at me and then strolls around the car to the passenger side.

What the fuck did I do? But by the time he slides into the passenger seat, I've tacked on a smile. After all, the man's aunt was just killed. The least I can do is be nice to him. "Where to—the hospital?"

"Actually, if you could take me over to my club that would be great," he says. "I can use a shower."

Damn. That *is* going to take me out of my way. "Sure. No problem." I slide my key back into the ignition, start up the car, and roll out of the parking lot. The silence becomes awkward. Once I reach the third traffic light, I sneak a quick peek over at him to gauge how he's handling things.

He's staring at me.

I give him a flat smile and then turn on the radio. I need to fill the silence with something. To my surprise, he immediately reaches over and turns it back off.

"I hope you don't mind. I don't want to deal with the noise right now."

"Of course. No. I understand." I fidget in my seat before adding, "I'm really sorry for what happened to your aunt. She was a great lady."

"Yes. She was."

Okay. That's short and to the point. I fidget some more. "Did they tell you what happened?"

"That some crazy hooligans shot up the church," he says, his expression unreadable again. "I heard that crime has gotten out of control in the area."

"Yeah." I struggle to match his emotionless face. "It's still weird. I saw her last week in church." I lick my lips nervously. "When was the last time you saw her?"

My heart hammers while I wait for his answer.

Diesel sighs. "I guess about a week ago. I took her home from the hospital and invited her to my club's opening."

My heart shoots up into my throat. *This lying muthafucka!* I take a deep breath and then remind myself not to get involved. Searching for something to do, I turn on the radio again.

He turns it back off.

"Sorry. I forgot," I say.

He doesn't respond. He simply stares.

Ignore him. I force myself to focus on the road, but after a couple of minutes, I buckle under the weight of his stare. I cut a look in his direction. "Can you please stop doing that?"

He doesn't say anything.

"I mean it. You're making me uncomfortable."

"Sorry. But . . . to ask me to stop staring is like asking me to cut out my eyes. You're beautiful."

Is he for real?

"Okay. Okay." He tosses up his arms. "I'll try not to stare."

"Thank you."

"But no promises."

He thinks he's being charming, but really he's coming off more like one of those creepy stalkers on the ID channel.

"So how are things with you and the, uh, boyfriend?" he asks out of the blue.

"My and Kalief's relationship is none of your business," I tell him. "I already told you that last night."

"Yes. Yes. I believe you said something about you being loyal." Amusement creeps into his eyes.

I grit my teeth. "Yes. I am."

"And what about *him*?"

The question is a punch in the face.

"I'm sorry. I didn't mean to hit a sore subject. I thought—"

"I really don't give a fuck what you think," I snap. "I'm not going to discuss my personal business with you. So drop it."

He holds up his hands in surrender. "You got it."

We ride along in silence for a full minute before he comes

at me from a different angle. "Now, if *I* had a woman like you, I wouldn't dare dream of looking at another woman."

I grind my teeth down another inch while my hands tighten on the steering wheel.

"I would shower you in diamonds, dress you up in all the fashion greats out of Paris and Milan. And there would be nothing I wouldn't do to make sure *all* your dreams come true."

These words find a chink in my armor. I sneak another look, and a bigger smile has eased onto his face. "Did you give this same line to that girl on your arm last night?"

"What girl?"

I roll my eyes. "Spare me. You're like all the other niggas out here, tryna run game."

"Nah. Nah. I don't have a girl—just a few friends showing me a good time in a new city. But if you say the word, my friend list will get much, much shorter."

"You need to learn how to take no for an answer."

"And you need to learn how to say yes."

I laugh.

"Finally. A smile." He pumps out his chest. "I was beginning to think that you really didn't like me."

A car horn blares. I glance up and see that a traffic light has turned green. As I ease off the brake, I flash the driver behind me the bird. "Calm down, asshole," I say, pretending to be annoyed when in truth I'm embarrassed that this man has me blushing.

Diesel laughs. He knows what's up.

I want to say something that will knock that smug smile off his face, but all my clever quips fail me.

Sensing an opening, Diesel leans closer. "I want to take you out."

"No," I croak—but there was a beat before I answered and he picks up on it.

"There's no reason to be scared. You know that you want to. I promise. I'll treat you like a queen."

Thank God, Club Diesel comes into view. "Here we are," I say, pulling in front of the building.

He doesn't make a move toward the door. "You should come in. I believe that I still owe you a check for last night's performance."

I perk up. I'd assumed that he paid Kalief, who was stalling on giving me and the band our money.

"It shouldn't take but a few minutes," he says.

I hesitate because I need my money. "All right. I have a few minutes."

19

Hydeya

"How long have you known that the chief is considering you to take over my job?" I ask Fowler directly. I cross my arms and prop myself against his cubicle wall.

"So she's talked to you?" He tosses down his pen and then looks up at me as if he's really not in the mood to have this conversation.

"Answer the damn question."

"This morning," he says. "I was gonna tell you at happy hour."

"Fuck you. Thanks for the loyalty." I push away from the wall and storm off.

"Hawkins, don't be like that." Fowler jumps to his feet and catches up with me. "I didn't go after the job. *She* came to me."

"But you'll take the job, right?" I challenge.

Instead of answering, he sighs.

"That's what I thought." I march into my office and plop down behind the desk.

"Why wouldn't I take the job?" he asks. "It's a promotion. It's better money, better pay—and I can do the damn job."

"And I can't? Is that it?" I challenge. "You know damn well how much I sacrifice for this. The hours I put in."

"And what? I play with my dick all damn day, is that it?"

"You're falling back on the dick jokes a little too soon, don't you think? The point is that I haven't been in the job long enough to warm the damn seat and now she wants to toss me under the fuckin' bus. That's bullshit."

"Dealing with bullshit is part of the damn job," Fowler counters. "And yeah, while you're like a hound dog on a trail, you don't do any of the political butt-kissing that comes along with the job. You and the hubby never attend any of the boring-ass political fund-raisers. I've never seen you at the department's Christmas parties, retirement parties—or even at the governor's parties, to kiss the ring. Hell, you don't even pay homage to any of the union functions either."

"What? I don't have time for all that bullshit. Look at my desk. I'm drowning in murder cases and everyone is pissed because I won't put on a damn dress and laugh at everyone's dumb jokes? I'm a cop, not a damn publicist or a fund-raising lobbyist."

"It's all part of the job. Captain Johnson ate that shit up," Fowler reminds me. "And so do all the assholes at the top of the food chain."

"Captain Johnson was a goddamn criminal."

"Maybe . . . but he knew how to play the game, which is why nobody wants you kicking over any unnecessary rocks on his case, just so you can watch the worms play."

A lightbulb clicks on over my head. "Oh my God. That's it, isn't it?"

Fowler frowns at my interrupting his lecture.

"This isn't about the murder count." I hop up from my desk, rush over to pull him into my office, and close the door.

"What are you doing?" he asks.

"Kicking over rocks? This is all about them forcing me to close the Captain Johnson case. Damn. She even said herself that she didn't want the investigation to fall down a rabbit hole—or not know who it may implicate—and blowback, and blah, blah, blah."

"So you did or didn't close the case?"

I cock my head up at him. "Will you please focus on the bigger picture here? Johnson couldn't have amassed all those drugs and weapons by himself. He had to have had help. It has to be a fucking ring of dirty cops here."

"So that's a no to you closing down the case?"

"I work cases. I don't parade around in ball gowns or brown up my nose while kissing political asses, remember?"

"That's not what I meant."

"That's exactly what you meant."

Frustrated, Fowler rolls his eyes. "All I'm saying is that the top brass are concerned about your lack of social skills. You've even admitted that you don't like dealing with the press—and it shows. You look like a deer caught in headlights every time you give a press conference. You're a great cop, but your presentation doesn't exactly exude confidence to a city under siege by gang wars."

"So that's a yes, you're going to steal my job?"

"I'm not going to steal—what the hell? Why are you jumping down my throat? Are you the only one allowed to have ambition around here? That's pretty fucked up. When you landed the job, I was happy for you."

"So I'm supposed to be *happy* that you're now trying to steal the job from me?"

"I'm not *stealing* anything. The chief came to me—not the other way around."

"Chief Brown is clearly looking for a fall guy—or woman—to pin the high unsolved homicide rates on. You do know that, right?"

"Do *you* know it?" As much as I want to believe my ascendancy within the department was due to my good record—I have more sense than that. My capabilities as an officer didn't have shit to do with my promotion. But now that I'm on this train I might as well ride it to the end of the line and then fall on my sword like a good soldier.

But I can't focus on that shit right now. I have to play the hand that I was dealt.

Fowler's anger cools. "Look. If you want to keep the job then you're going to have to learn how to play politics—and the first rule of politics is not to rock the boat. The chief told you to close the damn case—so close the damn case!" He brushes me out of the way and snatches open the door.

"Where the hell are you going?" I bark. "I'm not done arguing with you yet."

"I have cases to work too, you know. I'm going to head over to Shotgun Row to talk to that church volunteer, Josephine Holmes." Fowler sucks in a calming breath. "You want to tag along?" This is his weird form of a peace offering.

I'm not about to let him out of my sight. "Don't mind if I do."

Lieutenant Fowler turns onto Utah Avenue a.k.a. Shotgun Row. There are only a handful of brothers on the street. That's to be expected since it's still daylight. My gaze swings over to Momma Peaches's house and I wonder if Isaac has returned home.

"Let's stop at the Carver residence first," I tell Fowler.

"Why?"

"To speak with Isaac."

Fowler slams on the brakes. "What?"

I sigh. "With all the shit going on this morning, I forgot to tell you that Isaac was released from jail this morning."

"You *forgot*?" He stares at me up and down. "How the fuck do you forget to mention that King Isaac is back on the streets the same damn day his wife is killed and Python, rises from the dead?"

"C'mon. He had nothing to do with the shooting."

"How the hell do you know that?"

"Because he was with me at the time of the shooting. I

picked him up from prison, and had dropped him off when I got into that high-speed chase."

We glare at each other, the car charged with renewed anger . . . and distrust.

"So you and your father are back on good terms? When the hell did this happen?"

"Don't start," I tell him before he bounces onto my last nerve. He's the only one in the department who knows that King Isaac is my father—and now that he's going after my damn job, it's the perfect weapon at his disposal.

"I'm definitely going to need that drink after this shift," he says, easing off the brake. The second he pulls up to Momma Peaches's house, a fat knot lodges in my throat.

I hate doing this shit. I still haven't formulated a speech. I've delivered bad news to plenty of families in the past, but never to my own.

We climb out of the car, and when I'm about to knock, the woman on the porch next door speaks.

"Ain't nobody home."

We shift our attention to her.

"Are you sure?" I ask. The woman might not know that I drove Isaac here a few hours ago.

"Yeah. Momma Peaches is dead and her husband took off for the morgue hours ago."

Fowler strolls past me to hike across the street to Josephine Holmes's residence.

I ignore him so he can wallow in his feelings. Shit. He doesn't tell me every damn thing, so I don't know why he feels like he's entitled to know all my shit.

At this point, more neighbors mill outside, their attention locked on us. Nobody trusts the damn police anymore, not that I blame them.

Fowler opens the screen door and knocks. To our surprise, it swings open—but nobody is standing there. We exchange looks before reaching for our service weapons.

"Hello," I call into the house.

No answer.

We look at each other again, as if to say *"What do you want to do?"*

"Hello. Ms. Carter, are you in here?" Fowler shouts. "It's the police."

Silence.

I give Fowler the nod, and together we creep into the house. "I don't want to alarm you. I'm Captain Hydeya Hawkins with the Memphis Police. Lieutenant Fowler and I came to ask you a few questions." The silence grows deafening, the hairs on my body prickle. *I have a bad feeling about this.*

Inch by inch, Fowler moves two steps behind me. We've done this dangerous dance plenty of times in the past, but this number, it's a short one as we discover Josephine Holmes in her living room, face down, with the back of her head missing.

20

Cleo

I can't shake the feeling that my walking into Club Diesel is like strolling into the devil's lair. As I glance around, I hardly recognize the place. Without the wall-to-wall crowd of half-naked waitresses and dancers the place hardly looks the same.

"You know you helped my opening night to be a success," Diesel says, strolling ahead of me.

"I doubt that. I think you had more to do with that."

His deep chuckle rumbles throughout the club. "You have a hard time accepting a compliment, don't you?"

"That's not true, I . . ." I catch myself.

He stops and turns around. "Gotcha."

"All right. Fine. *Thank you.* I enjoyed performing here last night."

"So what do you say to being a regular here?"

"I, uh—"

"I know a star when I see one."

He's gassing me up again. I pump the brakes and put on my best poker face. "I'd say that I will have to get with my manager and run things by him."

"Ah. All roads lead back to him, huh?"

My lips twitch with a heavy smile.

He shakes his head. "It won't work."

"What?"

"You trying to hate me." He clasps his hands behind his back and flashes me his dimples. "I'm a charming cat." Without waiting for a reply, he turns and winds through the club.

I struggle to keep up with his long, confident strides.

"How long have you and . . . what's his name again?"

"Kalief."

"Right. Kalief. How long have you been together?"

"Professionally?"

We reach the back of the club and proceed to climb a set of stairs.

"Both."

"Not that it's any of your business, but we've been together since high school." *Now can I get my damn check?*

"Ah. So I'm going up against high school sweethearts. This is getting more and more challenging." He opens the door to his office and gestures me to go ahead of him.

When I walk past him, he says, "But no ring?"

I had a ring. Kalief pawned it two years ago.

"What's the holdup?" he asks as he crosses over to his desk.

"That's none of your business," I tell him, wanting to end this.

"Ah. We're back to playing the ice princess again." He grins.

I fold my arms and try to wait him out, but after a minute the game becomes stupid. "My money?"

"Oh. Yes." Diesel springs back to his feet. At the same time, he pulls off his bloody T-shirt and exposes his muscled body covered in tattoos, and a bleeding bandage on the back of his shoulder.

"What happened there?" I ask, forgetting my vow to keep my nose out of this man's business.

He turns his back away from me. "An old injury," he lies coolly.

Or you were shot inside of that church. Besides that, I have to admit that every inch of this honey-baked brothah is on point. I pretend to be unimpressed, but I'm sure the truth is written all over my face. More warning bells go off in my head and I take a step back toward the door.

Diesel grins like a slick panther, his eyes asking me whether I see anything I like.

My answer is to look away.

He chuckles. "I can't figure you Memphis girls out. Y'all stay hugged on these punk bitches that ain't got shit, but then when a real man wanna upgrade you, y'all act scared."

"I ain't scared of a damn thing. I just want my money."

He unbuttons his pants.

"What the fuck are you doing?"

"What does it look like? Changing." He opens a door off to his left and reveals a bathroom. "I have an important meeting to get to and I need to change." He walks into the bathroom and leaves the door open. "It should only take a few minutes for a hot shower." He turns on the water. "Of course, you're more than welcome to join me."

This muthafucka is playing too many games. I roll my eyes and give him my back.

"Just thought I'd ask." He laughs as he steps into the shower.

I don't believe this shit. I walk backward to the bathroom door and close it.

"Chicken!" he barks before his rumble of laughter comes through the door.

I roll my eyes. Alone in his office, I glance around and notice how pristine and orderly everything is.

I take a seat on the leather couch and wait. Outside the door, I hear a steady clack of high heels walking up the stairs. A few seconds later, a very curvaceous woman with model looks walks into the office. When she spots me, she stops.

"Oh." She tosses a look at the closed bathroom door. "I didn't know that, uh . . . Okay. I'll leave these on Diesel's desk." She walks over and drops off some paperwork.

I flash a smile, but keep my mouth shut.

"Don't I know you?" She cocks her head. "You're the singer, aren't you?"

"Yes. How are you? I'm Cleo." I stand and offer her my hand.

She nods, but keeps me hanging. "You're good."

"Thank you." I lower my hand while she continues to assess me.

The woman glances at the door again.

"He's taking a shower."

"I can see that."

She's jumping to the wrong conclusion. "I'm waiting for my check."

The woman lifts an amused brow.

"For performing last night."

"Oh?" Her other eyebrow rises up. "There must be some misunderstanding. Diesel wrote a check to your manager a few days ago. A, uh, Kalief something. Is that not your manager?"

"Are you sure?"

"Positive." She folds her arms. "I was there when he wrote it."

What the hell? "Do you work here?"

"Yes. I'm in charge of the girls."

"Ahh." Something tells me that she doesn't mean the waitresses and the dancers.

"See you around," she says and then exits the office without ever introducing herself.

Okay.

The shower shuts off. A few seconds later, Diesel returns to the office with a towel still wrapped around his chiseled hips.

"Good. You're still here." He grins at me.

"What kind of fucking game are you playing?"

"Excuse me?"

"Did you or did you not already pay Kalief for the band's performance?"

"Did I?" He pretends to think it over.

"You're too much. I'm out of here." I spin and head for the door.

"C'mon. C'mon. Don't be like that." He races to catch up with me; grabs my hand before I slip out the door.

"Don't touch me!" Angry, I snatch it back. "I don't know what kind of game you're playing, but I'm not fucking interested. In fact, you need to find yourself another singer."

"Whoa. Whoa." He jumps in front of me. "You're right. You're right. I'm sorry. I shouldn't have lied to you."

I try to get past him, but he blocks me at every turn. "Move!"

"Not until you say that you accept my apology."

Tired of his shit, I shove him as hard as I can.

He stumbles back, letting go of his towel.

It's impossible to avoid seeing the anaconda between his legs. I gasp and then race the fuck out of there.

"Cleo! Cleo!"

21

Shariffa

"Why in the fuck did you bring me here?" I ask as we pull up to a new crib in West Memphis. "I thought that you were taking me back home." I turn my nose up at the place.

Lynch cocks his head and gives me a flat look. "You know that I can't do that. Shit is still hot."

"So the fuck what? I have a psycho bitch stalking me out here. You're going to leave me to fend for my damn self?"

"Nah. I didn't say that shit. I'm going to assign a couple of my most trusted soldiers to stay out here and keep an eye out for you."

"Fuck that shit. *You're* supposed to be my nigga. You're supposed to protect me. Why the fuck can't I be with you?"

"C'mon, Shariffa. We've already been over this shit. You already know the situation back at the crib. I can't take you back there."

My mouth falls open. I can't believe the shit I'm hearing. "You're the muthafucka boss. You can do what the fuck you wanna do. You tell them purple niggas what's up and that be that. You ain't gotta ask their asses for permission."

He sighs and rolls his eyes like I'm getting on his fucking nerves or some shit. "You know that things are more complicated than that. My people think you brought all this heat on yourself and they don't see any fucking reason why they gotta get involved in your bullshit."

"You mean *our* people," I correct him. "They are involved because they are supposed to be our family. And on the streets, family takes care of family. That's the whole fucking point."

"Goddamn it, Shariffa. Why can't you do what the fuck I tell you to do? Why the fuck do you always make shit so damn complicated? You know why your situation is different. Why the hell are you forcing me to say it? Your shit is suspect because your flag ain't always been the right fucking color. And when you finally get the fuck out of your muthafuckin' feelings, you'll recognize the damn truth in what I'm telling you."

"I'm your fucking wife. How long do you fucking plan to hide me out here?"

Instead of answering me, he clamps his mouth shut.

"You don't fuckin' know, do you?"

"Shariffa, I—"

"I don't believe what the fuck I'm hearing." I stare at him as if it's the first time I've ever seen his ass. True. I've always had to push his ass to seize power and respect, but this shit is ridiculous. "You can't stash me out here forever."

"It's not going to be forever. I promise."

I want to believe him, but I feel like there is some shit that he's not telling me.

"C'mon, baby." He stretches his arm out to brush a curl of my hair behind my ear. "Trust me."

I shrink away from his touch. He may look like a big, strong man, but he's acting like a little boy. Not for the first time, but I miss being with a nigga like Python. He ran a tight ship—and no one dared to question his ass. His word was law. Same shit with the fucking Vice Lords. I can't imagine Fat Ace or Lucifer having to put up with the kind of bullshit I'm putting up with now. More and more I'm starting to see that the Grape Street Crips are nothing but toy soldiers playing at being in the game. I gotta figure out some fucking way to get this shit back on track, but how in the hell am I going to do that with this fucking crew?

"Hey. Look at me, ma," Lynch instructs. When I refuse, he leans over and cups my chin and forces me to look at him. "I need for you to trust me on this, Shariffa. I'm going to fix this shit. I need for you to give me a little bit more time. Can you do that shit for me, ma?"

"You ask like I have a fucking choice."

Lynch heaves out a deep sigh as his hand falls away from my chin. He's run out of fuckin' shit to say—and I'm fuckin' glad. There's not enough room in this vehicle to shovel more bullshit. "C'mon. Let's go inside and get you situated."

This time, he doesn't wait for me to respond before he opens his door and climbs out of the Range Rover.

"Can we go in too, momma?" Marcel asks.

I glance in the backseat where my boys' excited faces beam back at me. "I don't know. You'll have to ask your dad." I turn and open my door.

"Daddy! Daddy!" they shout until they gain Lynch's attention.

My nerves are frayed like a muthafucka so I march ahead into my new crib—or prison. I immediately wonder what bitch Lynch kept stashed up in this place, because I don't remember his ass ever mentioning having a place out here in this neck of the woods. The moment I walk in the door, my suspicion heightens once I pick up the subtle floral scent wafting throughout the place. As much as I stay on Lynch about his funky drawers and shoes he likes to leave all over the house, I know damn well his ass wouldn't know what the fuck a can of Febreze looks like.

"Mommy, Mommy. Daddy said that we can stay with you for a few hours," Marcel shouts.

They both wrap their small arms around my legs and squeeze so hard that I nearly topple over.

"Careful, you two." Lynch laughs. "You don't want Momma falling."

My smile melts off my face. "A *few* hours? Why in the fuck can't they stay with me?"

He huffs and then gives me a scalding look like my ass is a child or some shit. "You know that they have school and shit. Why are you asking me dumb shit?"

"Maybe because this whole thing is dumb. You kicked me out of my house and I'm not supposed to feel some kind of way about it? Where they do that at?"

"I'm tired of arguing with you, ma. You want my word to be law? Fine. You keep your ass right here like I fucking said and I don't fucking want to talk about it no more."

"I'm saying—"

"Shut the fuck up," he shouts so loud that the kids jump.

Julez starts crying.

"Are you happy now?" I kneel down and comfort my son until he stops crying.

Lynch paces back and forth like his ass is the one that's being locked in a cage.

Right now I can't stand his ass. It's clear that I'm going to have to take matters into my own hands. In order for me to go back home, I'm going to have to get rid of Lucifer. I swear that bitch isn't going to see my ass coming.

22

Hydeya

"**D**amn. People are dropping like flies out here," Fowler says, shaking his head as the forensic and paramedic teams arrive at Josephine Holmes's residence. "What're the odds that this shooting is related to the one at the church?"

Frustrated, I run my hands through my hair while trying to hazard a guess. "I don't know. Anything is possible." Which is true. Everyone on Shotgun Row is milling around in the streets. I catch a few of them questioning whether Fowler and I rolled in the older lady's crib and shot her ourselves.

Luckily there's enough people out here to set them straight before we have a riot on our hands.

"I don't know what to think," I tell him, though my gaze drifts across the street to Momma Peaches's house. I also don't want to believe that this would have anything to do with my father returning to the neighborhood. "But neighbors killed on the same day? It's a bit too coincidental." I glance over my shoulder back to Momma Peaches's crib.

"Let's split up and question the neighbors. The faster we get started the faster we can get this damn thing over with."

"Why? We already know what everyone is going to say."

"*I didn't hear shit or see shit,*" we say in unison.

As sad as that fact is, we start with the people, who are

watching our every move with hostile eyes. Sure enough. One by one, they repeat the same line of being blind and deaf. After a while, they walk away from us before we can fix our mouths to ask them a question. This part of the job is always heartbreaking.

I understand the mistrust. I'm a cop and I don't trust half the force. Racism, excessive force, deep-seated corruption—sometimes it feels as if I left one gang to join another one. This one is a lot more powerful than the Gangster Disciples.

By the time the last person on the scene flips me the bird, the sun is setting and my stomach is growling like a sonofabitch. "Shit. It's been a long damn day."

"Tell me about it," Fowler grumbles, slapping his steno pad closed. "How about that drink? You game?"

Before I can respond, a black '68 Dodge Charger rumbles down the street, snatching everyone's attention.

"It's him," a few excited teenagers say, pointing.

I recognize the car instantly. Isaac must have gotten his baby out of storage. When the car finally rumbles to a stop in front of his place, a crowd quickly gathers around him like he is an NFL star.

"Daddy's home," Fowler says.

I cut him a look to let him know that his joke isn't funny.

"Do you want to talk to him together or . . . ?"

"Nah. I got this," I tell him. "You can go on back to the station. I'll catch a ride back."

"Are you sure? I can hang out in the car."

"I'm sure," I tell him and stroll across the street. Fowler's heavy gaze follows me, probably wondering whether he should follow the order or not.

Isaac sees me approaching. There's a lifetime of pain, hurt, and mistrust flowing between us. Pain that neither of us knows what to do with anymore. We're two bad actors, waltzing around a stage, praying for a director to yell *"Cut."* But I still have a job to do.

"Hello, Mr. Goodson," I say formally in front of the crowd. "Do you mind if I come in and ask you a few questions?"

He shrugs his big shoulders. "Suit yourself." He turns and weaves his way through the crowd, which is shouting, "Welcome back, Isaac." And "Sorry about Momma Peaches."

If any of the shit is getting to him, it doesn't show.

"What's going on across the street?" he asks after we enter the house.

"You don't know?"

He faces me with a lifted brow. "Should I?"

There's no point in trying to read his sincerity because he could convince a pack of nuns that he's Jesus reincarnated if he put his mind to it. "Your neighbor Josephine Holmes had the back of her head blown off today."

"Josie?" He looks up toward the front window where he can see the yellow tape wrapped around the house. "What happened?"

"You tell me."

His eyes snap back to me. "You gotta be kidding me. You can't possibly think that I had something to do with it. I was down at the damn morgue, identifying my wife's body!" He stepped back and quickly grabbed hold of his anger. "Sorry. I shouldn't have shouted."

"That's okay. I . . . shouldn't have made the insinuation. It's just that a lot of shit has gone down on your first day back home." I swallow hard before adding, "I'm sorry for what happened to Maybelline. I know how much you were looking forward to you two having a fresh start."

He nods and then works his jaw for a few seconds, like he's having a hard time spitting out the words. When he looks up, his eyes are wet. "Thanks. I know that you never really cared too much for her, but—she really was a good woman. I didn't always do right by her. In fact, I did a lot of shit I wish I could take back." He hangs his head for a second so that he can gain control of his emotions again. "I wish I could've been a better man for her."

What about being a better man for me and my mom?

He looks up as if hearing my thoughts. "Sorry. I haven't been much good for any of the women in my life."

It's a backhanded apology, but I'll accept it. "What are you going to do?"

"Scrape up the money to put her in the ground, I guess. Give her a proper send-off." He walks over to a nearby chair and sits. "Have the police found her killer?"

"We're working on it. I'm sure we'll find him." Python jumps to the front of my mind. "I have a question for you."

"Shoot."

"You probably still have a few eyes and ears out here on the streets. You heard anything about where Maybelline's nephew, Terrell, may be hiding out?"

Isaac gives me a perplexed look. "Terrell is dead."

"No. I saw him this morning, right after I dropped you off, in fact. Chased him all over town and made the noontime news."

"Hmph." He gives me a half smile. "I still can't get over you being a cop."

"Captain," I correct him.

He nods, evaluating me. "You know what they say: Once you're in the Folks Nation you never really truly leave."

"So all that yack about you turning over a new leaf was bullshit?"

"Nah. Nah, princess. I'm keeping it one hundred. My bad-boy days are well behind me."

"You know that there's another saying: You can't teach an old dog new tricks."

Our gazes connect again. I make sure that he can read in my eyes that I'm not buying his bullshit—and that I'm going to be watching him.

"You don't believe that a man can change?"

"Men—yes. Snakes—no."

His head rears back at my blunt talk. He's never liked being challenged.

I stand and wait for the spiel about how he found himself, or better yet—found God or Allah in prison. He's going to give up this and that and blah, blah, blah. The convict anthem.

Isaac refuses to allow me to bait him into an argument. "You have every right not to believe me. All I can do is show you. You know, I spent ten years in that hellhole, thinking about the day my ass would get out and set shit right. In time, maybe you and your mother will find it in your heart to forgive me."

He walks toward me, but I instinctively back up.

"Sorry," he says. "I didn't mean to—"

"It's all right." I wave the shit off. "Back to Terrell. If you hear something, you'll call me, right?"

Isaac laughs. "I may have changed my ways, but that doesn't mean that I'm taking up snitching to police—not even to my daughter."

"All right. Well . . ." I glance at my watchless arm. "I gotta go. I have a lot I have to take care of."

His head bobs in understanding again while we finish out this bad acting scene. "Yeah. Well . . . thanks again for coming by."

"Not a problem." I start backing toward the front door. "I'll catch up with you later."

"You got it. I still got that rain check. You, me, and your white boy."

"His name is Drake."

"Right. Drake." He grimaces. "I look forward to meeting your husband."

I roll my eyes and exit the house. Still standing next to his parked car in front of the house is Fowler.

"What can I say?" Fowler grins. "I have a hard time obeying orders from female authority figures."

I should be pissed, but I'm actually glad that he stayed back. "You don't say." I walk out to the car and climb in on the passenger side. "Remind me when we get back to the station to write your ass up about that."

Fowler laughs and starts up the car.

23

LeShelle

"Hold still," I tell Python as I dig around in his thigh in the center of the living room, trying to remove the second bullet. I've played surgeon on these types of wounds for him so many times that it's almost second nature, but I'm having a hard time getting one of his wounds to stop bleeding. "I think this bullet shattered," I tell him worriedly.

"LeShelle, move your head. I can't see the television," Python complains.

I give him the are-you-fucking-kidding-me stare down, but he ignores that shit too. He's waiting for a newsperson to tell him something about the church shooting, but all any of them seem to care about is how he managed to elude the cops in two different states.

"Where's my fuckin' cell phone? What's taking Diesel so fucking long to call?"

There's no telling with that muthafucka. "Python, calm down. You're getting yourself worked up again." I pour another generous amount of peroxide around his thigh and go back to picking out chipped pieces of lead. After another thirty minutes pass, I voice my fears. "Maybe you should go see a doctor about this."

"Shhh. Shhh. Shhh. Here it is." He punches up the volume on the television.

"A community is in mourning after an elderly woman was found shot dead inside the Power of Prayer Baptist Church located off the 2400 block of Florida Street and East McLemore. The shooting happened this morning, not far from where this morning's police chase began. Police report the victim was pronounced dead at the scene."

Python and I both stop breathing.

I turn around from hovering over his thigh to face the television. *Did I hear that right?* Maybe they are reporting on a different church shooting? I know that it's highly unlikely, but my mind clings to the possibility.

Momma Peaches is dead—again.

Python completely loses his shit. He jumps up and starts punching the walls again. The place is already starting to look like a demolition crew has run through this muthafucka.

I rub his back, searching for the right words to say. In truth, I'm feeling some kind of way my damn self. Momma Peaches was tough OG. After all the shit she went through to now have to deal with this bullshit? The shit ain't right.

"I shouldn't have left her," Python croaks in regret.

"That shit wouldn't have changed nothing."

Bang! Bang! Bang!

"Who the fuck?"

Python struggles to stand.

I touch his shoulder and tell him, "I got it," before grabbing his gat from the floor and checking to see who it is. Ain't nobody supposed to be popping up at this bitch. Is it the police? The FBI? The TBI? If it's a Jehovah's Witness, they asses is about to get a face full of lead. After creeping up to the door, I look out through the peephole to see Diesel's shady ass standing there.

"Fuck. It's your damn cousin," I tell Python.

"Hurry up and let him in."

Rolling my eyes, I snatch open the door.

"Hey, Shelle," Diesel says, quickly shouldering his way through the door.

Shelle? Muthafucka, you don't know me like that. I peer out
the door to make sure that he's alone. I don't see nobody, but
remain on high alert, safety off. I trust this nigga about as much
as I trust my own damn sister.

"Why the fuck?" Python demands. "What happened? The
news got me fucked up."

Diesel pulls in a breath, but I note that he's careful in not
meeting Python's gaze. *Bad news—or this nigga is about to start
lying?*

"Sorry, cuz," Diesel says. "It wasn't but a minute after you
rushed out of the door before she was gone. There was nothing I could do."

Python drops and shakes his head. "Those dirty muthafuckas!" Pain and determination harden his resolve. "Blood or
no blood, that nigga got to pay for this shit."

Diesel bobs his head in agreement. "You know I'm here
for you, cuz. What the fuck you need, I got you."

"What I need is to see those niggas about this shit. Put the
call out to our top crew. I want to know where that cockroach
is at all times. I don't want his ass feeling safe at no time. That
includes them being locked down over on their turf on Ruby
Cove. You feel me?" Waves of sweat roll down Python's face
while his murderous gaze is consumed with pain.

"I definitely feel you." Diesel's pleased smile expands across
his face. "Welcome back, cuz. We're gonna take back these
fucking streets. No doubt." His gaze finally lowers to Python's
thighs and the mess of bloody towels littering the floor.

"You good, cuz. Do I need to send you one of my people
to suture you up?"

"Nah. I got him," I say, not wanting to take even a damn
glass of water from this nigga. I ain't missing how he's injecting
his ass into all our business. That whole *take back* bullshit. When
the fuck is this muthafucka going back to the A?

Diesel ignores me to look at Python.

"I'm good," Python tells him, placing a hand on my shoulder. "My old lady knows what she's doing."

Despite the vote of confidence, Diesel looks dubious.

Python dismisses the shit with his leg and says, "I don't understand why that grimy nigga would do something like that. If Fat Ace didn't want anything to do with his real fam, he didn't have to agree to the meeting."

I smother a smile. He's finally gone back to calling Mason by his street name.

"Fuck that muthafucka," Diesel says, shrugging. "We now know that we have to take him and his crew out."

There's that we *shit again.*

"Did she at least say anything before the emergency responders got there? Any clue to why the muthafucka did it?"

Diesel nods. "No, but she made me promise her something."

Python perks up. "What's that?"

"She wants us to get that muthafucka back."

I detect a false note in Diesel's voice—but his expression remains cool as ice. *Why the fuck is this nigga lying?*

"Done deal." Python and Diesel smack palms and bump shoulders to seal the deal. I see traces of my old man back. For that shit, I smile up at Diesel.

He stares back like I'm something nasty stuck on his shoe.

Qiana. How could I forget? This nigga knows my secret, and everything in his face tells me he's waiting for the right moment to get rid of my ass. *Tomorrow night,* I remind myself. Hack's Crossing. I'll get rid of Qiana *and* that damn baby.

24

Ta'Shara

I took the first two pills to calm my nerves. I take the next four to go numb. I can't stand the pain in my broken heart right now. I can't. I hate that this shit makes me weak. I'm beyond tired of feeling like a victim. A victim of life, love, and circumstances beyond my control. I should've listened to Reggie:

"Little girls like you drift in and out of my college classroom every year. Bright eyed and bushy tailed, and despite all the good-looking, intelligent brothers sitting right next to you in class, deep down you all want a thug. Some nigga that can't keep his pants up, body tatted, and brags about the fat knot of cash in his pants. Those guys think the money in their pocket makes them men and the guns they tuck at their backs make them even bigger men. Big men like your boy Profit are always being zipped up in body bags on the nightly news. If a few bullets don't get him, he is thrown in the back of one of the tax payers' patrol cars. He'll spend his youth behind bars.

"Of course, he'll ask you to wait for him on the outside. You with I don't know how many babies he'll put on you and his other women. And you'll try. But it gets hard being a single mother without a high school diploma or college degree. You won't find anyone who will pay a decent wage, so you will turn to the game too. You'll get your own knot of cash and a gun.

"Suddenly, you are a gangsta diva until a bullet or jail claims you too."

"That's not us. That will never be us," I said.

"No. Of course not. Your love is going to turn your gangster into Prince Charming and you'll ride off into that fairy-tale bullshit that you keep telling yourself."

But it *was* the kind of bullshit that I kept telling myself. I said that Profit and I were different until I fucking believed the shit. Now what am I going to do?

Closing my eyes, I lower my head beneath the steady stream from the showerhead. The hot water turned cold ten minutes ago and I'm barely aware that I'm turning into a human Popsicle. On the other hand, I prefer to freeze to death than go back out there and face Profit again.

For the first time in my life, I understand the concept of a "crime of passion" because I keep replaying seeing Profit kissing Lucifer, but instead of running back to our crib to put a gun in my mouth, I storm into that house and blow holes into both of them. Only then could they feel even the smallest bit of what I'm feeling right now.

I shiver while my fingers turn into soft prunes. It's time to step out of the shower and face my new reality. The drugs have kicked in because I'm moving in slow motion. My thoughts even sound drunk in my head. Small ripples of euphoria wash over me and I smile and ride the wave. For no reason at all, I hum to myself. I can get used to this feeling. When I was in the hospital, I hated being drugged up. Now . . . not so much.

I towel off, but then become fascinated by the Egyptian cotton. I don't remember it being so soft. It's amazing. After I finish drying off, I run the brush through my hair. That fascinates me too. At one point, it becomes difficult to remain on my feet. The floor keeps tilting from one side to the other.

Dizzy, I pop a squat on the toilet—only I did it too quick and become nauseated.

Damn. That shit is strong.

I chuckle—and then I can't stop.

Knock. Knock. Knock.

"Ta'Shara, are you all right in there?" Profit asks through the door. He twists the knob, but it's locked.

I laugh. *Serves him right.*

Knock. Knock. Knock.

"Baby? You've been in there for a while. We're going to have to get going."

Go away! "I'm coming," I shout back.

Silence. However, he doesn't walk away from the door.

"I said go!" I lean forward to smack my hand against the door and almost fall off the toilet seat.

"All right. I'll wait for you in the living room." He walks away.

I roll my eyes. "Silly rabbit. Trix are for kids." I have no idea what I mean by that, but it makes me giggle. But then the kiss replays and my eyes wet up.

When it comes down to it, Profit isn't any different than the rest of these niggas out here. That realization makes me feel so alone. I pull my gaze from the door to the mirror. The woman staring back at me is a complete stranger. Where did she come from? How did she get here?

A series of memories flash in my head. The night I was raped and branded like an animal. The vision of Profit being beaten and shot seventeen times. My descent into madness, my attempt to murder LeShelle. The ugly fight with my foster parents. The sight of their house burning to the ground. And the sound of LeShelle's laughter as she peeled off into the night. The murder of that store clerk. And lastly, Profit kissing Lucifer.

There's only so much shit that a bitch can take. As soon as I find a place, I'm out of this bitch.

I backhand my tears, and then push myself back up onto

my feet and, on rubbery legs, exit the bathroom. The black dress that I wore to my foster parents' funeral lays on the bed, ready to be worn to another funeral. I weave over to it, but I must've passed out for a few minutes because when I wake, Profit is rocking my arm, trying to get me to get up.

"Hey, baby. Wake up. Wake up."

I groan and lift my head.

"Here. I made coffee. Drink this."

"Coffee?" When I struggle to sit up, he helps me out.

"What did you take?"

I shrug off his touch. "Why do you care?"

He looks hurt by the question. "Of course I care."

He puts on his best puppy-dog expression, like that shit is going to fix something.

"Whatever."

"Don't you want to eat something before we head out?"

"I'm not hungry." As soon as I say the words, my stomach growls like it's filled with a pack of lions.

Profit's shoulders collapse. "Look, T. You have every right to be pissed at me right now. I fucked up and I'm sorry. The shit will never *ever* happen again."

Liar. How in the hell does he think that I can ever trust him again?

"But, baby, can we deal with this situation later? I got to bury my mom today—and this shit hurts like a muthafucka. Please. I know you understand."

I do understand. That's what makes this shit so fucked up.

After a long pause, he offers me an out. "Look. I'll understand if you don't want to go to the funeral. After all, you really didn't get a chance to get to know her."

No. That shit ain't right. I swallow my anger, but it's bitter going down. "I'll go."

Relief floods his face. "Really?"

I nod and that's all I'm willing to give him.

He sees that I'm not interested in continuing the conversation and moves away from me. "Okay. I'll let you finish getting dressed."

Instead of answering, I sip my coffee until he exits the bedroom. Then I slump in relief. Last night was the first time we slept in different rooms in this house. I took the bed while he lay on the couch. It was horrible—and the closest thing to drowning in a sea of loneliness.

Despite the number of pills I popped, sleep eluded me. I kept wondering whether he was sleeping—and if he was, who was he dreaming about?

The coffee turns into swill in my gut. I put it aside and force myself to get dressed. More than once Profit knocks on the bedroom door to see whether I'm ready. I try to pick up speed, but the drugs coursing through my body make it impossible.

By the time I leave the bedroom, Profit's irritation has left splotches all over his face—but he's not going to risk saying anything to me. He's also in the same suit he wore to Tracee and Reggie's funeral. A wave of déjà vu washes over me. Hopefully, we can get through this day without being arrested.

"Ready?" he asks.

"Yeah." He walks over to the door and opens it for me. For a brief moment, his hand brushes against my back—and I pretend not to welcome his touch. It's not fair that my body still responds to him. He no longer has the right.

I stiffen my resolve as he escorts me through the rain with an umbrella over my head, to the car. Once inside, Profit hesitates to start the engine. I glance over at him to see what's the holdup. There's a series of emotions playing on his face.

Without thinking, I reach over and touch his hand.

Surprised, he looks over at me.

"It's going to be okay," I say, referring to him getting through this day—but I think he misunderstands and smiles. I don't have the energy to clarify. Like him, I want to get through this day. I'll worry about moving out tomorrow.

25

Lucifer

Barbara Ann Lewis
December 3, 1961–January 28, 2012

Less than twenty-four hours after her passing, Dribbles is lowered into the ground. It's a small service, the way she would've wanted it. However, we couldn't have held it on a worse day. The sky is a grayish black and the heavy rain is freezing.

Mason is taking it hard. He hasn't eaten or slept, nor has he stopped blaming himself. "You can't change the past," he keeps mumbling. I know what he means. Whatever small chance that existed for him and his brother Python to reconcile is officially over. They will be enemies until the day they die. It's a shame, but I understand and will support my man in his decision. There will be no peace in the streets until he avenges his mother's death.

In the hours after the shooting, Mason's description of the man who'd actually shot Dribbles matched only one person: Diesel Carver.

My blood turned cold when I heard the name. Everybody in the South knows that nigga. He has amassed as much power as a real American cartel. The fact that he's even here is a reason to worry.

But Mason isn't worried. He's determined. Sadly, I know what that feels like. There isn't a day that goes by that I don't have my own homicidal fantasy about the last two grimy Crippette bitches who killed my brother Bishop. I promised Mason that I'd put my hunt on hold until I deliver the baby—but I'll get Shariffa and Trigger. They can bet money on that shit.

" 'In sure and certain hope of the resurrection to eternal life through our Lord,' " the pastor says, "we commit Barbara Ann Lewis to the ground. 'Earth to earth, ashes to ashes, dust to dust . . .' "

Mason's jaw clenches before he steps forward and shovels in one patch of dirt on top of his mother's casket. When he steps back, he hands the shovel over to Profit. When he steps forward to do the same thing, I catch Ta'Shara eyeballing the shit out of me.

Good Lord. As if I don't have enough problems.

I throw up a brick wall and tune the bitch out. Profit needs to handle that situation. Shit like this is the main reason why I don't hang with females: too much bullshit over little shit.

Mason moves to stand before the casket while pulling out the folded piece of paper that he spent all night writing and rewriting. However, he takes one look at the words scratched out on the page and then slowly puts it away. "There are no words that really describe my relationship with the woman who saved my life. Her blood may not run through me, but she was my mother—in every sense of the word. She may not have been perfect, but she truly tried to do the best that she could, given the circumstances. She really was a wonderful woman, though at times, she didn't believe it. There have been more times than I care to count where I had to take care of her. The times I had to pull the needle out of her arm or beat some brothah up for jacking her up—and never mind. No matter what the people said or the names they called her, I loved her. And I loved her and my pop, Smokestack, even more when they gave me a little brother." He looks up and winks at Profit. "It felt good, having him under my wing, showing him how to navigate through these mean streets. I say all of that to say—" He pauses to regain control of his emotions. "To say, that the one lesson that I've learned in life is that blood doesn't make you family. Love does."

The brothers share a smile.

"I don't hold out too much hope that there's a God. But if there is one, and there is a heaven, I hope that they look past my mother's circumstances and look into her heart—because there is no one with a bigger heart than Barbara Ann Lewis. One of her last acts was to try to right something that . . . that should've been left alone. There was a reason that she showed up at my real mother's house the day that she did. She saved me. Without her, I probably wouldn't be here. What happened at that church . . . should have never happened. We should've never gone." He wrings his hands for a while. "I'll miss her. And I'm going to set shit straight."

Mason looks over at me. "We're going to set shit straight."

I nod, letting him know that I'm down for however he wants to handle this vendetta, but in my heart, I can't help but feel remorse for how this whole thing turned out. The streets are going to get bloodier and I don't see how anyone can stop it.

26

LeShelle

I make it down to Club Diesel with a prepared speech scrolling through my head. I already know before walking in this bitch that I'm going to be engaging in the world championship of mind games. As far as I can tell, Diesel is the type of nigga that is always four chess moves ahead of the closest competitor. That shit worries the fuck out of me, especially since he could've outed my ass to Python the other night. The fact that he didn't tells me that there's a chance to negotiate. But what in the fuck could he possibly want?

It's four o'clock when Avonte, one of my trusted Queen Gs, pulls up to the back door. People are filtering in and out, getting ready for tonight's crowd. We slip inside as a stock boy exits the building with large empty liquor boxes. Winding our way through the back, I'm once again impressed with what Diesel has been able to throw together in such a short time. This joint is nothing like the Pink Monkey, which Python used to own. Besides, it being the place where I met Python, I never really cared too much for the place. Too many drunk niggas and too many pussies vying to get on. In retrospect, the Vice Lords did my ass a favor by blowing that shit up.

Exiting out of the back room, I hear a band practicing on

the stage. As I draw near, I'm surprised to see Cleo singing a Mary J. classic. I stop near one of the tables, stunned by the raw power of the girl's voice. By the time she's halfway through the song, the staff who were scrubbing tables and sweeping the floor have all stopped to listen. There is also another captivated fan: Diesel.

I watch him, watching her. There is no mistaking the desire written all over his face. Jealousy pricks my skin, which makes no sense. Despite his good looks, I can't stand this muthafucka. Game recognizes game. Cleo ends her set and the skeleton crew applauds, including Diesel. Hell. He even throws in a whistle too.

To my surprise, annoyance flashes across her face before she turns away. In the next second our gazes collide. Her annoyance transforms into anger. *Does this bitch know?*

Cleo cuts her eyes away to speak to her band.

I review what happened. I had my people imply that Essence's death was dealt at the hands of Lucifer. Has the truth gotten back to her? It's possible. I did blaze the bitch up in broad daylight with a gas station full of witnesses. Instead of being concerned, I shrug the shit off. It ain't like Cleo's ass is somebody. Yes. Technically, she's a Queen G, but I can't remember the last time the girl put in any work. The girl is a fucking nobody and I've already wasted two minutes thinking about her ass.

Returning my attention to Diesel, I cross over to his booth. When I spot Cleo's crackhead boyfriend, skinning and grinning in Diesel's face, I stand back and wait for the men to finish their conversation.

Diesel listens to Kalief's long-winded ass, looking bored as shit. Yet at the same time he seems to be evaluating the man. A few minutes later, my ass is bored. I know Diesel sees me over here, waiting to talk to him, but he doesn't appear to be in any hurry to finish up his conversation.

I huff and tap my foot. The blatant disrespect sets my blood boiling.

Damn. Even Avonte stays coughing and looking at her watch.

After five more minutes, my patience snaps and I march over and pop Kalief on the shoulder. "Get lost."

Kalief's head snaps up with an attitude, but once he recognizes me, he apologizes. "Oh hey, LeShelle. I didn't . . . how are you doing?"

"More moving and less talking," I tell him.

"Yeah. Yeah. I'm sorry." He glances back at Diesel. "I guess we can finish this conversation later?"

Diesel doesn't respond and Kalief is left to scamper off like a rat.

"Mind if I sit?" I ask, but drop into the seat without waiting for his response.

Diesel is still watching Kalief. "What the fuck does she see in him?"

"Who?" I follow his gaze and make the connection. "Cleo?"

He exhales a long breath and then slowly shifts his attention over to me. Unfortunately, he still looks bored. "To what do I owe this pleasure?"

"I need a few minutes of your time."

He leans back and rubs his legs. "Sure." He waves to a chick behind one of the bars. "Would you like something to drink?"

"Henny on the rocks."

When the chick arrives at our table, Diesel relays my order.

"Now that that's out of the way." His boredom deepens. "Talk."

"Okay. I'll get right to the point. What is your angle?"

"My angle?"

"Don't play me. We're both far from dumb. Why are you still here? Python is not going to hand you his throne. He's back in the game and he's in it to win it. So why don't you go back to your empire in Atlanta?"

"Atlanta. Miami. D.C. Richmond. St. Louis," he ticks off. "My empire spans a lot of places and a lot of businesses. Memphis is hardly a place one would install a throne."

"Then kick rocks," I counter. "If we ain't no damn body, why stay?"

"I came because I was invited and my cousin asked me for help."

"Now I'm uninviting you."

Amusement finally replaces his boredom. "I don't think that's quite how this works."

"Then what will it take to get you to leave?"

"Now why would I want to leave? I just opened this great club. I stand to make a lot of money. And money makes my dick hard. Do you want to feel?"

I clamp my mouth shut to prevent the yes from flying out of my mouth. Once the moment passes, I respond with a more poised, "I'll take your word for it."

The bartender chick returns with my drink. "Anything else?"

"I'm good," I say.

Diesel waves her off and then leans farther back in his seat. "I like Memphis. It's a nice, snazzy city. And a brothah like me is always looking to diversify."

"I don't trust you," I tell him, reaching for my drink.

He laughs. "*You* don't trust *me*? That's rich."

"Meaning?"

"Meaning, it's kind of like a pot calling the kettle black."

Our gazes battle each other from across the table.

"You aren't going to ask me?" he taunts. "Or do you already know what I'm talking about?"

With my heart hammering inside of my chest, I ask, "What are you talking about?"

Diesel's smile blooms wider. "I'm talking about your little secret; only, it's not too little. Is it?"

"Spit it out," I say. "You're dying to say her name."

"I have two names. Qiana Barrett and Yolanda Terry."

Though I was bracing myself, my heart still bottoms out.

"You can't imagine my surprise when Qiana told me about y'all's deal. Scandalous. Queen Gs and Flowers crossing color lines and striking deals? The next thing you know, cats and dogs will be fucking together." He snaps his fingers. "The only thing is, I don't really give a fuck about you tampon soldiers offing one another, *but* this one bitch was carrying my cuzzo's seed. She was due any day. That's some cold shit."

"What do you want?"

"Now my cuz may not earn no father of the year awards, but blood is blood."

"Blood is overrated." I gulp down more of my drink.

"Well, at least you're not going to insult me by denying the charge."

"I don't have to deny it. You don't have any proof. Python isn't going to take the word of some wilted Flower on the wrong side of the tracks."

"Are you sure about that?" He sits up while his smile keeps creeping wider.

"Positive."

"Hmph. Then it sounds like you don't have anything to worry about."

A migraine hammers my temples while my hands grow slick with sweat.

Diesel cocks his head. "What's the matter? You don't look so good."

"You don't want to do this," I warn. "You're fucking with the wrong bitch."

He lowers his arms from the back of the booth and leans toward me. "Don't I?"

With nothing else to say, I drain the rest of my drink and climb out of the booth.

"Leaving so soon?"

"Fuck you."

"Aww. Don't be like that. We're family. Remember?"

I signal to Avonte from across the club and then march out of the club, all the while flashing him the finger. *I have to get rid of Qiana and that damn baby. Now!*

27

Cleo

I watch LeShelle storm out of Club Diesel, feeling like a fucking punk. That evil bitch killed my sister and she marches around town without a care in the fucking world. The shit isn't fair.

"Are we going again?"

I jump. "Huh? What?"

Practice," Joe asks. "If we're taking a break right now, I have an errand I have to take care of."

"Yeah. Sure. Let's break for an hour," I tell him and then stroll off the stage. It was getting a little uncomfortable performing in front of Diesel anyway.

I wish I could quit this job, but since Kalief has already spent the money, I have no choice but to fulfill the one-month contract.

On top of that stunt Diesel pulled in his office, I keep wondering about Momma Peaches's shooting. I have yet to see any proof that he even gives a damn about her death. At the same time I can't believe that he would actually have anything to do with the shooting. After all, she's his aunt.

"Sounding good, baby." Kalief cheeses at me the second I slip off the stage.

I swallow back my annoyance as he wraps his arms around

me. However, when I pull back, I peep the perspiration beading his forehead. I glance in his eyes and see that they're dilated.

Fuck. He's high.

Kalief sniffs and wipes his nose. "Hey. You got a few minutes? I need to talk to you."

Sighing, I already know that I'm not going to like whatever he's got to say. "What is it, Kalief?"

He fidgets around on his feet while he tries on a different smile. "Look. I know that this is going to sound crazy, but don't say no until you hear me out."

"No," I say, shutting him down.

He jams his fists on his hips. "I haven't told you what it is yet."

"You don't have to. I know you—and the answer is no."

Kalief's fake jovial smile evaporates. "C'mon, Cleo. I need you to be serious."

"I was being serious," I tell him. "Whatever it is, my answer is no." I step around him, but he snatches my wrist. When I try to jerk free his grip tightens.

"Let go," I hiss.

"I'm not finished talking with you."

We wrestle over my arm for a few seconds before I give in.

"All right. What is it?" I snap. The sooner I let him say his piece, the sooner I can end this.

"I . . . I need for you to go out with Diesel Carver," he says.

I wait for the punch line. When it's clear that there isn't one, I burst out laughing.

"I'm not joking," he says. "I need for you to do this."

"What? Why?"

He works his mouth, but no words come out.

Something is up. I square back around to stare at him. "What aren't you telling me? What did you do?"

He continues shuffling his feet, but his hand remains locked on my arm.

"Kalief? Spit it out."

"I owe him some money."

"What do you mean? How much money?"

"Look, Cleo. Please. Do this for me, okay? I promise that I'll make it up to you."

"Do what?" I cock my head and try to figure out what he's not saying—but I'm not liking where my thoughts are leading. "Are you fucking trying to pimp me out?" I snatch my arm free. "I don't fucking believe this."

"Cleo, you don't understand. I owe him."

"Then you fuck him." I spin around and march off. "I'm outta this bitch. I quit. And YOU'RE FIRED!"

Kalief races after me. "Cleo. Cleo. Come back here!"

This time he grabs my upper arm, but when I spin around, I slap the holy shit out of him.

He backhands me and I hit the floor, my face stinging from the blow.

Kalief drops down beside me. "Cleo, I'm so sorry. I didn't mean to do that."

"Get away from me." I scramble away from him.

Kalief's face falls as his hands drop to his sides.

I don't know how he does it, but I actually feel sorry for him. When he looks at me again there are tears in his eyes. "Cleo, I wouldn't ask you to do this if it wasn't important. Please. Do this for me. You—you won't have to sleep with him. He wants to take you to dinner. That's all."

Tears burn the backs of my eyes. What kind of man would ask his girl to do something like this? At the same time I can see in his eyes that he's scared.

"How much money do you owe him?"

Kalief's gaze drops again.

"How much?" I repeat.

"You don't want to know."

I press my lips together and shake my head. But my tears still fall.

"I'm sorry," he whispers, and reaches for my hand.

"I promise you that after this, I'll get my shit together. I'll go to rehab. I'll quit cold turkey. I'll do whatever you want. I promise."

Disgusted, I pull myself off the floor and walk away.

"So you'll do it?" Kalief calls after me.

I ignore him while tears skip down my face.

"Cleo? Cleo!"

28

LeShelle

One stop that I've been dying to make while I'm back in Memphis is a trip to Fabdivas Hair Salon. It's the best place to announce to the other Queen Gs that momma is back. The amount of gapes and wide-eyed stares when I walk through the door is enough to boost my ego into the stratosphere.

When the initial shock wears off, two dozen Queen Gs jump to their feet and bum-rush me with a million questions.

"Bitch, you back?"

"Where have you been?"

"Did you hear about Momma Peaches?"

"Who the fuck is this Diesel muthafucka?"

I hold up my hands and laugh. "All right. All right. Calm the fuck down. Can't a bitch just come in here and get a blowout?"

One bitch ain't hear that. "Girl, they saying that King Isaac is back."

"What?" I twist up my face at the scrawny chick rocking a head full of Rainbow Brite hair colors.

"Yeah. People are saying that he's out of jail."

"Girl. You need to stop listening to rumors. He got like another year or so," I tell her, wanting to mush her in the face.

"But Chantal said he got out early."

"Don't you think I'd know if King Isaac was out?" I ask her.

She buttons those big-ass lips of hers and blinks those equally big eyes at me.

"Exactly." I look around for my favorite hairdresser, Nekeva, standing at her station. "Can you squeeze me in? I got something special planned with my *husband* tonight."

"Yeah, girl. You know I got you." She pops the mousy trick who is sitting in her chair on the shoulder.

The girl screws up her face. "What? I was here first."

I head to Nekeva's chair, but before I reach the disrespectful bitch, a group of Queen Gs snatch the girl with a head full of creamy crack out of the seat. When she tries to buck again, she gets smacked dead in her mouth.

I fucking love and miss this shit. Within seconds of my ass being planted in the chair, the owner, Ms. Anna, is handing me a glass of pink Nuvo and asking whether I'd like to get a mani/pedi too.

However, the buzzing Queen Gs don't stray too far away.

"So everything is still cool with you and Python?"

"Are you guys coming back to Shotgun Row?"

"When is Momma Peaches's funeral?"

I sigh and tell the girls that nothing has changed and that Python is definitely still running the Gangster Disciples and Diesel ain't no damn body. He's a temporary fix to a temporary problem.

Then the complaints start about how all the gang wars are affecting everybody's pockets and niggas ain't eating like they used to. Did I know that Fat Ace was back and did I know that Lucifer was pregnant with his baby?

On and on until my ass has a damn headache. They follow me from the chair to the bowl to the damn dryer. The best that I can tell them is that we are going to turn everything around—but they act like they didn't hear shit. The complaints continue.

Nekeva hooks my shit up. It's been a while since I've had my do done. I love the way my girl fixes my shit so that my hair hides my damaged ear from when LeShelle tried to chew the damn thing off. Of course when she asks what happened, I give her the mind-your-own-damn-business stare before she shuts the fuck up.

By the time Avonte and I roll out, my Queen G crown is tilted to the side. Python and I have a lot of work to do when we move our operation back to Memphis. When muthafuckas start bitching about their money, trouble is usually not too far behind. It also makes me wonder what the fuck Diesel has been doing if not feeding these niggas in our absence.

As Avonte rumbles through the streets, I recognize the area where Python bought a few of his exotic pets. With it being a minute since he had one of his beloved snakes, I have the idea of surprising him when I return.

An hour later, I leave Reptile Emporium with a handsome Burmese python in a cage. Avonte doesn't look too thrilled to have the snake in her car, but she manages to keep her mouth shut and delivers me back out to West Memphis promptly.

"Do you still need me tonight?" she asks, referring to my meet with Qiana at Hack's Crossing.

"Definitely," I tell her. "And I need you to get a couple of Queen Gs that you trust to keep their mouths shut."

Avonte nods.

"No. I mean it," I tell her. "I don't want anybody asking a whole lot of questions. Just bitches who know how to follow orders. You got me?"

"Got it."

I slap the top of the car's roof and watch Avonte pull off. A weird, ominous feeling comes over me. It's strange because it comes out of nowhere and before I can question it, it's gone.

29

Ta'Shara

I'm sorry that Profit lost his mom. I hate seeing how it's tearing him up inside—*but* I'm unable to comfort him. I know that shit makes me an asshole, given how he was by my side when Reggie and Tracee were killed, but I can't help how I feel.

That kiss.

It's been two days and I can barely stand to look at him, just like I can't stop all the questions looping in my mind. The number one question is *why?* And *when?* As in when did he stop loving me? When did he start being attracted to *her?*

I replay all those times when Profit pretended to hate or resent Lucifer. Was all that shit for show—for my benefit?

And what now? What are we supposed to do now—*pretend* like the shit didn't happen? I can't do that. I won't do that.

For now, Profit is huddled up with his brother Mason in our living room. I'm still trying to get used to calling him that. He's always been Fat Ace—the dangerous and notorious Vice Lord gangster who was second only to Python, the Gangster Disciple. I watch the brothers, bonded in grief, as they try to come up with a plan to avenge their mother. Behind me in the kitchen is Lucifer, strangely playing the role of happy homemaker as she serves bottles of beer and a variety of snacks. Who in the hell can eat?

When I'm not watching the brothers, my gaze creeps over to Lucifer. More now than ever, I study everything about her, especially her growing belly. More questions pop and roll around in my mind. *What if?*

No.

I shake my head and then try to shame myself for even thinking this shit, *but* anything could've happened while I was in the hospital and Lucifer thought her man was dead. Anything.

My heart sinks even lower and when Lucifer approaches me with the last bottle, I snatch it from her hand and then wait to see if she says anything. She doesn't—but she gives me a stare-down that *feels* like an ass whupping.

I glance away and clench my jaw. There's no sense in my ass trying her. She could take me with little effort—pregnant or not. Again, I can't bottle what I'm feeling—but clearly neither her or Profit wants their lip-lock session to get to Mason. *That's* the battle that's raging inside of me right now. Why should I be the only one suffering from their betrayal? Why should I be the only one in pain?

My gaze zooms back over to Mason, whose head is bowed and shoulders slumped. He's still blaming himself for Dribbles's death.

"I should have never agreed to go to that damn meeting. It wasn't going to accomplish or change anything. Muthafuckas can't change the past."

He's not talking to me, but his words crush me all the same. I don't know how many times I've wished that I could go back and this time pay heed to Essence's words and ignore Profit's ass the minute he told me who his people were. If I had, she would still be here—and me and LeShelle would—what? Still be sisters? Do I miss that?

Kind of.

It's hard being at war with someone you've spent your whole life loving. Before this past year, LeShelle had always been my protector. Sure, she's rough around the edges, but it's only because she has been through so much. I loved her and I thought that I understood her. For years we bounced around from foster home to foster home. I can't begin to count the number of nights I lay awake, frozen, as men crept into our rooms and raped my sister. In the earliest years, LeShelle would fight and then cry into the pillows next to me. After a while the fighting stopped and then later so did the tears. Before long, LeShelle was hard and jaded. And she would often warn me that one day, when I developed my tits and ass, those foster daddies would start coming for me.

She was right.

One night when we stayed with Ms. Ruthie and her white husband, Abdul, shit went seriously left. Before it all went down, LeShelle had asked me to run away with her, but my young mind didn't understand where we would go. It was so dark and scary outside—gunshots were always popping off. And at that time, I thought crackheads were zombies looking to eat children's brains. I don't know where in the hell I got that shit. But LeShelle must've had some type of premonition, because a few minutes later, Abdul crept to our room smelling like he bathed in cat piss and beer. We both dove under the covers and I could hear LeShelle praying, *"Please, God. Not this shit again."*

God never answered LeShelle's prayers—but I'd hoped that that time he would . . .

"Hey, li'l girl." He felt around and then snatched down the blanket. "Whatchu doing hiding under there?"

"What do you want?" LeShelle hissed.

Lying frozen in my own bed, my tears felt as if they had transformed into battery acid. They burned so much.

"C'mon, girl. You've played this game before. Anyone

can take one look at you and know that your cherry was popped a long time ago. Ain't that right?"

I peeked from underneath the covers to see LeShelle and Abdul wrestle. I wanted to scream for him to get off of my sister, but my throat had squeezed shut and I couldn't get a single sound out. What if he turned his attention from her to me? I actually thought that shit, as well as "Better her than me."

"Get off of me!" LeShelle twisted and kicked.

"Aww. You're a feisty bitch, huh?"

They continued wrestling until Abdul got tired and then cold-punched my sister as if she was a grown man. LeShelle went still, allowing him time to snatch off her nightgown. Then he suddenly had something in his hand, but I couldn't tell what it was until he said, "You better be nice to me or I'll cut this hot li'l pussy up."

A knife! My heart dropped and I couldn't swear that I was even breathing.

"You know in some parts of Africa men cut the girls' pussies to stop them from becoming whores." He laughed. "Maybe I'll do the same thing to you."

LeShelle whimpered, but she didn't say shit.

"That's it. I love it when you li'l bitches fight back."

Don't fight. Don't fight, I kept thinking.

I convinced myself that LeShelle must've heard me because she went ahead and let him climb on top of her and hump so hard that the bed banged against the wall.

"Ah, shit. Ah, shit," Abdul moaned. That, and, "I love fuckin' black pussy." He kept at it for a long time.

I cried. Why couldn't he leave us alone?

Suddenly, the bedroom door burst open and Ms. Ruthie snapped, "Ain't you through yet?"

Abdul kept humping away. "Does it look like I'm through? Aw, shit. I'm about to cum."

"It's about time. You've been in here almost an hour."

"Ah, shit. Ah, shit. This bitch got some tight shit. Ruthie, you just don't know. Ah, shit."

"What? That fast bitch? Please, tell that shit to some-body else." She puffed on her cigarette. *"What about the other one?"* she asked. *"You test her out yet?"*

My heart dropped clear to my toes. I was next.

"FUUUUUUUCCCK," Abdul roared.

LeShelle's entire bed shook.

"Shit. It's about time," Ms. Ruthie huffed. *"Now c'mon. You done played long enough."*

Abdul grunted. "Damn. You ain't going to let me catch my breath?"

"If you're talking then you're breathing. Now c'mon."

He sat up. "I haven't played with the other one yet."

"It's late. Now bring your ass on."

"Dammit, Ruthie." He stood from the bed and shuffled to the door. *"You said I could do both of them."*

"Don't get mad at me because you spent all your time with the slutty one," she argued back. *"Do her tomorrow."*

"Fine. Tomorrow then." At long last, they walked out of the room and closed the door.

LeShelle and I listened as they headed back to their bedroom. Neither of us moved or said a word until we were sure Abdul and Ruthie were back in their own bedroom.

Finally, I was able to move. I popped up out of bed and raced to turn on the lights. "Shelle, are you okay?"

She didn't answer.

"Shelle?"

"Yeah. I'm all right," she lied.

I didn't know what to do so I said, "I'll go get you a washcloth." I turned to run, but she quickly snatched me by the wrist. *"Wait until they're asleep. We don't know if they'll creep back out."*

"And grab me?" I asked in horror.

LeShelle didn't answer.

"He's gonna beat me and stick his weenie in me, ain't he?"
LeShelle shook her head.

"But he said—"

"Don't worry about what he said. I'm going to take care of it."

"But—"

"Hey." She grabbed my chin and forced me to look at her. "Don't I always take care of you?"

I nodded.

"Then leave it to me." She sucked in a deep breath. "Go back to bed."

"Don't you want me to help you clean up?"

"No. I can take care of myself. Go!"

I hesitated.

"Go," she hissed.

I slunk back to bed, crying as I crawled under the sheets. At some point I fell asleep—but I was jolted back up when Ms. Ruthie screamed, "WHAT? WHAT'S GOING ON?"

I kicked off the covers and hissed, "LeShelle. LeShelle, are you awake?" When she didn't answer I rushed to turn on the light again. But this time, LeShelle wasn't in her bed. Scared as shit, I kept hearing thumping and crashing.

"You little bitch," Ruthie shouted.

I knew then and there that LeShelle was in trouble. I unglued my feet from the floor and took off running from the room. In Ms. Ruthie and Mr. Abdul's room, I see that big woman wailing on LeShelle. In the corner, Abdul rocked back and forth, his pajamas covered in blood.

I had to do something or Ruthie was going to kill LeShelle. On the floor was a bloody knife. I didn't stop to think. I raced for the knife and then plunged the damn thing into Ruthie's back while she was still wailing on LeShelle, who had passed out.

"Aaaaaargggh!" Her head spun around like a damn

demon. I yanked the knife out, but before she could launch at me, I swung it back down and buried the blade in her left titty. "Oh fuuuuck," she wailed, stumbling backward. Her eyes locked on to the knife handle sticking out of her chest, like she could hardly believe that it was there.

I couldn't believe it either. I caught movement from the corner of my eyes and jumped. But it was that ugly-ass orange cat, Milly, that Ruthie loved so much. I don't know what made me do it, but I calmly walked back over and snatched the knife out of Ruthie's chest. She fell to the floor right next to LeShelle.

"You're a dead little bitch," Ruthie croaked, feebly trying to plug the hole in her chest.

I walked over to the cat with the bloody knife, cooing, "Here, Milly. Come here, girl."

The cat stared at me. "Meow."

I smiled and then promised her with my eyes that I wouldn't hurt her.

She stood still with her back hunched up but she allowed my blood-stained fingers to rub her soft fur. A couple of seconds later, Milly relaxed. That's when I slit her throat.

"Noooooo," shouted Ruthie.

I stared at her, cocked my head, and then threw her dead cat at her.

It must've been all too much for her because she slumped over, passed out.

I glanced down at LeShelle and then finally dropped the knife . . .

A knock at the door snatches me out of the past and lands me back in my present hell.

"I got it," Lucifer says before I can climb up out of my seat.

Who in the fuck does this bitch think she is? She's running *my* crib like it's her own. I give Profit a sharp look, but he turns his head from me like his ass doesn't want to get involved.

"Yo, T. We . . . Oh, hi, Lucifer."

I glance up to see Mack, Romil, and Dime crowded around the door. Their gazes all shoot toward me. "T," Mack shouts. "Can we holler at you for a minute?"

"Now is not a good time," Lucifer tells them.

I pop up out of my seat. Who the fuck does Lucifer think she is—my mother? "Yeah. I got a few minutes," I say, over-riding her.

Lucifer slices a look in my direction, but I ignore her *and* Profit as I march toward the door. If he isn't going to check Lucifer then he sure in the hell ain't going to check my ass.

Lucifer moves away from the door.

I step outside and close it behind me. "Yeah. What's up?"

"What the fuck do you mean, what's up? Why didn't you fuckin' tell us about what happened with Emerald and Nisha at that liquor store?"

I glance over to Dime.

"The shit is all over the fucking news. They say that the cops got video."

Video? Fuck. I didn't even think of that shit. Hell, I haven't thought about any of that crap since the whole Profit and Lu-cifer shit. I glance over my shoulder and even the thought of going back in there gets my temples throbbing.

"Yo, do me a favor. Take me over to y'all's crib for a few. They got some family shit that they're dealing with."

Mack looks at her girls and then shrugs. "Sure. C'mon."

30

Lucifer

I turn at the sound of footsteps behind me.

"Where's Ta'Shara?" Profit asks.

"She left."

"What?" He opens the front door as Mack pulls out of the driveway. "Yo, T. Wait up!"

There's a brief pause but then Mack hits the accelerator and the car peels out with a cloud of smoke jetting out of the exhaust.

"What the fuck?" He turns toward me. "What got into her?"

I shrug.

He stares after Mack's vehicle as if he's unable to process what the fuck happened.

I toss a glance over my shoulder to make sure that Mason is still settled in the chair in the living room before stepping outside and closing the door behind me. "Look. You need to get your fucking girl in line."

He frowns at my pointed finger. "I'm not a fuckin' child."

"No? Okay. So what do you want to do? You wanna go in there and tell your brother how you came on to me?"

"I didn't—"

"What?" I step forward, ready to break his fucking neck.

"Are you going to try to play crazy? You're going to say that I'm making this shit up? Is that what you're telling me?"

He finally clamps his mouth shut. "It was a mistake."

"You damn right it was a fucking mistake. A *huge* mistake. Like the one you made when you started fucking the enemy."

"What?"

Pissed, I pop him upside his damn head. "Do you *ever* fucking think? Look at all the bullshit that's happened since you hooked up with that girl. But, hey. It's not my business. But what is my fuckin' business is whether the bitch knows how to keep her mouth shut. She said that she saw your slick move yesterday morning at my crib. The bitch was crazy enough to step to me over the shit, and I swear to God she was seconds from blabbing that shit to Mason. And what the fuck do you think is going to happen if she does that shit, huh?"

Silence.

"See. That's why I can't stand being around bitches. They stay all up in their feelings waaay too goddamn much. I don't like that you put me in this fucking position where I gotta keep a secret from my fiancé. It's like I did something wrong. If I tell him, he'll probably try to fucking kill you—or me, thinking I did something to lead you on. And as bad as that shit is, it would be fucking *worse* if Ta'Shara said something to him first."

"All right. All right. I get it. I'll handle it."

"You better."

"Ta'Shara won't say shit. I promise. I'll talk to her."

I glare at him, wishing like hell that I could trust his ass to handle the situation—but I know how emotional bitches can get. As long as Ta'Shara stays all up in her feelings, she's a fucking threat to me and mines. "All right? Talk to her. Handle it—because you won't like it if *I* have to do it."

31

Ta'Shara

"Yo, T. Wait up," Profit shouts.

Mack brakes.

"No. Don't stop," I tell Mack, seeing Lucifer step out of the house and stand next to Profit. My gut loops into a giant knot. "I don't feel like dealing with his ass right now."

"Ooookay," Mack says, shifts into drive, and then floors it out of Ruby Cove.

I resist the urge to turn around. I don't have to. I feel Profit's heavy gaze on the back of my head. *Fuck him*. I can't get his betrayal out of my head. I doubt that I ever will.

"Trouble at home?" Romil asks.

None of your damn business. I close my eyes and lean my head back. It's either that or start crying—and I'm not about to do that in front of a bunch of bitches that I hardly know.

Romil gets the hint and drops the damn subject.

"Damn, T. I didn't know that you were a stone-cold killer," Mack says, puffing on a blunt as she corners out of Ruby Cove. "Dime told us how you took out that sand nigga at the liquor store."

"Saved our fuckin' asses is what she did," Dime says, nodding. "I ain't never seen no shit like it. The bitch was calm, cool, and collected as she capped that racist muthafucka. Shit went down so fast, my head is still spinning." She laughs as she reaches for Mack's blunt.

"Is that shit true?" Mack asks.

I peel open my eyes and meet Mack's gaze in the rearview mirror. She's looking at me with amusement mixed with admiration. "I did what I had to do," I say simply.

Mack's smile stretches wider. "See. I knew that I liked your ass for some reason."

Minutes later, we pull up to another brick home surrounded by dead grass and four cars with their hoods up. I'm the last one to climb out and as I trail Dime into Mack's place, I note the number of stray dogs and cats patrolling the area.

"T, you want to hit this?" Romil holds out the shrinking blunt.

"Sure." I don't even bother asking what the fuck is in the shit before putting it to my lips. I hope that it's strong enough to stop all the questions racing around in my head and to numb the pain in my heart.

Inside Mack's crib, we maneuver around stacked boxes and a pile of shoes. The air is also infused with strong incense, probably to mask the underlying smell of mildew from the brown carpet. Instead of giving a damn, I take another pull from the blunt and enjoy the feeling of a few brain cells melting.

Romil hits the Bose stereo and an old Snoop Dogg joint blasts through the speakers.

Mack directs me to the black sofa.

I plop down, still all in my feelings. I don't know what to do or where to go. I don't want to be the kind of bitch who lets her man disrespect her and put her through all kinds of bullshit in the name of love. Profit was supposed to be different. Our love was supposed to be different.

"You know, petal, you should look into hanging with me and my girls. We could use a bitch with your skills. NawhatImean? I'm talking about making some real gold coins. None of these scraps that the big dogs let fall off of their table."

I don't know what the fuck she expects me to say to that, so I tug another hit on the blunt before passing it to Dime.

Dime nods, grinning. "You should do it."

Do what?

"Check it. I know that with you being all booed up with Profit you probably ain't exactly hurting for paper. *But* take it from us, it don't hurt for a bitch to be stacking her own paper on the side. For emergency. You feel me?"

"Real talk," Romil says, pulling out a small brown vial. "Brothahs in the game are always hollering about having a ride-or-die bitch on their arm, but that don't necessarily mean that their asses will remain loyal—or free. You gotta remember that niggas get locked up in the regular out here. You have a backup plan if Profit ever gets locked down?"

I shake my head.

"Hmph. Neither do most of these wifey-bitches flossing on their man's dime. A bitch always gotta have her own shit stacking. You feel me? At any moment, a trick can be broke, busted, and disgusted."

I nod. They are making a whole lot of sense right now. With Reggie and Tracee Douglas gone, LeShelle and I beefing to the death, what the fuck do I have to fall back on? *Nothing.*

I avert my gaze so that she doesn't know how close to home she's hitting. At this point, my entire life depends on Profit: the roof over my head, the food I eat, and any money I need for personal shit, I have to ask him for it. "Yeah. Yeah. I feel you."

"Good. So are you in?" Mack asks, dipping the blunt in the vial.

"What's that?" I ask.

"Oh, this?" She holds up the vial and shakes the brown liquid inside. "This is *wet.* You ain't ready for no shit like this, li'l petal."

"Stop calling me that," I snap, irritated. "That bitch calls me that and it gets on my nerves."

"Stop calling you what? Petal?" Mack asks, laughing. "That's what we call all you new Flowers. At least until you've proven yourself."

"What happened to all of that smoke that you blew up my ass a few minutes ago?"

The girls look at each other and come to some kind of silent agreement.

"When you're right, you're right." Mack laughs, taking out a new blunt and dipping it into Romil's vial. A few seconds later, she puts a flame to the tip and inhales. I watch her and her girls pass the shit back and forth. A wave of curiosity and jealousy washes over me. I don't like being left out.

"I'll take a hit."

They all snicker.

"What?"

"Nothing. Nothing." Mack shrugs. "If you think you're woman enough to handle it then . . . be my guest." She passes the blunt.

There's something about the look on her face that gives me pause. I stare at the wet blunt and then ask, "What did you dip this into?"

"A little PCP," Romil says. "This shit will get you higher than you've ever been in your entire life. Are you sure that you want this?"

Is she fucking kidding me? "I can handle anything you throw my way."

"Then let's get you wet, baby." Romil passes the wet blunt to me.

They're all laughing when I take my first puff. The second I hold that shit in my lungs, I can feel the room breathe. Literally the walls grow spores and I can see it expand and contract. "Oh shit," I moan, already unable to feel half of my face. In the next second, I can hear the hair growing out of my scalp. "Oh shit."

"That's right. Don't fight it. Ride the wave."

Ride the wave. Ride the wave. Parts of my body start tingling. Shortly after, *every* part of my body tingles. After a full minute, I can't describe how good I feel. I brush my hand across my arm and then become fascinated by how smooth my skin feels. Is it that new cocoa butter I've been using, or the bath oil? I keep caressing myself and wondering how come I've never noticed this shit before.

Dime laughs. "Somebody is feeling good."

"Huh?" I glance up and laugh.

"What's so funny?" Dime asks.

I slap my hand over my mouth but still manage to laugh even louder.

"What?" Dime insists.

"Your head," I blurt out.

"What about it?"

"It's so fucking big."

Mack and Romil join in laughing while Dime flips us the bird.

"Whatever, bitch," Mack says. "You know your ass got a big head. Don't play."

Dime finally smiles. The music is turned up, and we go through a case of beer before we decide to have a twerk-off. Since I've never done the dance before, I come off looking corny as shit. However, Dime and Romil put the game on lock. Their round booties bounce so good that I end up making it rain with the fifty bucks I have on me.

Determined to win the contest, Mack jumps up on her coffee table and makes her shit clap so hard that it sounds like her ass is applauding itself.

"WINNER! WINNER!" Romil and Dime shout, throwing their money all over Mack.

The Bose changes CDs and then Trey Songz croons at us.

"Aw. That's my joint," I announce, throwing my hands up and joining Mack on the table. We dance . . . and then we grind. It's harmless fun so I don't take offense to Mack's hands

being on my hips and then on my titties. Somewhere along the
way, the temperature jumps thirty degrees. "Fuck. It's hot in
here."

My new friends giggle.

"What? Aren't you guys hot?"

"We can stand to crack a few windows," Mack finally
agrees.

Dime gets up to do that, but she moves way too slow and I
start removing my shirt.

"Make yourself comfortable." Mack laughs.

"Don't mind if I do."

Dime and Romil laugh.

But I don't give a fuck about these hoes. I'm still mad
about . . . about . . . about some shit. For a few minutes I
struggle to remember what I'm supposed to be upset about,
but instead break down, giggling.

"Awww. Somebody is feeling good."

"Fuuuck. Yeah." I roll my head back and ride the wave like
a fuckin' surfer.

"So are you down or what?" Mack asks.

"Down with what?" I ask. "Y'all ain't saying shit about
how we're supposed to be making this gold coin."

"Don't worry. We'll tell you about it later. We got to make
sure that you're a down-ass bitch first."

"Meaning?"

"Meaning that you know how to keep your damn mouth
shut. If we cut your ass in, it's some serious shit. We can't risk
having a weak link in the chain."

The girls fall silent as they cast their eyes in my direction.

I look around because I know that they can't be talking to
me. When I realize they're serious, I crack the hell up.

Mack frowns. "Bitch, we ain't fucking around."

"Whatever. I ain't begging you bitches for a fuckin' job—
and I ain't cosigning onto no stupid shit either."

"It's not stupid. It's foolproof," Mack insists. "When the time is right and you've proven yourself to us, then we'll cut your ass in on it."

If she thinks my ass should be grateful for what scraps her crew is talking about, she's mistaken.

"So what's up with you and Profit?" Romil asks. "Y'all already hitting a rough patch?"

I open my mouth to blab how much Profit ain't about shit and we may break up when I remember the number one rule when it comes to new girlfriends: Keep them out of you and your man's business. "Nah, girl. We good. I just wanted to get out of the house for a few. NawhatImean?"

"I feel you on that," Dime says. "Niggas nowadays can stress a sistah out—always wanting to be up under them and shit. Can't a bitch breathe? Damn."

We laugh and it feels good to finally be surrounded by friends.

32

LeShelle

Python is back.

I return to the crib to see that he's already up and moving around. He looks like he's still in pain, but he's doing what he's got to do. I'm not going to worry about the fever in his eyes. I'm sure in a few days that he'll be able to shake that shit off. Meanwhile, he's inhaling a plate of food like he ain't ate shit in weeks.

"Morning, baby. I left you some food on the stove."

"Nigga, you cooked?" I walk into the kitchen to verify the shit myself. "What's the fucking special occasion?"

"No occasion. I got up early 'cause I got some business meetings lined up today. Gotta get our shipments and arms back up so I can get more money in our soldiers' pockets."

I like the sound of that shit. "Oh yeah?"

"Yeah. I sent June Bug and Kane to round up the chief enforcers and deputies. Time to do some restructuring and take back some of the land we done lost."

"Does that mean we're going back to Shotgun Row?"

"Naw." He shakes his head. "Not with this mug shot. Pigs will pick my ass up before we even get in the door good."

My smile falls.

"But we're going back to Memphis," he says, turning my

smile around. "There's this one crib that I've been eyeballing that may be perfect and off the police grid while we rebuild."

"Oh yeah?" My nigga is finally saying all the shit I want to hear.

Python waves me back to the dining room table and then pats his lap for me to take a seat. "Thanks, babe."

"For what?"

"For keeping your damn foot up my ass these past few months. If it hadn't been for your damn stubbornness, we'd be sipping on margaritas in Tijuana or some shit."

"Nah. That shit will never be me." I tug on his ear and then plant a fat kiss on his lips. "But I'm ready to ride by your side and take these damn streets back."

"That's what the fuck I'm talking about." He winks and then smacks me on my ass.

Kane does his special knock on the door, letting us know that it's him.

"I'll get it." I don't want Python overexerting himself. I open the door and, sure enough, Kane and June Bug rush inside, both looking as though they've seen a ghost. "What the hell is wrong with you two?"

"King Isaac wants to see you," Kane announces, stumbling over his own tongue.

"What?" Python and I say in unison.

"He's out." June Bug bobs his head. "He got out two days ago. When we rolled over to Shotgun Row, he told us that he was handling Momma Peaches's funeral and that he wanted to meet."

Python pushes up onto his feet. "Where at?"

My mind races. *What the hell does this mean? Has my king been bumped down to a prince? I now have two muthafuckas crouching in on my territory? What kind of shit is this?*

"He gave us an address for a warehouse out in Frayser."

"Let's go," Python says, wincing in pain as he walks.

"Wait. Without me?"

"It's not just business," he says, dropping his gaze. "I wanna know what he's doing about Momma Peaches's funeral arrangements. You know that everybody that's anybody is gonna be there. I wanna make sure that he sends her out the right way, know what I mean?"

I study him. "You're not thinking about going to the services, are you?"

He sighs. "I wish—but that's off the table. The feds would love for me to do something that damn stupid."

"Mind if I play tag?" I've never met Python's stepfather. He's been behind bars the entire time that we've been together. Of course the streets stay talking about the days when King Isaac ran shit with an iron glove. The way that some folks tell it, you'd think all his folks in the GD Nation feasted like royalty and lived off streets paved in gold.

When Python stepped up, he had some big shoes to fill. This past year has been the only hiccup. But now that his head is on straight, nothing can stop the Folks Nation from beating back the greedy Vice Lords.

Python surprises me by agreeing. "You wanna come, you can come. The old man probably will want to meet you anyway."

"Cool."

Frayser is a small town south of Memphis. It's an economic wasteland where the majority of the residents live well below the poverty line. The place also has enough abandoned buildings that are perfect for our purposes.

The second we cross the city line, danger clogs the air. Niggas that ain't got shit don't blink at killing a muthafucka just because it's Tuesday. I keep my eyes and ears open to every dreads-wearing muthafucka who turns his head our way when we roll by.

"Shelle, relax," Python says, reaching over to rub the tension out of my left shoulder. "We good."

We pull up to a redbrick warehouse that's at least a hundred years old. "How in the fuck did y'all find this place?" I ask, climbing out of the car.

"There you go, worrying about the wrong damn thing again." Python wraps his meaty arm around my neck and then tucks my head under his arm like it's a fuckin' football.

"Let go." I tug on his arm, but he chuckles while he drags me to the door and releases me. Then his mood slowly turns more sober.

June Bug pulls open the building's heavy metal door. The rusty hinges squeak and groan in protest, announcing our arrival.

My stomach twists into knots. It's been a long time since a muthafucka has made me nervous. I'm about to meet a legend in the game.

I follow Python as he limps across the threshold, while Kane takes up the rear.

"Is that my boy?" A voice booms like a clap of thunder.

Python chuckles under his breath. When we turn a corner, there, standing in the center of this huge dusty warehouse, is King Isaac.

My heart quickens. He's an imposing figure, an inch or two shorter than Python, but with muscles a good couple inches bigger. He also has the sexiest bald head I've ever seen and his rich chocolate skin is tattoo-free.

"My boy!" He throws open his arms and the two men embrace. There's no mistaking the genuine love between them. As they pull back, they take a few minutes to assess each other.

"You're looking good," Python praises.

"Can't say the same for you," Isaac says honestly. "You seeing anybody about those nasty burns?"

"Yeah. My old lady here is handling it."

Isaac casts his gaze in my direction.

I flutter on a nervous smile and pray that he doesn't hear my heart galloping in my chest as he walks over to me.

"So you must be LeShelle," he says, smiling down at me. "I've heard a lot about you."

"I heard a lot about you too."

An awkward silence fills the space between us before he asks, "So are you going to give your new father-in-law a hug or not?"

"Of course." I throw my arms around him and note how good he smells.

The men face each other again and Isaac is the first to approach the subject of Momma Peaches. "I'm sorry about your aunt. You know that she loved you like a son. And I love you like a son. You know that?"

Python nods. "Yeah. I'm really going to miss her. I can't believe I'm going through this shit again. Losing her twice is hard." He breaks eye contact to shake his head. "I wish that I'd gotten to the church sooner. I would've prevented this shit."

Isaac's face wrinkles. "What are you talking about? You were there?"

"Yeah. I rode out to meet Momma Peaches and . . . well, she arranged a meeting with that nigga Fat Ace."

Isaac's face turns into a sheet of rock. "Fat Ace . . . with the Vice Lords? Why the fuck were y'all meeting him?"

Dread starts to creep up my spine. I don't want to hear Python start up that "brother" crap again.

"Spit it out. If that nigga got something to do with my having to lower my baby into the ground, then I'm gonna see him for it."

"It's a long fuckin' story." Python looks up and asks, "Wait. Didn't you talk to Diesel?"

"Why in the hell should I have talked with Diesel?"

"He stayed behind at the church," Python says. "He was with Aunt Peaches when she passed away."

"The first I heard of it," Isaac says. "When word got back to me, her body was headed to the morgue."

Python nods. "Sooo . . . you'll take care of the funeral arrangements? She deserves a nice send-off."

"Of course." Isaac breaks out a wide smile. "I'll give her the best farewell party the hood has ever seen."

"Thanks."

The men share warm smiles. They clearly want to say so much more about the woman they both loved and now have to figure out how to live without.

Isaac says, "I wish that I'd always done right by her." He gets a faraway look as if his thoughts are tumbling through the past. "I've made a lot of mistakes in my time . . ."

Python waits him out to see if there is more to the sentence. When Isaac remains silent, Python asks the question that hovers at the top of his mind. "So are you back in the game?"

Isaac's smile returns as well as a twinkle in his eyes. "A Gangster Disciple never quits the game. He's in it until the world blows. You feel me?"

"I hear that." Python and Isaac slap palms.

My heart sinks. My king has been officially demoted to a prince.

"So tell me. Why is Diesel in town?" Isaac asks. "What the fuck does he want?"

Python sighs and shrugs. "I was in a tight spot when I got blasted to number one on the Most Wanted list. I needed someone that I could trust. The folks I trusted are no-longer breathing. The whole structure got shaky." He shrugs again. "I figured that I could rely on family to get me through a rough spot."

Isaac shakes his head. "Son, there are some branches on the family tree that you don't fuck with. You trim or prune those muthafuckas. And Diesel is one of them."

Python tries to shrug it off. "Look. I know that you don't really care for him—"

"I'm not the only one," Isaac says. "Your Aunt Peaches never trusted him either. She always said that something wasn't right about the boy. I got to tell you that some of the shit I've heard about him over the years don't sit right with me either. Now I know you may feel differently since you'd go down to Atlanta and visit every spring break when you were a kid. You know him on a different level. But I don't trust that boy worth a damn. And he has another muthafuckin' thing coming if he thinks he's coming to *my* city to take over.

33

Ta'Shara

Tonight me and the girls are going to check out Memphis's newest hot spot, Club Diesel. This morning when Romil told me where we were headed, I snatched a handful of bills out of Profit's pocket while he was staring dead in my face, and I refused to tell him what I needed the money for. I then took his car and rolled my ass to Saks for a hot dress and my first pair of Louboutins.

Dime and Mack insist on giving me a two-hour makeover while we get ready at Mack's crib. When they finish, my face is *beat*, according to them.

"Damn, girl, you're going to get some niggas shot tonight." Mack laughs when I exit her spare bedroom to spin around in my new ensemble.

"Yeah. Profit ain't going to like niggas checking you out," Romil tosses in.

I wave off her comment. "Chile, please. Ain't nobody thinking about Profit's ass."

"Damn. It's that serious?" Dime asks. "When in the hell are you going to tell us what the fuck is going on with you two?"

"Hmph." I roll my eyes. I ain't crazy. I'm not letting these girls in my personal business.

"All right. Whatever." She waves me off, pretending like she ain't still dying to know. "I know I'm going to do me and get some tonight."

We laugh because every time we go out, she says the same thing and I have yet to see her pull a man. But it's all been in good fun.

Tonight we're celebrating the state dropping its case against me in Kookie, Reggie and Tracee's death. Like Mack said, those pigs didn't have shit on me. They knew that shit when they embarrassed me and hauled my ass out of my foster parents' funeral service in front of the entire family.

And as far as my real crime, the murder of the liquor store clerk, I haven't heard a peep. Hell. I still haven't even told Profit about it. Why should I? He's so damn good at keeping secrets. I should have a few of my own.

Life with Profit hasn't turned out like I've always dreamed it would. We walk on eggshells around each other. He keeps asking for forgiveness and pleads nightly to crawl back into our bed. I shut that shit down. How could I let him lay with me and dream about *her*? I'm not trying to be a bitch, it's just how I feel. What would've happened if Lucifer hadn't turned him down? Would he have left me for her? Double-crossed his brother?

That thought keeps me awake at night. He's fucked up if he thinks that I'm about to be his fuckin' consolation prize. Maybe when the pain stops, but that isn't happening either. At the moment, as far as I'm concerned, "we" are a wrap. Even though I, technically, still live with him, I spend all my time with my girls. They are my new family.

"What you need to do is stack your own money," Mack tells me. "I don't know what's going on with you and your man right now, but take it from me, these niggas out here ain't loyal. And you never know when one of them is about to be locked down and you're stuck out here defending yourself. If I've seen it once, I've seen it a million times. Bitches get booed up, think their asses are King Bey and Jay-Z, making it rain in all the stores. The nigga gets capped or locked up, and then that balling bitch is on the street corner, sucking dirty dicks to pay her light bills."

"Real talk," the girls cosign.

"The real lesson from King Bey is to hustle for your own shit. Don't let what some nigga brings home be all you have to eat, you feel me?"

"You're right," I agree. "I need to get a job. But who in the hell is going to hire me? I don't even have a high school diploma." *Shit. I was going to be a fucking doctor.*

My girls burst out laughing.

"What's so funny?"

Romil shakes her head. "You. Ain't nobody talking about getting no W-2. We're talking about you making some real money. Easy money." She slides two perfect lines of coke onto a mirror.

I smile. The girls know what I need for a little pick-me-up. The coke has replaced my bottles of Xanax, Inderal, and Tofranil that my doctors had placed me on since leaving the hospital. To be real with it, the street shit is much better in controlling my anxiety and keeping me numb to the bullshit that has become my life.

I drop my head and vacuum up the pretty powder. Instantly, my nose blazes up, but my fucking high is instant. "Whooo!"

The girls laugh as I climb to my feet and start shaking my ass. "We're going to party tonight."

"And you know this, mannnn," Dime says in her best Chis Tucker voice.

The party train ready, we dance our way out to Romil's black Range Rover and pile in.

"You know you should come work for us," Mack says, settling down beside me in the back. Dime takes the front seat next to Romil.

I frown over at my girl. "Shit. Now that I think about it, I don't even know what the fuck it is that you do."

"I make money. Daaamn good money," she brags. "Don't let the middle-class crib fool you. My shit is all the way fucking right."

"All right. I'm listening." I sniff and rub my nose. "What kind of work are you talking about?"

"I run a few businesses, but my most profitable shit is this credit card situation I got set up. The money is fuckin' sweet."

"Oh yeah?" I ask, intrigued. If I can make my own money, then I can move out and find my own place.

"And the shit is easy. I got girls who work all over town supplying us with people's names and social security numbers, right? And what we do is open a few credit accounts in their names. My main nigga, Harlan, has the hook-up with this small lender company that secures us some open-line credit under muthafuckas' names, and *cha-ching!* Bitches are paid." She pops her fingers and wiggles her ass.

I laugh, but shake my head. *Credit card fraud?*

"Whatcha think?"

"Sounds interesting," I say, not wanting to fuck up our vibe. "Let's talk about it later."

Mack bounces her head to Snootie Wild's latest hot track. "That's my muthafuckin' nigga," she says, bouncing her head.

I laugh because she says that shit about every damn song. The rest of the conversation we have during the ride flows in one ear and out the other. My buzz is on point. I don't know who Mack knows, but we blast to the front of the line at the club and are ushered through the velvet rope by a winking security guard.

"You ladies enjoy yourselves."

I giggle and whisper loudly to Dime. "He didn't even check my fake ID."

"Shhhh." She smacks me on the arm and glances over her shoulder to make sure no one heard me. "What the fuck?" She laughs. "You're going to get our asses thrown out of here before we even have our first drink. C'mon here." She grabs my wrist and tugs me deeper into the crowded club.

"Damn. This joint is nice," Romil says, sidling up to the first bar we come to. "These niggas in here got pensions and shit."

"It's nice," I agree, taking it all in and hoping that they don't plan on staying hugged up at the bar all night.

"Wanna dance?" a rich baritone asks from behind.

"Yeah," I answer before turning around and seeing who asked. It doesn't matter because I'm already having a hard time standing still. But lucky for me, my new dance partner is a fine chocolate brother with a white-picket-fence smile.

"Be back," I tell the girls and bounce off to one of the club's many dance floors.

Between the music, the coke, and the nigga grinding on my ass, I'm flying high and not worried about a damn thing. Three songs later, me and my dance partner are damn near fucking on the dance floor. His thick-ass dick is grinding on me *that* hard. I'm sweating so hard that my damn roots are kinking up, after my girls spent so much time ironing the shit straight.

"What's your name, shawty?"

"Shawty?" I laugh. "Where are you from?"

"Atlanta," he says, grinning. "You?"

"M-town, baby. All the way."

"And that name?"

I peep out his fine frame and estimate that he has a good seven to eight years on me. And though he's GQ'd up, I sense that he's a thug to his core. "Ta'Shara," I finally tell him.

"Ta'Shara," he repeats, pressing his hand against the small of my back.

"And your name?"

"My government name is Benjamin, but my friends call me Beast."

"Beast?" I laugh while getting all warm and tingly. "And why do they call you Beast?"

He nuzzles his head in the crook of my neck to whisper, "Because I'm a beast with everything I do."

Shit. I think I just came. I lean back and he allows me to ease from his strong embrace. "Well, Beast, you're gonna have to put you on a leash for a minute while I take a trip to the ladies' room."

His handsome face twists into a frown as he pulls me back even closer for another good two-step grind. "Mmmm. I don't wanna let you go."

The way his voice drops into a deeper baritone is sexy as hell. "I'll be back," I promise and manage to pry his arms from around me. Our hands remain linked together until I move out of his reach.

I float on a cloud as I maneuver my way off the dance floor in search of a bathroom. Before I know it, Dime and Romil flank me.

"Damn, girl. Who is that fine nigga?" Dime asks. "He was all up in your business."

"Girl, bye." I giggle.

Romil shakes her head. "Nah, girl. She ain't lying. I think I got a Plan B pill in my purse. Do you need that shit?"

"Y'all stupid." We locate a bathroom and push our way in-side. The place is packed, but the line seems to be moving at a steady pace. After a quick piss and hand wash, we are ap-proached by the bathroom attendant, who offers us a bit more than sanitizer and breath mints.

Dime waves her ass off, not wanting to sample some ran-dom's product. Romil and I are curious and buy a couple of packets of nose candy from her. We quickly rush back into one of the stalls and pull out our hand mirrors.

"Damn. That's some good shit," I marvel the second the candy hits my system.

"Oh. Fuck. Your nose is bleeding."

"Really?" Laughing, I reach for the toilet paper to fix the problem. When we exit the ladies' room and blend back into the crowd, I'm mentally fucking gone. I dance with a handful of random men and even a few chicks before Beast finds me again.

He says something. I laugh. I don't know what the fuck is going on. I'm feeling too fucking good.

Suddenly, Mack snatches me by the arm. "Girl. Profit is in here looking for you!"

"What?" I glance around and then jerk my arm back. "So?" I try to return to dancing with Beast.

Mack ain't having it. "So. Your nigga looks hot to death. We got to get you out of here." She tugs on my arm again.

"Bitch, let go!"

"Is there a problem?" Beast asks, stepping up.

"No. I—"

"TA'SHARA!"

My small group turns their heads and sure enough, Profit and a cluster of Vice Lords come blazing toward us.

Disloyalty

34

LeShelle

Hack's Crossing Park

"**I** knew I couldn't trust that bitch," I fume, glancing at my watch every other minute. "You give people an inch and they want to take a fucking mile. Now those kiddie bangers got me out here looking like Boo Boo the Fool.

But I ain't got muthafuckin' time to be chasing bitches all over Memphis like a human GPS. I clench my teeth as I hear the invisible ticking of the clock. Diesel is going to make his move any day now—probably after we bury Momma Peaches.

It works to my advantage that King Isaac has planted new seeds of doubt in Python's mind about his shady-ass cousin. If we get into a situation where it's my word against Diesel's over the Yolanda hit, my word will carry more weight if there are no snitches and no new baby with Python's fucking DNA breathing.

My blood pressure rises. If given a choice I'd take the dead baby over revenge with those Flowers. Python will never believe the word of some crumpled-up Flowers anyway. *The baby. I just want the baby.*

An hour passes. Two hours.

Avonte and her girls Myeisha and Erika, who are also trusted Queen Gs, keep blowing up my phone almost to the point where I start entertaining the idea of putting a bullet in their skulls.

Goddamn it. I stomp my way out of the park and meet up with my girls.

They all sense that I'm in a foul mood and don't say jack shit to me. The whole ride back to West Memphis, I plot my next move, knowing that it needs to be swift.

"Avonte, I need you to do some investigating for me."

She looks up at me in the rearview mirror. "Sure. Whatcha need?"

"Does your little sister have a Morris High School year-book?"

"What year?"

I shrug. "Last year."

"Yeah. I think so."

"Good. Bring it to me tomorrow. I need to flush Ms. Qiana out of hiding. The best way to do that is to reach out and touch those two bitches she rolls with."

Avonte nods. "Sure thing."

I'm fairly certain that I can identify the two girls that were with Qiana the first night we met. Once I know who they are, I can damn well find them. *Time to show these tricks why no one fucks me over.*

35

Ta'Shara

"Oh shit," Mack swears, but remains rooted by my side.

Profit's rage has transformed his face. Visible veins are pulsing out of his neck and the side of his face. "What the hell do you think you're doing?"

"Calm the fuck down. You're causing a scene," I tell him.

His arm snakes out so fast to snatch me up that it's a blur. "Come on. We're leaving."

He manages to drag me a couple of feet before I buck. "I'm not ready to go!"

"I didn't ask you what you were ready to do," he snarls, pulling me again. "We're going home."

"Let go!" I jerk harder, but when he doesn't let go, Beast steps up.

"Is there a problem?" He towers at least two inches over Profit and sports more muscle.

"This ain't got shit to do with you, bruh. You need to back the fuck up," Profit tells him, clearly not ready to take any shit.

"The lady says that she's not ready to go." Beast nods to someone off in the distance.

"Fuck off!" Profit throws the first punch and then all hell breaks loose.

"Profit! Stop it!" I attempt to jump in between the two, who are throwing powerful blows, but brothers that ain't got shit to do with what's going down start popping caps.

Screams go up and people scatter out of the way. Everything spins around me like a Ferris wheel. Minutes later a bloody and pissed Profit is dragging me out to the damn car.

"Are you fucking happy?" he barks, slamming the door and then rushing around the car as the sound of police sirens fills the night.

Once Profit jumps behind the wheel, I light into him. "Don't blame this shit on me. Nobody asked your ass to go barging in there and acting like a goddamn fool."

He jams on the accelerator. "You like to play games now. Is that it?" he shouts. "I got niggas coming at me left and right talking about how you and your girls are all up in the club. My own muthafuckin' family punking my ass about how I can't control my ol' lady. And tonight, muthafuckas hitting me on my cell telling me how you fucking some nigga on the dance floor."

"That's bullshit," I shout back. "I can't control what the hell comes out your gossiping bitches' mouths."

"T, I saw the damn nigga all up on you with my own damn eyes."

"You didn't see shit!" I whip my head around and stare out the window like a petulant child.

"Is that how the fuck you're rolling now?"

"What, a bitch can't go dancing?"

He works his jaw. "I swear to God, I feel like bouncing your ass out that goddamn window."

"You ain't going to do shit." I rock back in my seat and cross my arms.

His head whips in my direction. "Who the fuck *are* you?"

I roll my eyes and pretend like I don't know what he means, but he's not going to let it go.

"Really. I need to know. Because I've been operating under the illusion that you just needed some time to work out your anger about the whole Lucifer situation and *then* we were going to work out our issues."

"*Our* issues?" I ask. "I didn't stab you in the back."

"I've apologized for that shit. How long are you going to hang that shit over my head?"

"As long as I fucking feel like it! I'm not anybody's god-damn consolation prize."

"So what you saying? Huh? You want to squash this shit and go our separate ways?"

It's my turn to grind my back teeth instead of spitting out some shit that I can't take back. In my head, I'm flooded with memories. How we met. How I lost my virginity. How he used to sneak into my bedroom at the Douglases'. Prom. We used to be so good together, but shit has gone downhill for a long damn time now. When do you throw in the towel? When is enough enough?

Despite my ass trying to stay strong, my eyes fill with tears.

"You want out?" he asks again.

I don't know what the hell I want. The rest of the ride to the crib is quiet and uncomfortable.

Profit suddenly leans over to get a better look at me. "What the fuck is that?" He wipes a trace of white powder from my nose.

Defensive, I smack his hand away. "Don't touch me, you goddamn cheater." Once I throw one punch, I can't stop.

With one arm, he tries to block me the best he can. The car fishtails in and out of the lane.

"Goddamn it! Stop it!" He pushes me one good time and I go flying back to hit the back of my head on the passenger-side window—hard.

"Fuck!" The shit hurts. I grab my head, but my ears won't stop ringing. Tears flow, fast and heavy.

Profit's voice softens. "Are you all right?"

"Go to hell." For the rest of the ride, I remain huddled in my seat, crying as quietly as I can.

"Why are you doing this to us?" he asks.

I sniff and wipe my eyes. "There is no us."

He nods. "You're damn right."

36

Cleo

"**A** hundred and seventy-eight *thousand* dollars?" I reel. How in the fuck does Kalief owe Diesel that kind of money? The shit doesn't make any kind of sense. And why is it up to me to pay his fucking debts? A point that I keep telling his ass, but he keeps blowing up my damn phone.

I can't believe that he's seriously trying to pimp my ass out. Sure. There are other Queen Gs who get tossed around from nigga to nigga for shady-ass shit, but that ain't never been us. I'm not a damn moll and I ain't a broke-down thot twerking in the VIP room like they used to do over at the Pink Monkey.

Niggas have taken this whole *ride or die* too muthafucking literally. For years, I took pride in not being one of these hard-core chicks. I'm a Queen G mainly because of family history and my address. Niggas can't survive out here without having to rep *somebody's* flag. That doesn't mean that my ass is squeaky clean, but I've never done anything that would land me in our modern-day concrete plantation.

And I'm not going to be stuck at my grandma's crib for the rest of my life either. I'm gonna roll up out of this bitch with or without Kalief's help. I figured that he would take the hint when I refused to return to Club Diesel, but that move infuriated him. The boy started blowing up the business phone at my fast food job while I was working a double. The shit got so bad that the manager wrote my ass up.

Kalief got my ass on the phone then—and I ripped him a new fucking asshole. Don't mess with me and my paper, even if the shit is barely above minimum wage.

Today is my first day off in two weeks and I'm enjoying this shit, despite the screaming kids running throughout this bitch. I run a bubble bath and turn off my phone. Two hours later when I turn the muthafucka back on, I have sixty-seven fucking missed calls. Sixty-seven. Where the fuck niggas do that shit at?

Knock. Knock. Knock.

I glance over to my bedroom door to see my brother, Kobe, standing at the doorway. "What?"

He holds up his phone. "Will you *please* call your nigga Kalief back? Bruh is whining like a bitch all over my voice mail."

I sigh.

"I mean it, Cleo. This shit is getting damn ridiculous. What the fuck did y'all fall out about now?"

"We broke up."

"Again? Don't y'all do that shit every other week?"

I roll my eyes, hoping he'll get the hint to back off.

"What happened this time?"

"You wouldn't believe me if I told you."

On cue, Kobe's phone rings. He glances at the ID screen and huffs out a long breath. "This nigga here." He shakes his head. "What do you want me to do?"

"Ignore his ass."

"I've tried that shit, but I can't have a decent convo with bae without this nigga beeping in every other minute. You need to handle your fucking business and get this muthafucka off my phone." His phone stops ringing and mine blows the fuck up.

"*Talk* to him," Kobe shouts, mean-mugging me like I did something to his ass.

"Fine." I swipe my finger across my screen and answer the call. "What is it, Kalief?"

"Why the hell ain't you been answering my calls?" he snaps.

"'Cause I already know what the fuck you're going to say—and I ain't interested. How many times do I have to tell you that?"

"Damn, girl. What's the big fucking deal? It's one date. It ain't like I'm asking you to sleep with the nigga."

"Does that shit even sound right to you?" I challenge him. "One date to wipe out a hundred and seventy-eight thousand dollar debt?"

"He likes you."

"I don't *like* him. And listen to you. I'm supposed to be your fucking girl, not your fucking ho. Are you putting any thought into how this shit makes me feel?"

"Cleo. Cleo. You're blowing this shit way out of proportion. Just think of this shit like it's a business dinner."

"Kalief—"

"Hear me out. We ain't talking about a regular bitch-ass nigga in the industry. We're talking about a *made* nigga. His ass say jump and niggas start bouncing. Nobody asks how fucking high—or any of that shit. I *promise* you Diesel can get you on. Period. Do you know how many bitches would kill to be in your position?"

"Yeah. The same bitches who are always trading pussy for studio time—or for whack-ass beats. Nobody is ever going to take my ass seriously if I have to fuck every nigga in the industry. We've both seen this damn movie before. I'd rather keep rolling goddamn burritos for the rest of my life than have to owe Diesel Carver for a muthafuckin' thing. If you were a *real* manager, you'd keep this damn nigga off my ass instead of trying to sell it. If you were any kind of *boyfriend* you would've throat-punched that muthafucka for even suggesting some wild-ass indecent proposal.

"But *nooooo.* You're too busy gambling and throwing money up your goddamn nose, thinking that I'm going to pay the fucking tab. Well, you can miss me with all that shit."

"Oh. Oh. So now I ain't been out here busting my ass, tryna get you on?"

"That's exactly what I'm saying. It's time for me to cut my damn losses and toss your ass deuces. You ain't shit. You ain't never been shit. And you ain't never going to *be* shit."

"That's cold. After all we've been through? I thought you were my *ride or die.*"

"Fuck you. You wanna pay off your damn monies? *You* fuck his ass."

"I done told you that it's just dinner."

"C'mon, Kalief," I say, stomping my foot. "Either you're stupid as hell or you think that I am."

Seeing that he isn't getting anywhere with me with a lie, he changes it up. "All right. I ain't shit. Happy?"

Silence.

"You have no idea how much it hurts me to have to ask you to do this shit. The truth of the matter, Cleo, is that I fucked up. I ain't got the money to pay this nigga back. And it's well-known that brothas that come up short with his ass turn up missing. Is that what the fuck you want? You can't giggle over a damn lobster dinner to save my ass?"

"Why didn't you think about all that shit when you borrowed the money or smoked his shit?"

"I did think about that shit, but c'mon. You know I got a damn problem. You don't think that I don't try to beat this shit every muthafuckin' day? I hate that I still got this monkey on my back. And I hate that I have to ask the one person I love most in this world to do this for me. But I'm not asking anymore. I'm begging. Either you do this or I'm dead." He breaks down.

I pull the phone away from my ear and shake my head. This can't be my life.

"Cleo, please. I promise if you do this, I won't ask you to do another thing for me. Please. One dinner."

I grit my teeth while angry tears sting my eyes.

"Please, baby. Please."

No. No. No.

"I'll go to rehab. I'll get into whatever program you want. I'll get clean. I swear."

I slam my eyes shut and try to hang on to my resolve—but listening to Kalief starts tearing me up inside. "All right. One date."

37

Ta'Shara

When we reach the house, I jump out of the car before Profit shifts the car into park. I'm in luck that the front door isn't locked because I have no idea where my purse or keys are at. I blaze straight to the bedroom and once again start grabbing all of my shit. The party is over and we can stop with all the charades.

I should have left days ago. My sticking around has only made shit worse. My anger has blossomed into hatred.

Profit is silent when he enters the room, but I can feel his heavy gaze. It isn't until I've gathered all my shit out of the closet that I realize I'm hoping he will say something just so we can go for round two. I don't care what he saw tonight or whether I was wrong or if I'm too fucking high to process everything. It's still his fault and I hate him for it.

I start cramming shit into bags. My bags. His bags. It doesn't fucking matter. I move over to the dresser and start snatching my shit from there as well. All the while, Profit doesn't say shit.

It isn't long before his silence starts riding my last nerve. When I can't stand it any longer, I spin around and face him. "Are you just going to stand there?"

Instead of barking back, Profit pushes away from the door and storms away from the bedroom. "I'll call you a cab."

His words are like a punch to the gut. More tears spring to my eyes, but I make sure that those muthafuckas don't fall. *Fuck him.* I return to shoving shit into bags. I race to the bathroom for my toiletries. It doesn't seem like I can move fast enough. But everything stops when I catch a glimpse of myself in the mirror.

"Shit." I look like shit and quickly hand-iron my wild hair back down. But my eyes are dilated, red and swollen, there's still powder on my nose, and I have raccoon eyes from my smudged waterproof mascara. *Oh my God.* I try to fix it, but there's no fixing this.

I lean back against the wall and then slowly slide down to the floor, sobbing. *What have I done? What am I going to do? Where the fuck am I going to go?*

Bam! Crash! Smash!

Profit is tearing up the living room.

This is rock bottom.

38

Lucifer

"**P**ush. Push," Dr. Modi coaches from between my legs.

I'm baptized in pain as I grind to get this baby out of me. But no matter how much I grunt, curse, or scream, the baby refuses to budge. I stop for a second to try to catch my breath. Unbelievably that shit makes the pain worse.

"It's okay, Willow. You got this."

I look over, expecting to see Mason holding my hand, but I'm shocked to see Bishop—complete with the left side of his head blown off. I don't freak out. In fact, I'm happy to see him.

Bishop smiles. "Now push."

"I-I can't," I whine. I've never whined a day in my life, but here I am drowning in this pain. I also never cry, but there's twin waterfalls rushing down my face. Something has to be wrong. I feel like I've been at this for hours if not days. "I've changed my mind. I don't want to do this anymore."

Bishops laughs. "It's a little too late for that."

That's not what I want to hear. "But there's something wrong. I know that there's something wrong."

"Push. Push. Push," Dr. Modi shouts.

I grab hold of Bishop's hand, take a deep breath, and push, grunt, and scream all over again.

"Here comes the head," Dr. Modi cheers. "Push."

"Wait. Mason. Where is Mason? Where did he go? The baby can't come until he gets here."

"Push!"

I don't know where the strength comes from, but I bear down and I give it everything I've got until I feel the baby's body slip out between my legs. I collapse in a pool of my own sweat—but then I realize something is wrong. The entire room has gone quiet.

"W-why isn't he crying?" I ask, glancing around.

Bishop is gone.

Mason glares down at me. "He's dead. What did you do?"

"What? That can't be." I try to sit up and see for myself, but all I see is blood. So much blood. Then I see him. A tiny deformed body that is turning a darker shade of bloodred with each passing second.

"Noooooo!"

I bolt straight up in bed.

Mason does the same thing, grabbing his 9mm from beneath his pillow, ready to blast the thing or person that ain't supposed to be there. He comes to his senses at the same time I realize everything was a dream.

"Fuck!" I fall back against the pillows and suck in deep breaths.

"Everything cool?" Mason asks, still alert and armed.

"Yeah. I-I'm . . ." Hell. I don't even know what to tell him. Instead, I climb out of bed and head to the bathroom.

"Willow?"

"I'm fine." I wave off his concern. "Go back to sleep." I enter the bathroom and close the door behind me. He must be wondering what the fuck is wrong with me, but I'm chalking this shit up to hormones. That's got to be it. I even try to review the dream while emptying my bladder—but it's pointless. None of it made any sense. I mean, why would Bishop be there? He's dead.

I reach for the roll of toilet paper and wipe.

Blood?

My heart jumps into my throat. Why is there blood on this toilet paper? I try to tell myself that I'm not seeing what I think I'm seeing. I quickly discard the toilet paper into the bowl and then snatch myself another long strip of Charmin from the roll and wipe myself again. *More blood.*

I suck in a deep breath. "Don't panic," I say, even though I'm already in the midst of a full-blown panic attack. I jump up and scramble to find a box of pads that I'm not even sure I have. Under the sink, the étagère, and the linen cabinet— nothing. That can't be right. I haven't had a cycle in six months. There should be something in this muthafucka.

Bam! Bam! Bam!

"What the fuck are you doing in there?" Mason thunders. He opens the door without waiting for an answer and catches me on my hands and knees, looking behind the Clorox, Pine Sol, and Tilex. "What the—?"

Bang!

I knock the shit out of the back of my head on the pipe under the sink. I climb out, glaring up at him. "What the fuck? Can't I piss in private?"

"You piss under the sink now?" he asks, confused. His gaze drifts over to the bloody water in the toilet bowl. "What the hell is that?"

"Will you get out of here? I'll be out in a minute."

Mason's eyes get big as fuck. "Are you bleeding? Why the fuck are you bleeding?"

"I'm sure that it's no big deal," I tell him, even though I'm not too damn sure of a damn thing my damn self. "I'm looking for some . . . some . . ."

"Some what?" he asks, frustrated.

"*Pads!*" My face heats with embarrassment. I don't discuss personal shit like sanitary napkins with anyone, let alone my man. And he's staring at me like I sprouted a second head. "Get out. I know I got some around here someplace."

Mason snaps out of whatever trance he's in, grabs my hand, and snatches me off the floor.

I don't even have time enough to complain before he tosses me my clothes and hauls me out of the house. He drives me to the crib where Profit and Ta'Shara are shacked up.

Bam! Crash! Smash!

"What the fuck?" Mason abandons knocking on the door to charge right on in.

We catch Profit in the middle of the living room, throwing a vase at a nearby wall.

"What the hell are you doing?" Mason thunders.

A startled Profit spins on his heels, whipping out his gun.

Mason quickly steps in front of me to block a potential shot. "Yo! Whoa!"

Recognition slams into Profit. "What the fuck?"

"That's what I asked you," Mason says. "Put that damn thing away."

Profit lowers the gun and apologizes.

I look around. It looks like a tornado blew through this muthafucka.

"You a'ight, bro?" Mason asks. "What got you so fucking heated?"

We step farther into the house. I close the door behind me.

Profit looks around like it's the first time he's seen the destruction. "Uh, it's, uh, nothing," he lies.

"It looks like you're either handling some bullshit or some bullshit is handling you," Mason comments.

His brother gnashes his teeth, but then gives the coffee table a good damn kick.

"Where's your girl?"

Profit rakes his hand through his hair as if that was a difficult question. "She's in the back."

Mason cuts me a look and I know he wants me to go
check on her.

"I'll be right back."

He nods, but at the last second grabs hold of my wrist.
"Make sure that you also ask her for those, uh—you know, for
your situation."

My situation? "Yeah. Yeah. I got it." I pull away, rolling my
eyes. Shaking my head as I make my way back to their bedroom, I can't help but dread this coming conversation. The
master bedroom door is open and the first thing I see are bags
crammed with clothes all over the floor. *What the fuck?*

"Ta'Shara?" I lean my head inside of the door. "Girl, are
you in here?"

I hear someone whimpering or sniffling in the adjoining
bathroom. *Aww. Shit.* I'm not in the mood to be dealing with
another emotional female. I got my own damn problems. I
stand at the door, weighing my options. I could tell Mason that
the girl doesn't have what I need and book our asses out of
here. But my conscience makes a rare appearance and tells me
that I can't do that. The next thing I know, I'm huffing and
rolling my eyes as I stomp my way over to the bathroom.

After one knock, I push open the door to see Ta'Shara sitting on the floor with her legs pressed against her chest and
her head lying on her knees. She looks like a hot-ass mess.

"Are you all right in here?" I ask.

She lifts her head and looks at me. I know immediately
that the girl is as high as a kite.

"What the hell do *you* want?"

My conscience poofs up in smoke. "The attitude is getting
old," I tell her.

She waves me off like I'm an insignificant fly buzzing around
her head. "Go away."

"Bitch, either you got a new set of balls or you got a fuck-ing death wish."

She looks me dead in my eyes. "No offense, but fuck you."

"Okay. That's your last muthafuckin' one. Mouth off again I'll slice out your damn tongue. Got it?"

She keeps her chin up and her anger visible, but she's not dumb enough to call my fucking bluff. Finally she looks away. "What do you want?"

I spot a box of Kotex pads and snatch the bitch up without asking for permission. "Not a damn thing."

She looks at me like I've lost my mind, but it'll be a cold day in hell before I ask this girl for a damn thing. As I storm back across the bedroom, I'm counting to ten.

"Wait," she calls after me.

I pull up, but don't turn around.

"Have you and Profit ever . . ."

Slowly, I spin around. "Have Profit and I what?"

"You know."

Suppressing the urge to curse her out, I take a breath be-cause clearly the girl is in pain. Suddenly I remember all the times it tore my heart out as I stood by and watched Mason date one bum bitch after another before he finally bought a vowel and got a clue about our love. No matter how I feel about this girl, she's still new to this life.

"Listen to me, because I'm only going to say this once." I wait until our eyes connect. "No. Hell no. And not even if he was the last brother walking." *Ok. Technically that was three times.* "Profit is practically my annoying teenaged brother."

She nods.

"Are you good?"

Ta'Shara hesitates. "The thing is I don't know whether he looks at you simply as his sister."

The misery etched into her face tugs at me again. "He said it was a mistake," I tell her. "I believe him. I don't know what that kiss was all about and to tell you the truth, I really don't give a damn. But let me give you a little sisterly advice about men. They fuck up—constantly. You gotta figure out whether you can learn to love him despite all of that. Now I'm not saying that you have to stand around and take it. At the end of the day, you got to do what's best for you. If you love him, fight for him. If you're not sure, you need to figure it out." I glance down at her bags and then turn and walk out of the bedroom.

In the living room, Mason and Profit are sitting across from each other with their heads bowed. When I walk in, Profit lifts his head and looks like an abused puppy. Him and Ta'Shara belong together, but they probably have a long road ahead of them before they figure that out again.

"Everything cool?" Mason asks, spotting the box in my hand.

"Yeah. Let's go."

Mason stands and then looks down at his brother. "Are you going to be all right?"

Profit nods.

"All right. You know that I'm here for you, little bro."

Profit comes to his feet with a gloomy smile and walks us to the door.

"You know I'm always here for you," Mason adds. The look on his charred face reads that he wishes he could fix whatever is wrong between the two young lovers, but he realizes that they need to find their own way.

39

Ta'Shara

Profit pads his way to the bathroom and leans his body against the door's frame.

I don't bother to hide that I'm throwing myself a pity party. "Did you call the cab?"

"Yeah," he answers softly. "It should be here any moment."

I nod, having run out of things to say. The silence is excruciating. I want him to leave me alone, yet I also want him to stay and help me figure shit out.

"Do you have any money?" he asks.

"I think I have a couple of dollars in my purse."

He reaches into his pocket and pulls out a knot of cash. First, he peels off a few bills, but then ends up handing me the whole damn thing. "Here. This should tide you over."

I remain stubborn. "I don't want your money."

"Take it," he insists.

After backhanding the next wave of tears, I swallow my pride and accept the bundle of cash. "Thanks."

Silence.

I pull myself off the floor and finish cramming the rest of my shit into the bags.

"Are you finished with these?" Profit asks.

I nod and he picks them up and carries them into the living room. I follow him with the last of my stuff. It's another twenty minutes before a pair of headlights sweeps across the window.

Profit looks out and announces, "Your taxi is here."

Struggling to keep it together, I start picking up the bags again.

"Here. I'll get those," he says, rushing over.

When I exit out of the house, my eyes burn and my heart feels as if it's being squeezed inside a vise. The driver sees the bags and pops the trunk. Once the bags are put away, I creep to the cab's back door while searching my brain for something to say.

Profit opens the back door and then shifts his weight nervously on his feet.

Unable to take the awkwardness any longer, I decide to keep it simple. "Bye."

"Do you know where you're going to stay?" he blurts once I climb into the backseat.

"I have an idea."

He waits, but once he sees I'm not going to tell him where I'm going, he nods again. I reach for the door, but he continues to hold on to it. But when he can't settle on what it is he really wants to say, he settles for, "Take care of yourself."

"You too." I tug on the door just as he releases it.

"Where to, miss?" the cab driver asks.

I give him Mack's address.

He frowns. "That's a few blocks from here," he says, confused.

"There's a hundred bucks in it for you."

He perks up then. "All right then." He shifts the car into reverse and pulls out of the drive.

Profit stands in the front yard, watching.

As the cab pulls away from Ruby Cove, I tell myself, *Don't look back.*

It's the hardest thing I've ever done.

40

LeShelle

Oak Court Mall

I hate the fucking mall—especially on a damn weekend. It's filled with kids, crowding the food court while they peep each other out like a damn meat market. The thought of picking this bitch Adaryl out of the crowd is already giving me a headache.

"Are you sure that this bitch is here?" I ask Avonte.

"Yep. She works at Foot Locker."

At least that'll make it easier. "All right. Let's do this shit."

We all pop out of Avonte's car and head into the mall. The second I step into the place it completes my nightmare. Out-of-shape security guards, old people walking laps, weak men with weak game winking and trying to holler at me. And, of course, the teenagers. Fast girls dressed like mini transvestites and the boys still wearing their pants damn-near down to their ankles, with their caps twisted back. But no flags hung from their back pockets. Nowadays you have to get up close and personal to read brothahs' tats.

The same game, but with a twist.

Myeisha taps me on the shoulder and then points to a bitch up ahead leaving the Foot Locker. "There she go."

The second I spot her a shot of adrenaline shoots straight to my pussy and a smile stretches across my lips. We follow close behind Adaryl as she makes her way toward the food court. We got to play this shit right; despite this mall being sketchy as hell, it's probably filled with cameras.

With my patience wearing thin, we stalk Adaryl while she hooks up with some friends, none of them Qiana or Shamara. Thirty minutes later, Adaryl puts away her tray and heads toward the girls' bathroom alone.

"Let's roll."

Avonte, Myeisha, and Erika stand and follow her. Once we push our way through the door I shout to the other occupants, "You bitches, get the fuck out!"

Adaryl whips around, sees my face, and tries to make a run to barricade herself in one of the stalls.

Avonte grabs her by the collar while Erika and Myeisha usher everyone out the door.

"Please. Please," Adaryl cries. "I don't want to have anything to do with this."

I shake my head at her terrible lie. "That's not how I remember it. I recall *you*, Shamara, and Qiana approaching *me* to strike a deal."

Myeisha locks the bathroom door.

Adaryl panics. "It's Qiana you want. I don't even fuck with her no more."

"Aww. You girls had a BFF spat?" I ask in a fake sympathetic voice. "That's too bad." I cock my head. "But *we* still had a deal," I remind her. "I kept my end of the deal. And you bitches pulled a fast one on me. That doesn't seem fair, does it?"

Tears flow down Adaryl's face like a waterfall.

"I asked you a question."

"N-no. But Qiana doesn't even have the baby no more."

"What?" I cock my head. "What did she do with it?"

"I don't know. I swear. The cops came snooping around and she had to stash him somewhere—but she didn't tell anyone where."

I stare at the girl, weighing whether she's telling the truth.

"I didn't think so—but the thing is: I had a talk with your girl Qiana, and she was supposed to set shit right with me the other night. Did she tell you about it?"

More tears. "I-I'm sorry."

"Sorry that you left me standing there all night like a damn fool? C'mon. You know I can't let you bitches play me. What if that shit got around? I have a reputation to protect. You understand that, don't you?"

"Please. Please. Don't kill me."

"Kill you?" I laugh and then look to my girls, who awkwardly sputter out a few chuckles. "No. No. I'm not going to kill you. Don't be ridiculous. I need to send a message to your friend Qiana. That's all."

Adaryl's tears slow and her breathing eases. "Really?"

"You can carry a message for me, can't you?"

"Y-yes. I can do that."

"Good."

I look up at Avonte, who produces a bowie knife and hands it to me.

Adaryl freaks.

"Hold her down," I order.

"No. Wait! Please! No!"

I place the blade under her chin. "Shut the fuck up!"

She clamps her mouth shut, but still whimpers loudly.

"Your ass needs to be happy that I'm gonna let you walk your bony ass up out of here. You start screaming like that again and I might change my mind."

The whimpering stops.

"Now are you right-handed or left-handed?"

"R-right."

My smile broadens. "Good. Now to show you how much

of a reasonable person I really am, I'm going to let you keep the fingers on your right hand."

More tears.

"Left hand," I bark to Avonte and Erika.

They quickly jerk the girl's hand down on the bathroom counter. Remembering how Qiana had begged for time, I relent. Maybe the girl really does need more time to bring the baby from wherever she stashed him at. "And as an added bonus, tell Qiana I'm going to give her a little more time to retrieve that baby. Two weeks. That's all."

I place the blade over the middle three fingers. "This is going to hurt like hell," I warn her and then chopped those muthafuckas off.

Adaryl screams.

41

Qiana

GG, Li'l Bit, and I comfort a near hysterical Adaryl. Her left hand is fucked up. LeShelle left her with two digits: her thumb and pinky finger. It gets me thinking of how lucky I'd been in the back of that cab.

"She wants that fucking kid," Adaryl snaps. "Give him to her."

"She is going to kill him," I say.

"So? It's either that or she'll kill all of us."

"Shhh." I glance over my shoulder while we're nestled behind a curtain in the Emergency Room. "You want everyone to hear you?"

"I don't give a fuck," Adaryl says. "Look what she did to my hand in broad daylight at the fucking mall. She knows our names and where we live." She glances at Li'l Bit. "You too."

Li'l Bit swallows hard and looks ready to faint.

GG steps in. "So what does she want you guys to do?"

"She set up a second meeting at Hack's Crossing Park. She also gave you two more weeks to retrieve the baby from wherever you stashed him at. But if we don't show up this time and that pop-up bitch is coming for us."

"Okay. We'll get you out of here," GG says.

"The nurse says to wait here. I have to file a police report. I couldn't do it at the mall since I passed out."

"Are you crazy?" I hiss. "You can't file a damn report. We're already on the cop's radar for that hit."

She frowns like she hadn't thought about that.

Still bickering and arguing, me and my girls, Li'l Bit and Adaryl climb into my SUV after leaving the hospital.

"I don't understand why we don't give her the real baby," Adaryl says. "We done played that bitch LeShelle twice already. She's going to go all psycho on us if we try to do it again."

I sigh. We've already been over the plan to have a full posse in place so that we can gun LeShelle down and walk away. But Adaryl keeps poking holes in every plan we give her.

"Where is the baby anyway?"

"Don't worry about it. He's safe." The less information she has, the better.

My aunt Kathy has Jayson. She lives on the other side of town and didn't ask too many questions when I gave her Jayson. She's never had a baby of her own and practically looked at the child like an early Christmas gift.

"I have a bad feeling about this," Adaryl says every other minute.

"Will you *please* shut up? You're really working my nerves."

"Well, I guess we wouldn't want that, now would we?" She sneers.

"Bitch—"

"Whoa. Whoa," Li'l Bit shouts, tryna keep her eyes on us *and* the road. "You two calm down. We all need to stay calm so we can get through this shit."

"We're driving straight into a trap," Adaryl mutters, twisting in her seat. "What?" she snaps when I twist around and stare at her.

"You really are working my nerves."

"So what?"

"Okay, you two. Let's act like grown bitches and squash this shit," Li'l Bit whines.

We don't hear a word our girl is saying. "What the fuck is your problem?" I snap.

"*You* are my damn problem," Adaryl barks. "The muthafuckin' police have been to my house *twice* asking me about Tyneshia's ass. When was the last time I saw her? Why didn't I report her ass missing? What was her relationship to that other dead bitch you carved up? Tyneshia's people live right next door to me and are lookin' at me sideways because they *know* Tyneshia always mobbed with us—and there you were chillin' with a baby everybody knows you didn't shoot out your fuckin' pussy."

"Just y'all and GG even knew I had him."

"Plus Tombstone *and your dad,* Nookie, *and* the train of senior citizen crack hoes he deals with," Adaryl reminds me, "and everybody at that muthafuckin' Flower party last week. I heard them talking about it. They think Tombstone has a baby momma floating around somewhere and dumped that baby at y'all doorstep."

"What?"

"Yeah. Lucky for you"

I relax.

"We're on our home turf, but don't act like snitches aren't real," Adaryl adds. "They *are*—and they have jacked up many of our plans for niggas who thought they were too slick by half. It's a matter of time before that new captain of police and her gang of storm troopers take they asses down to Ruby Cove and toss us into a cell so dark and deep that muthafuckas are going to forget that we were ever born. Frankly, we should've murked that li'l nigga when we had the chance."

"Don't put this all on me. You had your chance to kill him and you couldn't kill his ass either," I remind her.

"None of us did. But that didn't stop you from smoking Tyneshia's ass."

"Fuck that twenty-dollar-weave bitch," I shout. "I never

liked her ass no ways. She hung with our ass for five goddamn minutes and was already tryna rise up."

"You mean you felt your follow-the-leader position was threatened with our dumb asses, so you popped off and got us in some real shit. Look at my goddamn hand!"

"Pump the brakes on all this whining. For real," I warn. "Weren't you the one that wanted to be a street bitch—a real gangsta bitch?"

"For the Vice Lords? Hell fuckin' yeah," Adaryl says. "But for *this* bullshit—hell no!"

For a hot second, I envision blasting this bitch's head clean off her shoulders.

"Well?" Adaryl challenges me. "What the fuck you wanna do?"

"Chill. All this shit is going to be over soon."

"Fuck that." Adaryl unhooks her seat belt. "Li'l Bit, pull over."

"No." My hand goes to my burner before I even have a chance to think about it. "Keep driving."

Adaryl's gaze zooms to the gun in my hand. "What? You're going to shoot *me* now?"

"We're going to stick to the goddamn plan. When we're done, everybody can go their separate ways. Cool?"

Adaryl shakes her head. "You ain't hearing shit. LeShelle ain't going to let us walk away. We know too much."

"She's right." Li'l Bit chirps her two cents. "I'm starting to get a bad feeling about this too."

The mutiny is complete.

"Pull this bitch over. I want out. Li'l Bit, you can hang with this crazy, scarred-up bitch if you wanna, but you can count me out. Deuces."

Li'l Bit eases her foot off the accelerator.

I swing my burner to point it right at her head. "Don't you stop this car," I threaten.

Shocked, Li'l Bit's eyes triple in size. "Are you crazy?"

"Hell yeah, she's out of her damn mind," Adaryl yells. "I told you this shit for months!"

"Shut the fuck up." I swing the gun toward the backseat of the car. "I'm sick of your ass. Who the fuck told you that you were running shit?"

"Nobody elected your ass to run shit either," Adaryl barks.

I spring up out of my seat, my gun now trained on this reckless bitch who's begging for a bullet. "I don't need an election. I run this shit. Always have and always will. Play your position."

"Fuck you!" Adaryl thrusts her .38 in my face with her good hand. "I'm tired of *your* shit. Just because Tombstone got rank, don't mean your ass is somebody. You wanna pop off? Then let's do this shit."

"Y'all quit it!" Li'l Bit shouts, easing her foot off the accelerator again.

"Didn't I tell your ass not to stop?" I make the mistake of turning my attention back to Li'l Bit because Adaryl's stupid ass chooses this moment to fire.

POP! POP! POP!

"BITCH!" I shoot back.

POP! POP!

Adaryl ducks to the floorboards while my bullets shatter the back window.

"Quit it! Quit it!" Li'l Bit slams on her brakes.

I fly backwards. My head hits the windshield and my back slams against the dashboard. Tires squeal and in the middle of the craziness, I drop my gun and hear it go off one last time before we fly off the road and roll down an embankment that seems to go on forever. Then suddenly everything stops. The car. The screaming. The shooting.

Everything.

42

Lucifer

King *Isaac.*

His name is rumbling in the streets again. This on the heels of learning that Diesel Carver has transplanted from Atlanta. Add an angry Python and that makes three powerful legends suddenly on the scene. How could a massive invasion on our territory not be too far off? From my left Mason's snoring deepens. I'm glad that he's finally getting some sleep, but at the same time, why the fuck is he sleeping when we're being surrounded by enemies and we don't have a new arms dealer lined up?

And I'm in this condition.

I toss and turn for more than half the night while Mason finally sleeps like a baby. Pregnancy doesn't agree with me. I do manage to fall asleep briefly, but I wake up frightened, and then for hours I can't shake the ominous feeling that has somehow crept into my bones. That can't be good.

When Mason wakes, he catches me frowning and rubbing my belly.

"Is everything cool?" he asks.

"Huh? Oh. Yeah." Since that doesn't sound too encouraging, he continues to stare at me. "You'd tell me if there's something wrong, right?"

Depends on what it is.

"Right?"

"Mason, please. I'm just cranky, all right? And it's hot in this bitch. Are you sure the damn air conditioner is working?"

"Yeah. But if it'll make you feel any better, I'll go and check." He climbs out of the bed and pads out into the hall to check the thermostat and the vents. "I feel cool air," he hollers back.

I roll my eyes and wish that I could crawl out of my skin.

Mason walks back into the bedroom, takes one look at me, and asks, "How about I fix you a bowl of ice cream?"

"I think I just fell in love with you all over again," I blurt out, unsure why I feel like I'm on the verge of crying. *Crying.* I rarely fucking cry.

"Okay. It's settled. Ice cream for breakfast." He slaps his hands together and makes a mad dash to the kitchen.

I push myself up from the bed. When I do, I feel a sudden drop. That startles me. "What the fuck?" When nothing else happens, I breathe a sigh of relief. In that moment, my fear forges a special bond between me and my child. The fear that something may be wrong or something may have happened to him.

Until this moment, being pregnant has been just my state of being—and yes, I felt some kind of way about being inconvenienced. But the thought of there being something wrong terrifies me like nothing in the streets ever has.

"Okay," Mason says, returning with a big ol' grin on his face. "I got your favorite: Rocky Road." He takes another look at my face. And he sees my watery eyes. "What happened? What's wrong?"

"Nothing." I swipe the tears from my eyes.

Mason stares with two bowls of ice cream in his hands, like he's too scared to move.

"I just felt the baby kick. That's all."

"Oh yeah?" He puts the ice cream down on the dresser

and rushes over to have a feel for himself. But he waits and waits, and when nothing happens, his smile drops again.

"Maybe you'll catch it later," I say.

Disappointed, he nods and stands. "We got to get you an appointment with a doctor. I can't believe that you haven't done that yet."

"Can you hand me my ice cream before you turn into my mother?"

He grabs the bowls. "I'm just saying."

"Yeah. Yeah. I'll call someone today."

"Who?"

"I don't know. I'll look in the phone book or Google it, I guess." I plow my first spoon of Rocky Road into my mouth.

"You're going to get some random?" he asks, twisting up his face.

"What? You got your favorite ob-gyn doctor on speed dial or something?"

"Nah. Nah." He shrugs. "I thought you and your girls kinda shared that sort of information."

I stare at him.

"I mean, surely one of the Flowers can recommend a doctor."

"I wouldn't know since I don't hang out with the Flowers." I give him a *what the fuck* look.

"Okay. Don't get like that. You know what I mean. We should get someone with a proven record."

"How much skill does it take to stand between my legs and play catch?"

He cocks his head and stares with his mismatched-colored eyes. "Will you get serious? It's not going to kill you to act like a female for the next couple of months. That means going to a doctor and letting him check out your lady parts."

To avoid snapping back at him, I shove more ice cream into my mouth.

"Don't act like I'm wrong or I'm being unreasonable."

"Okay. Okay." I roll my eyes. "I'll . . . ask around."

He smiles. But he waits until I'm practically inhaling my creamy breakfast before he hits me with his next request.

"I need for you to go see Smokestack," he says.

I groan. "I'm sorry. It seems like lately every time I see him, I'm the bearer of bad news for him."

"I understand. But I really need you to do this. He's gotta have a contact for our people to get more guns."

He has my full attention. "So you're worried about King Isaac being back on the streets?"

"More than worried. The timing with this Diesel character *and* Python simmering out there?" He shakes his head. "We got to be on our p's and q's on this shit. I want our people armed to the teeth if need be."

I nod. "Okay."

"And take Profit with you."

"What?"

"Look. It's way past time for me to start grooming him for leadership. In this game you never know. I may not always be around. He's got to be ready to step up."

I know he doesn't mean it the way I took the statement, but it still hurts. Mason meets my gaze. "I love you, baby, but you can never be king—only queen." He crosses over to deliver a kiss. I'll admit it: it does make me feel better.

"So you'll do this for me?" he asks.

I hesitate a second too long.

"When are you going to tell me what the hell is going on between you and Profit?"

I choke. "What?"

He leans over and lightly whacks my back until I can breathe again. "You good?"

I nod.

"Cool. Now about Profit—and before you fix your mouth to say *nothing*, I'm not blind or stupid. *Something* is up."

Oh fuck. I don't know whether I have the energy to come up with a lie that I can remember—and given how salty Ta'Shara has been behaving, I need to think my answer through.

Mason's stare intensifies. "Are you two still fighting about that night I went over the bridge? Do you want me to talk to him?"

I relax. "No. I don't need for you to fight my battles."

"Well, I don't want him stressing you out. There's no reason for him to still be upset about that. I'm back. Everything is cool."

"Give him some more time. He'll come around," I say, sighing and mentally kicking myself.

Mason weighs my words. "All right—but if I see him stressing you out again, I'm gonna step to him and set him straight."

"Deal."

He gives me another kiss and then places his hand on my belly. Again, the baby doesn't kick and he has to walk away with his ice cream, disappointed.

43

LeShelle

I haven't been catering to my man as much as I should. Given the amount of stress that we've been going through this past year, we've been feeling the cracks in our foundation, but we're finally back on the same page. I sent Kane and June Bug to Bath & Body Works for some bath soaks, body scrub, and a few more supplies so I can give him a nice mani and pedi.

I know that I'm running the risk of going overboard, but I'm so damn happy to have my real nigga back that I might also throw in a private strip show before I really put it on him. Once I get the candles lit and the rose petals tossed, I change into a black silk teddy and half robe, and then call Python into the bathroom.

He takes one look around the bathroom and cocks a curious smile. "What the fuck is all this?"

Smiling, I walk over and take him by the hand. "This is all for you."

"Yeah? Did I forget that it's my birthday or some shit?"

"No. I just wanted to do something nice for you." I tug his suspicious ass inside and then help him remove his shirt. Then I run my fingers over his muscled and tattooed chest. My nigga may be ugly as sin, but he also has the body of an African god.

"Now that you got me up in here, whatcha gonna do?"

"I'm going to treat you like the king you are." I unhook his black jeans and then slowly slide down the zipper. We usually go at it hard and rough, but tonight I want to slow shit down and seduce my man. I glide my hands to each side of his hips and then tug his jeans and boxers down his legs. As I kneel in front of him, his cock springs up and pops me on the chin.

"It looks like someone is happy to see you," Python says, smirking. "Are you ready to eat the cake, Anna Mae?"

"Not yet." I wink up at him. "I like my dessert after the meal." But to tide him over, I take hold of his thick dick and plant a kiss against the fat mushroom head.

"All right, momma. I'm gonna let you do you and enjoy the show." He steps out of his clothes.

Standing up, I remove my robe and allow a few seconds for him to drink me all in. The lace on the front of my teddy does a good job of hiding the rash of keloids across my chest, courtesy of Ta'Shara's failed murder attempt. Regardless, I'm still flawless judging by my husband's hungry gaze. I take him over to the tub and tell him, "Step in."

For once, he follows directions and sits down. "Awww. This feels nice."

"You like that, baby?" I ask, kneeling down next to the tub.

He leans all the way back and closes his eyes. "What's not to like?"

"Good."

"Are you going to join me in here?"

"I already had my bath." I reach over for the new mesh sponge and then douse it with liquid soap. I wash his body in small circular strokes, taking my time to make sure that I get every inch of him. The shit starts feeling so good to him that he starts humming. That's when I surprise his ass and bust out the bowl of grapes.

"Oh. You're on this shit." He chuckles before plucking a few and popping them into his mouth.

"I want to make you feel good," I tell him. "After all that's gone down, you need to relax and recharge." His crooked smile gets my heart fluttering a bit. "Welcome back."

Python knows exactly what I'm talking about. "Yeah. I guess I was trippin' on some bullshit," he admits. "Muthafuckas can't change the past. What's done is done. I know that shit now."

Our eyes lock and for the first time in a long fucking while I feel as if we're one.

"Thanks for hanging in there with your man. I'm going to do right by your loyalty."

"Does that mean that we're going to start fighting for what's ours again?"

He nods. "We're going to take our shit back and then we're going to snatch everybody else's shit too. You feelin' me? You down?"

My smile widens. "What the fuck do you think?" I set the grapes aside and start soaping his two-tone dick as it juts above the milk-colored water like a chocolate éclair.

"Mmmmm." Python sinks lower into the tub and spreads open his legs so I can make sure he gets as clean as a whistle. In no time, he's moving his hips in time to my rhythm. With my free hand, I reach for the bath oil and then use that mutha-fucka like a lube.

Python looks like he's ready to lose his shit when I slow everything waaay the fuck down. "Ah. I knew that your ass was going to start playing games."

"Yeah? But isn't this a *fun* game?" Leaning over, I pour everything that I am into a kiss because I want him to truly feel me. The shit must feel good to him because the next thing I know his wet hands wrap around me and I'm pulled into the tub with him.

Laughing, I splash down next to him. "What are you doing? This is silk."

"I don't give a fuck about that. It's coming off any damn way." He hooks one finger around one, thin spaghetti strap and then snaps that muthafucka off with no effort. "I appreciate you pampering your man, but the best way to spoil my ass is by giving me some of that bomb-ass pussy you got." To make sure that I didn't misunderstand his direct ass, he cups my pussy and gives it a firm squeeze. In response, my clit pounds against his palm like a jackhammer. Next thing I know there's a whole lot of splashing going on as the teddy is ripped from my body. There's no need for foreplay because I'm already adding my special honey into the mix.

With one powerful stroke, I'm impaled on his cock. The shit feels so good that my head immediately lolls back and my eyes roll around in my head. Once my pussy adjusts I start rolling my hips.

"Yeah, baby. That's what the fuck I'm talking about. Ssssss." Python caresses my breasts for a moment, before pinching the nipples.

I hiss my damn self. The harder he pinches, the higher my nut rises.

Loving the sound of my pleasure, Python pushes himself up from the water to latch his mouth around one of my throbbing nipples. The instant his teeth skim across the delicate skin, my pussy squirts all over his dick. In no time at all his hands make their way around my body and my ass cheeks inch wider and wider.

I know my nigga like the back of my hand. I know what he's feigning for. My pussy may be great but my ass is like fucking heaven to him. Still rocking my hips, I feel one of his fingers slide in through the back door.

Then another.

Before long, I'm wide the fuck open: on my knees with my face pressed against the cold water knob and my ass up in the air, getting pounded hard.

"Awww. Fuck. Yesssss. Ssssssss." Python slaps my ass so hard that I jump and squirt some more. Nigga turns my asshole into a crime scene before he nuts so fucking hard that I feel that shit gushing all up in my belly.

And our asses ain't nowhere near done.

We stand up together and turn on the shower to rinse off. But minutes later, our wet, naked bodies are falling onto the bedsheets, ready for round two. Instead of looking around for a belt buckle, Python snatches the cord from the nightstand lamp and wraps that shit around my neck like a fucking noose.

I don't panic or lose my cool because this strangling shit ain't fuckin' new to me. Back in the day when we first hooked up, I thought the muthafucka was sick, and this li'l freak nasty shit that he was into was something that I had to endure to be his new queen. But over time, I started liking the pain and then loving it. There is something about playing with death that makes muthafuckas feel more alive. That's the best way to describe it. And if you're doing the shit with a nice cocaine kick: paradise.

"Ssssss." We're in the fucking zone. No one and nothing exists but us and this moment. Once again, I feel like I would lie for this nigga, kill for this nigga, and even die for him. And right now, with a dildo in my pussy, his fat cock in my ass, and a cord wrapped around my neck, I *know* that he feels the same fucking way.

44

Qiana

I wake up screaming. The pain in my leg is excruciating. I fight like hell to move it, and then when I realize that maybe I shouldn't, the pain gets worse. Soon the screaming and crying uses up my energy and my lungs start burning. I swear, if that damn Adaryl isn't already dead, I'm going to fucking kill that damn bitch. Closing my eyes, I tell myself to rest for a few minutes. Instead I nod off. When I wake the second time, it's to the sound of GG's panicked voice calling out to me.

"Qiana? Can you hear me? Say something if you can hear me."

The most I can do is groan.

"Oh, thank God," she pants, relieved.

Mentally, I struggle to pull it together. "My-my leg is stuck," I say. "Can you help me move it?"

"Hold on."

She moves around outside of the vehicle, and then nothing. "Hello? GG, are you still there? Hello?"

She latches hold of my foot and another scream rips from my soul. Mercifully, it only lasts for a minute and I'm able to breathe again.

"Can you move now?" GG asks.

I'm certain I can't, but try anyway. Surprisingly, I'm able to move an inch—and then another one. Within seconds, hope reignites and I'm able to pull myself through the shattered window.

A thunderclap booms as I crawl into a field of muddy grass. GG rushes to my aid and tugs me the rest of the way. I glance back over my shoulder to see the car sitting on its roof. "Damn." I look around. "Where's Adaryl and Li'l Bit?"

GG clamps her mouth tight and shakes her head.

What the hell is that supposed to mean? I swipe a hand across my brow and notice the scrapes and gashes across my arms and hands.

"They're dead," GG croaks. "Both of them."

"What? Are you sure?" I stare back at the car again and spot Adaryl's mangled body in the front seat. She must've been what had my foot trapped in the front of the car. A few feet away from the car, lying in a disjointed heap, is Li'l Bit. Her dead, sightless eyes staring up toward the graying sky.

"What the hell happened?" GG asks. "Who the fuck was shooting in the car?"

The argument replays inside my head, but I'm not taking the blame for this shit. "Adaryl fired first," I say, which isn't a lie. "She got cold feet about the plan and started tripping."

"Goddamn it," GG swears under her breath. No doubt, she regrets getting herself involved in my shit now.

"What are we going to do now?"

She shakes her head. "I don't know. Let me think."

I look at her, ready to hang on her every word. I have no clue what to do other than eat a damn bullet my damn self or wait for LeShelle to do whatever the fuck she's going to do. I'm almost past fucking caring.

A car speeds past on top of the embankment. Sooner or later someone is going to spot us and stop or call for help. The same thought must've crossed GG's mind.

"Okay. Let's get you out of here. There's nothing that we can do for your friends now." She squats down beside me. "Can you stand?"

I look at my foot with doubt, but I have to try.

GG helps me up. I place nearly all my weight on the good leg, but when I have to take that first step, I almost face-plant back into the mud. But my girl catches me and helps me up the hill to her car. By the time we get inside we're both sweating up a storm.

"I'll take you home, get you cleaned up, and figure out our next move. Okay?"

Of course, I agree. I'm all out of ideas.

45

Ta'Shara

Life at Mack's place continues to be one big party. I'm glad because I need this shit in order to survive my broken heart. One part of me screams for me to forgive, but another won't let me. Maybe this shit is all my fault—for clinging onto Profit like he was a life raft. Maybe I've become too needy—too clingy.

Mack is right. I need to become more independent. Stack my own paper. Have my own identity. For the moment, I'm living off the knot of cash that Profit gave me and I'm ashamed to say that I've spent most of that on drugs.

It's not a habit. I can quit at any time. But right now I have no desire to be all up in my feelings twenty-four hours a day. Feelings lead to tears and I'm all cried out.

"So are you going to get in on this or what?" Mack asks, referring to her great credit card scheme.

I sigh, still not feeling her big moneymaker, but what the fuck else am I going to do? "I guess I can check it out," I tell her. "See if I'm any good at the shit."

The girls break out into huge smiles.

"Trust me," Mack brags. "It's the easiest shit you've ever done."

"We'll see," I say, accepting the wet blunt being passed by Romil.

This shit gives me an incredible high. I don't know why Mack thinks this is the best time to go over step-by-step how we jack people's social security numbers and what not, because everything she's saying is going in one ear and out the other. I get a rhythm going on, knowing when to nod and when to say, "Uh-huh."

When my body gets to tingling real good, I tell one of the girls to turn the music up and I start shaking my ass.

"Looks like someone is ready to hit the clubs again tonight," Mack says.

"Yeah. Maybe we can find that sexy-ass nigga you were dancing with at Club Diesel again."

I blush, remembering Beast. "He was fine."

"Uh-huh," Dime cosigns. "He's the perfect brother to get your mind off Profit."

My mood sours. "Why the hell did you have to bring him up for?"

Mack joins in. "Hell. You probably gotta worry about him rolling his ass up in there again and dragging you out."

They laugh at my expense, sounding like a pack of hyenas.

"Girl, don't make that face. You know that nigga is still hung up on you. People peep you two rolling around this hood, trying not to trip over each other's bottom lip. It's fucking sad."

I clamp my mouth shut and seethe. It's not their fault. I still haven't told them what went down between Profit and me.

Mack stays on a roll. "You know y'all still love each other. I don't see what the problem is."

Dime chirps up again. "Yeah. My nigga, Big Boy, says Profit is keeping to himself and acting like he don't see none of the neighborhood thots tryna push up on him."

"What?"

"Girl. These thirsty bitches don't play. If there's an available dick on the market, they're going all in on that shit."

"Fuck available. Thots be checking the locks on the shit that's locked down, too." Romil laughs.

Dime suddenly gets religion. "Amen and amen."

"Will you please change the damn subject?" I growl. I'm already having a hard time getting that damn kiss out of my head. I don't want or need to add images of a line of hoes rotating in and out of our bedroom.

"All right, girl." Mack shrugs. "Don't say that we didn't warn you. Out here, a good nigga is hard to find."

I roll my eyes and reach to take another hit on the blunt, but as high as I am, I can't get the nightmare images of Profit fucking every girl in a ten-mile radius out of my head. I hop up on Mack's coffee table and try to dance Profit out of my system.

Suddenly there's a knock at the front door.

"I'll get it," Dime says, stubbing out the blunt and running toward the door.

I go back to my blissful dancing until I hear Qiana Barrett screech, "WHAT THE FUCK IS *SHE* DOING HERE?"

46

Qiana

My gaze bounces around Mack's living room. I can't believe what I'm seeing.

"What the fuck do you mean?" Mack asks. "She's here because I invited her ass here. Check the fuckin' address. This is my fuckin' crib."

I snap my jaw shut and then turn toward GG. "This was a bad idea. Let's go."

She gives me the stink eye. "And then do what? The clock is ticking, remember?"

She's right. My heart drops. If we don't ask her girls for backup, we're left to deal with this shit by ourselves, which means I'm a dead bitch.

"So what's up?" Mack shouts. "Are y'all comin' in or are y'all trying to heat the outside?"

Despite being in a desperate situation, I tug GG's arm for us to leave, but she shrugs it off and crosses the threshold. I have no choice but to follow.

"It's about damn time," Romil says, shaking her head. "Y'all want a beer or something?"

"Sure, that'll be great," GG answers and then looks at me.

"Yeah. Fine."

"Well, don't do us no muthafuckin' favors." Romil wrinkles her nose. "What the hell is wrong with your foot?"

"Nothing," I lie, holding on to GG's arm.

GG leans over and whispers, "Chillax. We need them, remember?"

My gaze shoots over to a smirking and dancing Ta'Shara. I hate this bitch. And as far as I'm concerned, she's the damn reason that I'm even in this predicament, her crossing color lines and flaunting her and Profit's relationship in my face every time I turn around.

Ta'Shara stops dancing and stares me down. "Damn, bitch. Snap a picture or something."

Dime snickers. "She either wants to kiss you or fuck you. I can't tell which."

Bitch has gotten bold as shit.

"Here you go, Q." Romil hands me a beer. "Make yourself at home."

I look around but don't know where to sit. In fact, I feel out of place—period. And they're supposed to be my people. Not Ta'Shara's.

"What the fuck are you twisting your face for?" Mack barks. "You got something to say about my place?"

"No. No." I glance over at GG, who's eyeballing me to behave. Swallowing back my irritation at Ta'Shara's presence, I drop down into a La-Z-Boy that has definitely seen better days but is still comfortable.

"So what brings you two bitches here?" Mack asks. "This ain't normally your neck of the woods."

"We came by to ask you guys for . . . help."

"GG!"

"What?"

She can't be this fucking clueless that she's about to blurt out my business in front of every damn body.

"Huh. This looks serious." Mack's gaze shifts from me to GG. "What's up? I'm all ears."

"Well. It's personal," GG says, glancing toward Ta'Shara.

Mack, Romil, and Dime all turn toward Ta'Shara.

"What? Y'all want me to step out or something?" she asks.

"Yeah, Einstein," I sass.

Mack faces me and folds her arms. "She ain't gotta go no damn where. She stays here. Anything that you got to say, you can say in front of her."

What? She and Profit not together anymore?

"Well?"

"Oh. Fuck this shit." I push out of the chair and hobble a bit. "I'm out of here."

GG leaps up and grabs my arm. "No. Wait."

"Don't let the door hit you where the good Lord split you on your way out," Mack says.

"See? They aren't even interested in helping me." Saying that shit makes me tear up. I'm not so stupid to not realize that my ass is fucked. I'll have to meet LeShelle without a plan and without backup.

My distress must show because Ta'Shara suddenly says, "Nah. It's good. Y'all talk. I gotta piss anyway." She jumps off the coffee table. "I gotta pee."

Mack smacks the girl on the ass as she turns and sashays away.

What the fuck? The girl has only been a Flower for a hot minute and she's already in deep with GG's clique. My blood boils as I watch Ta'Shara disappear down the hallway.

"Q, child. You're gonna have to get over your li'l beef with our girl. She's one of *us* now," Mack says, grinning.

"Get over it?" I yell. "Look at my fucking face." I point to the twin gashes on my face. "Would you get over this shit?"

Mack shrugs, unmoved. "You stepped to the girl first."

"You're going to choose a damn Queen G's word over mine?"

"She ain't no Queen G. Never was."

"The bitch's sister is the head bitch in charge of those blood clots!"

"You mean the bitch's sister who's been tryna kill her this past year? That bitch?"

That put a pause in my anger.

Mack continues. "Regardless, you gotta squash the shit. You can figure out how to do that shit on your own time. Me? I like her. She's cool."

"And a great muthafuckin' shooter," Dime adds. "You should've seen how she took out that sand nigga at the liquor store."

"What?"

"Saved our asses," Dime says, seeming to have a hard time keeping her head from rolling around her neck. "You really need to give her another chance. You probably have more in common than you think."

I'm in the fucking twilight zone. What was once up is now down and vice versa.

"So what the hell did y'all come over here for—other than to fuck up my damn high?" Mack asks.

GG and I cut a look to each other. I still have a bad feeling about this.

"We need backup," GG blurts out. "We have ourselves a little situation."

"What kind of situation?"

GG looks at me again and my stomach twists.

"Well? You gonna speak or what?" Mack snaps.

"With, um, LeShelle Murphy," I say. "Well, I . . . I sort of . . . did something I shouldn't have—and now if I don't give her what she wants by tonight, she's going to kill me."

"Whoa. Whoa." Mack holds up her hands. "Slow down. What the hell do you mean, you did something you shouldn't have? What did you do?"

Romil and Dime lean forward and stare at my mouth. But

suddenly I can't get my tongue unglued. After all, I killed one of our own.

"Shit. SPEAK!"

GG jumps in. "She made a deal with that crazy LeShelle."

Silence.

"Okay. You two bitches are working my nerves. GG, you're my girl, but really? Either spit it out or get the fuck on."

"I struck a deal," I say, my heart racing. "If she took care of someone for me then I would murk someone for her."

Silence.

"I know it was stupid and I probably wasn't thinking straight. But now I'm in some serious shit. And, well, GG thinks you girls can help me."

"I don't understand," Romil cuts in. "Why didn't you murk the bitch you wanted to murk—or ask us *then* to help you?"

"Because . . . Lucifer gave the order that the bitch couldn't be touched."

"Oh shit," Dime says, her neck still bobbing around. "You violated Lucifer's order? Have you lost your mind? Do you know what the fuck she'll do to you if she finds out?"

My eyes wet up. This is not going at all how GG told me it would go down. *What are we going to do if they turn me down— or worse, turn me over to Lucifer?*

Before I can stop them, tears slip down my face. "I fucked up, okay? I shouldn't have asked LeShelle to kill that grimy bitch Essence. But she violated *all* the fucking rules by going to see Profit while he was laid up in that hospital. Since when in the hell do we protect Queen Gs and shit? The bitch was an enemy and flaunting it in my face that she was allowed to sniff around Profit. So, yeah. I saw an opportunity to get rid of her and I took it. But then LeShelle found out that I didn't kill the baby too, and now she wants me to give her the baby Saturday night at Hack's Crossing—but I know that if I show up, she's going to kill him *and* me."

"And who did you murk for her?" Mack asks, ignoring the second half of my rant.

I swallow and shrug. "Some pregnant yellow bitch that was fucking her man."

Mack, Romil, and Dime rush toward me. "That's where that fuckin' baby came from?"

Dime looks blown away. "Was that the same bitch that they were talking about on the news? You sliced that baby out of a damn corpse?"

"No." I shrug and shuffle my feet. "I sliced him out first."

"Daaaaamn. That's some cold shit." Mack steps back and studies me.

"They found Tyneshia Gibson's body with that girl," Dime says. "She do that damn job with you?"

I swallow.

"What happened?" *Lie. Lie. Lie.* "I, uh, I mean . . ." I glance over at GG for help.

Mack cocks her head. "Don't tell us you had something to do with her death, too."

Ta'Shara's voice slices through all the bullshit. "*You* had Essence killed?"

Everyone's neck swivels to an angry Ta'Shara. She looks like she's breathing fire.

"Answer me, you low-life bum-bitch. You had my best friend killed?"

"Aww. Shit," Mack huffs.

"Fuck that bitch—and *fuck* you too."

In a flash, Ta'Shara flies across the room.

Hell, I barely have time to put my hands up before she's on my ass like white on rice.

"BITCH!"

I back up but my weak foot gives out and we fly over the arm of the La-Z-Boy. When I hit the floor, the air is knocked out of me. Before I can replace it, Ta'Shara's fists crash against my jaw in quick succession. I swing back, but the bitch blocks my punches to deliver more blows. In no time, my mouth fills with blood. *Where the fuck is GG? Why in the fuck she ain't getting this bitch off of me?*

"No. No," Mack snaps, holding GG back. "We're going to let them hash this shit out for once and for all."

Ta'Shara lands another punch and fuckin' stars dance around my head like a fuckin' cartoon. It's almost as if this bitch has superhuman strength and I'm a fucking punching bag, unable to land a single blow—then the bitch snatches a handful of my hair and tries to snatch me bald.

"Aaargh! Get this fucking bitch off of me!"

BAM!

Ta'Shara punches me in the mouth. Clearly, I'm not going to get any damn help. I buck, kick, and do everything possible to get Ta'Shara off of me, but it's not fucking working. Heart racing, I expect at any moment she's going to slip out her blade and slice me up some more—if she doesn't kill me first.

A few times, I catch the glassy rage in her eyes. Is she high on some shit? Are they going to let her fuckin' kill me?

"All right. That's enough," Mack says. She and the other girls pull Ta'Shara off. The girl is still scrapping to get back at me.

"I'm going to fucking kill her!" Ta'Shara roars.

I scramble back across the floor, staring at the bitch. She's possessed or some shit. "She's fuckin' crazy!" I wipe the back of my hand across my throbbing lips and to no surprise see a trail of blood. "Look at what the fuck she just did."

"Calm down," Mack orders. "Nobody is going to commit a damn homicide up in here today. We're all on the same team."

"The fuck we are," Ta'Shara shouts as she attempts to rush me again and it takes all four of them to hold her back—barely.

I relax.

Out of the blue, Ta'Shara grabs hold of a liquor bottle, breaks free, and launches toward me.

Unable to move on my foot, I'm a sitting duck when she smashes that shit over my head, knocking me senseless. I drop like a stone as my head explodes in pain.

"SHIT!" GG cries.

I reach up and touch the side of my head. More blood.

"You're a piece of shit," Ta'Shara rages.

Get up! Get up! But my legs won't work. *What the fuck?*

GG and her friends struggle to hold Ta'Shara back.

I try again, but bump into a table where a Bose stereo and about twenty-odd lit candles topple onto me. A white light flashes—then an indescribable pain shoots across my body.

FIRE!

My ass is on fire.

"Holy shit!" Mack shouts. "Somebody get some fucking water!"

But everybody stands there stunned as shit with their goddamn mouths open.

Frantically I swat at the flames but they only seem to grow bigger. "AHHHH! Help me! Somebody help me," I scream, flailing around in circles. I can't tell what the fuck those non-helping bitches are doing, but I keep spinning around and then I break for a run—going straight through the back glass door. More pain. The fire keeps burning and then pain grows so intense that I give up and black the fuck out.

47

Hydeya

"**W**e got her."

My head snaps up from my desk and I stab Lieutenant Fowler with a look. "We got who?"

He steps into the room, grinning from ear to ear. "Qiana Barrett. Her tire tracks came back a perfect match for the Yolanda Terry–Tyneshia Gibson case."

I pop out of my seat and retrieve my service gun from the top drawer. "Don't fuck with me. Are you fucking with me?"

Fowler slaps the tire forensics report on my desk. "I wouldn't fuck around with something like this. We *need* a win."

About a month ago, Fowler and I paid that mouthy Qiana Barrett a visit after a tip from Tyneshia Gibson's parents. They grew suspicious when their daughter's supposed *good* friends failed to come to the funeral. After I did some digging, I discovered that whenever Tyneshia was arrested, the same three girls the Gibsons named were hauled off to jail with her: Adaryl Grant, Shamara "Li'l Bit" Moore and Qiana Barrett. Everything about Qiana—and her brother, Charles—rubbed me the wrong way. Finally, it looks like we can close a case around here.

There's been so much murder and mayhem since I first got the case that I do feel a little guilty that it hasn't remained on the top of my list. Now we can get justice for Terry and Gibson. I only hope that we're not too late to save the baby who was cut out of Yolanda.

I scan the report and flash Fowler a smile. "Good work."

"I do what I can," he says, winking.

"You think that she'll turn over on her accomplices?" Fowler asks as we head out of my office.

"We sure as hell are going to find out. Let's get that warrant."

Fowler holds up the warrant. "I'm already ahead of you. Judge Oxford signed off a few minutes ago."

I pause in surprise, but then force a smile on my face. "Well, let's go pay Qiana Barrett a visit."

Thirty minutes later, Lieutenant Fowler and I lead a train of police squad cars over to Ruby Cove. Heads turn and neighbors spill out of their houses when we roll to a stop at the Barrett residence.

My adrenaline pumps petro as Fowler and I climb out of the car and then hammer on the front door. It takes a full ten minutes before it's opened. Charles Barrett's imposing physique fills the doorway.

"You again."

I wave the warrant in front of his face. "Gotcha a gift." I slap it against his chest and shove him back from the door.

"What the fuck is this?"

"What does it look like? It's the warrant you wanted. Qiana is wanted for the murders of Yolanda Terry and Tyneshia Gibson."

His head snaps up. "Tyneshia?"

I nod. "If she's caused harm to Ms. Terry's baby, there'll be a third count."

"Baby?"

"Yeah. Ms. Terry's child was sliced out of her belly the night she was killed."

The color drains from Charles's face.

"Where's your sister, Qiana?"

Before answering, he glances over the warrant. When he looks up, he shrugs his shoulders. "No idea. She's not here."

"Right." I wave the rest of the team into the house. "I'm sure that you won't mind us taking a look for ourselves."

"I mind—but do what you got to do." He slaps the warrant back against my chest.

Out of reflex, I grab his wrist and twist that muthafucka behind his back and jam him up against the wall. "Careful. You wouldn't want me to bring you in for assaulting a police officer."

"Like I said: Do what you have to do," he growls.

"If you insist." I go for my handcuffs when he bucks. I put a knee to his groin, which drops him like a stone. I'm not the bitch to be fucking with.

"What the hell is your goddamn problem?" he yells.

"At the moment: you." I turn to my team. "Search this place from top to bottom."

They get to work.

Within seconds, a woman's high-pitched screams fill the house.

"What the hell?" I hand Charles over to another officer and then go and check out what all the commotion is about.

An older woman wrapped in a dingy bedsheet races down the hall.

"Ma'am, ma'am. Calm down."

She looks far from calm—she's close to being hysterical. "What the hell are you cops doing here?" she screams, with her lace-front askew.

An even older man, in a wheelchair, powers down the hall spitting and yelling at us too. "You dirty pigs get the fuck out of my house! You ain't got no right. Y'all need a fucking warrant to be up in here."

I turn back and swipe the warrant up from the floor by the

door. When I slap the warrant into his lap, he stops yelling in midsentence.

"What the fuck is that shit?"

"We're looking for Qiana Barrett. Are you her father?"

"Yeah. I'm her damn daddy. What's it to you? Qiana ain't here, so get the fuck out."

This family is already riding my last nerve. "Where. Is. She?"

"I. Don't. Fucking. Know. Now get out."

"Keep searching," I tell everyone, but I suspect that her family is telling the truth.

"All clear," the officers shout as they finish searching each room of the house.

Fuck. With the element of surprise gone, Qiana's family now has the advantage. Qiana Barrett will likely stay in the wind for a long damn time.

Shit.

48

Ta'Shara

I rewind the tape in my mind several times and I still can't process Qiana catching fire and then running through the back screen door, screaming. Her voice is still ringing inside my head.

Once the shock subsides, the other Flowers finally rush to help their blazing member. By the time Mack gets the water hose going, Qiana has stopped moving and her screams have stopped.

Stunned, everyone freezes in their tracks and stare down at the smoldering body.

She's dead. There's no doubt in my mind. Everyone tends to die around me. Instead of joining the crazy scene out back, I drop to my knees. *This can't be my life.*

"This bitch is gone." Mack's declaration wasn't necessary.

"*This* is going to be some fuckin' shit right here," Dime adds.

They all stand over Qiana's body, equally shocked.

I have no idea how long we all stay like this because time seems suspended.

Eventually, Romil asks, "What the fuck are we going to do?" She looks at Dime. Dime looks to Mack and Mack stares at GG.

GG turns in my direction and stares as if it's the first time she *truly* sees me. "You. You're just as fuckin' *evil* as your damn sister!"

I smile as if it was a damn compliment.

GG charges toward me, but before she gets one foot back into the house, two gunshots ring out.

I jump, shocked.

GG hits the concrete patio face first.

The only sounds in the backyard were the water soaking into the ground from the water hose and a couple of crickets serenading each other.

When my eyes travel in the direction from where the shots were fired, they clash into Dime's determined face.

"I owed you one," she says simply.

"Holy, fuckin' shit," Mack says. "What the fuck . . . ?" She moves her mouth some more, but she's at a loss as to what to say.

"Tombstone is going to fucking kill us," Romil says, blinking out of her trance.

"How in the fuck are we going to tell him that we killed both his sister *and* his girlfriend?"

"I ain't telling that nigga shit," Mack says. "Fuck. I'm not even sure what the fuck happened. I just reacted. Besides, that muthafucka ain't gonna hear shit we got to say."

I shrug. "Qiana was an accident."

Mack laughs. "How in the hell is bashing the bitch over the head with a bottle of liquor and then shoving her ass into a table full of candles a fuckin' accident?"

My face heats. "I didn't knock her into those candles. Her clumsy ass did that shit." Even as I say the words, I'm not sure whether I believe them. If I hadn't hit her over the head, her ass wouldn't have backed up. Simple as that. "She had that shit coming. She had my best friend killed," I add.

"By *your* sister," Romil tosses in.

"And?" I challenge. "My sister and I are two different

people—and on opposite sides of the color lines—or did you forget?"

They shrug.

"Then tell him *I* did it. If he has a beef or a problem with it, he can come see me or Profit about it." For the first time, I'm actually cloaking myself in Profit's protection—and by extension, Mason's and Lucifer's. Who was Tombstone any damn way—Lucifer's driver? I've only been an official Flower a couple of damn months and I have more power than he does.

Mack holds up her hands in surrender. "Calm down before you get an internal war going. I'm saying what other muthafuckas are going to say. Regardless, I don't think that it's going to make a damn difference to Tombstone." She looks over to Dime. "GG brought her here for help."

"GG also knew that the bitch killed one of our own. I knew Tyneshia. I used to babysit her ass. When the girl turned up missing, Qiana never said a muthafuckin' word. Who the fuck makes a deal with the head bitch of the Queen Gs any damn way? A muthafuckin' traitor."

That shut the fuckin' conversation down.

Dime and I stare at each other. At the end of the day these two dead bitches' blood is on our hands.

"We get rid of the fuckin' bodies and we keep our fucking mouths shut." She finally shifts her gaze to Mack and Romil. "Y'all got a problem with that?"

Mack's gaze rakes Dime up and down. "Don't come at me sideways. Ain't nobody said that they had a problem with shit. We're all in this together, regardless."

"Does anybody else know that they came here?" Romil asks.

Mack shakes her head. "We'll find out sooner or later. Right now we got some fuckin' cleaning to do." She storms back into the house, stops in front of me, and offers me her hand.

Another understanding flows between us and I know without a doubt that she has my back. They all do. My heart swells with emotion. Yes, I've already been accepted as a Flower, but now I'm a part of a real sisterhood.

It feels good. I accept her hand and she pulls me up to my feet.

"A drink first—and then we clean this shit up."

Everyone agrees. But one drink turns into three.

Hours later, Mack and Romil show Dime and me where they keep the cleanup kit in the garage. Clearly, this isn't the first time that Mack has cleaned up a crime scene. Her kit even includes the type of body bags forensic teams and emergency responders use to transport bodies.

There is no time to ask a lot of questions. After packing the bodies, we load them in GG's whip.

"You drive," Mack says, tossing me the keys.

"To where?"

"I'll tell you when we get there," she says.

I climb in behind the wheel.

"You do know what this means, don't you?"

"What?"

"We now know exactly where LeShelle will be Saturday night."

49

Hydeya

"You look as though you could use a drink," Fowler says, propping himself up against my office door.

"I can always use a drink," I tell him and then hold up more police reports. "Two more homicides. Care to guess their names?"

Fowler sighs. "Someone I should know?"

"Yep. Adaryl Grant and Shamara Moore."

"Holy shit!" He straightens up.

"Exactly." I slap the reports back down onto my desk. "It's like playing Whac-A-Mole with all these cases."

"Was Qiana Barrett with them?"

"No. But get this: There was a child's car seat with a baby doll and a sack of baby clothes found at the scene."

"But no baby?" he asks, looking as confused as I feel.

"Noooo baby." I shake my head. "You gotta love this city."

"What the fuck is going on?"

"You tell me and we'll both know. However, don't dismiss Ms. Barrett completely. One of the guns found at the scene has her fingerprints all over it."

"So she *was* there?"

"Seems like a safe bet. Won't know until we find her."

"So was it a car accident or a shooting?"

"Apparently both." I pull a deep breath and then look at my empty coffee cup. I really could go for a drink, but the paperwork keeps calling my name. "Just when you think you have one case figured out, the muthafucka unravels in front of your eyes." Realizing that I'm about to go on a tirade, I clamp my mouth shut. Fowler is no longer one I can vent my frustrations to. I look up and finally notice the package in his hand. "What's that?"

"What? This?" He holds up what looks to be a King James Bible.

"Yeah."

"It was found at the Carver crime scene. I was about to take it back down to the evidence room."

"And the Bible is evidence of what?"

"That she carried one." He looks at me and then back down at the holy book. "You think your father would want it?"

"If he doesn't curl up and hiss from the sight of it."

Fowler laughs. "Still not buying that 'turned over a new leaf' spiel, huh?"

"I learned a long time ago to believe nothing I hear and only half the shit I see."

"That's a good policy." He walks over and places the good book on my desk. "I doubt that it'll be missed. You should give it to him."

"Yeah?" I'm tempted.

"I think it'd be a nice gesture."

"All right. Thanks." I open my desk drawer and place the Bible inside. If anything, it'll give me an excuse to drop in on Isaac again.

"So about that drink?"

I hedge.

"C'mon." He winks as he backtracks toward the door. "My treat."

"I don't know. I got a lot of work I need to get done—and I have a husband who would probably like to see me every once in a while."

"Hydeya, I hope that regardless of what goes down that me and you are still cool. At the end of the day, we're friends. Right?"

I nibble on the inside of my bottom lip.

"We've been partners for a long time—and we've been through a lot of shit to let this situation bust us up."

He's right. *Damn it.* We've saved each other's ass too many times to count, but it's hard knocking that damn chip off of my shoulder.

"Say yes and I'll buy the first *two* drinks."

"Two? Hell. In that case . . ." I stand from the desk and grab my jacket. "Let's go."

Twenty minutes later, we're hugged up at the bar at Alex's. The age-old bar isn't really my taste. The split-level establishment was once a brothel and is now known for its greasy burgers and dingy vibe. This place, with a jukebox loaded with rock 'n' roll classics, isn't exactly my sort of bar. So, of course, most of the cops at the precinct love the place. By default, we come here a lot.

Fowler throws back shots of tequila and I order an old-fashioned.

"Not that you asked for my opinion," Fowler says, jump-starting the conversation, "but I think that you're being hard on yourself."

"Is that right?"

"Yeah. We both know that we can't control what the hell goes on out here in these streets. The city is flooded with illegal arms, people are crunked up on one drug or another. And the city officials keep promising Joe Citizen that they can fight the war on drugs with no money and fewer officers—then they throw up their hands as if they're shocked—shocked, I tell you—that the shit doesn't work."

"True."

"Our problem out here isn't gangs, it's capitalism. Plain and simple. Supply and demand. I read the other day that the global drug trade is a 321 *billion* dollar industry. These gangs out here don't own any fuckin' poppy fields or ships or subs— however the fuck they manage to get the shit over here. All we do is lock up muthafuckas at the low end of the totem pole and think we're doing something. How the hell do we ask folks who ain't never had shit and that we block every way we can from getting shit to walk away from the only damn thing that put money in their pockets? That's the damn dilemma.

"People are only looking for an escape from their shitty lives, and frankly, there are times I don't blame them. But then the same people riding our asses about making shit safe are the ones with brothers, sisters, mommas, daddies, and cousins contributing to the problem. The damn war on drugs has been going on since the damn *Nixon* administration. Do you realize how long that shit is?

"Nah. These streets were bad *with* Captain Johnson and the streets are bad without his ass. If you ask me, the chief is just spinning her wheels, looking for someone to blame so that the damn mayor stays off her ass. You're hard on yourself because you take this shit personal when *none* of this shit is personal."

"Is that your roundabout way of telling me that when you take my job, it's not personal?" My face heats.

"And when the next muthafucka takes it from me, I won't take it personal," he says, shrugging.

"Nice try." I drain my drink, but it does nothing to cool me down. "I know that you gotta do you and everything, but I don't think none of this has anything to do with our high homicide numbers. The chief didn't get twitchy until I told her about where my investigation into the Johnson case was headed. She shut me down before the investigation ever got started."

"Perhaps." He nods, his eyes drooping low with his fifth

tequila shot. "But let me ask you this: What does taking on the department actually look like to you?"

"What do you mean?"

"What do you hope to achieve? What's victory? Even if what we allege is true and Captain Johnson was neck-deep in the game, think about all the politicians with their photo-ops and media kits, shaking that man's hand. You don't think, as the young kids say, that they are going to feel some kind of way about letting you bring down his heroic image? You can't do that without dragging them down. And to what point? The man is dead. You want to dig him up just so you can put his corpse in a jail cell?"

"Don't be ridiculous."

"No. I'm trying to understand where you're coming from. I know you want to make your mark—or get your own shine—but as your friend, I'm telling you that you're going about it all wrong."

He's right. And I know that he's right—but damn.

"Look. I don't have a dog in the fight. But I know what happens to cops when they don't toe the line." He pauses to take another shot. "My father was a cop down in South Carolina. His partner got snatched up in an excessive-force charge after gunning down an unarmed black kid. My pop agreed with the charge and told his higher-ups that he believed that his partner was out of line that night and murdered that defenseless kid.

"The hell he caught for being willing to testify against his partner also put our whole family at risk. They came at him with every fucking thing that they could think of for going against one of their own. Just like a street gang, loyalty means everything. You *know* this."

I do.

"Then one night the pressure really got to my father. He drank a whole bottle of Jack Daniel's just so he could get

enough nerve up to eat his gun. He'd rather do that than actually get up on that stand and testify."

I watch Fowler and feel his pain. I knew that Fowler's father was a cop, but I'd never heard this story before. "You always said that your pop died a hero in the line of duty."

"In my book, he did. I don't care about the lies they told
about him after the fact. He tried to do the right thing and
where did it get him?" He shakes his head. "If you really pur-
sue tryna find where Captain Johnson's rabbit hole leads you,
you're just asking for trouble."

I soak in Fowler's warning while grudgingly admitting to
myself that he's right—again. I hardly have the kind of power
to protect myself from any potential blowback. Yet, Captain
Johnson's case still keeps me up at night.

"Let it go," Fowler says. "Take it from me, it's not worth it.
And you'll get to keep your job."

50

Cleo

"Wow, Cleo. You look like a princess," Kay, my seven-year-old cousin, coos, looking up at me.

"Thank you, baby." I slowly spin around in the gold-beaded Givenchy dress that Diesel Carver had delivered to my house, feeling every bit like a fairy-tale princess. I can't get over how beautiful this dress is. He must've spent a fortune. I never heard of a man sending a woman such an expensive dress to wear for a first date. At least not in real life. I might've seen it in a movie or something.

Kay watches me with big, moon-sized eyes. "I wish that I had a dress like that."

I smile. "Maybe one day you will."

My youngest brother, Freddy, knocks and then whistles low. "Now that's a damn dress." He crosses his arms and looks at me suspiciously. "Who is this nigga you're going out with anyway?"

"None of your business," I tell his nosy butt before reaching for the matching clutch bag.

"The hell it ain't my business. Random muthafuckas need to go through me or Kobe around here. We need to make it clear to this knucklehead that if something happens to you there will be problems and complications to the nigga's breathing habits. You feel me?"

He's serious. We all feel that we dropped the ball when we lost Essence. As large and as close as our family has always been, we should've kept a better eye on her. Her last prom was when everything changed. Her best friend, Ta'Shara, had been beaten, raped, and then transferred into a mental hospital. Essence moped around the house and then was suddenly doing favors for that evil bitch LeShelle.

One day, she'll get what's coming to her. I just hope that I'll be around to see it.

"So?" Freddy probes. "Who is he?"

Sighing, I give up the details. "Diesel Carver."

"Say what?" He cups his ear like he's suddenly hard of hearing. "I know I didn't hear that shit right."

"Freddy—"

"KOBE!"

Aww, damn. It's about to be an emergency family meeting. "Freddy, don't start flipping out."

"Don't start—Do you know who that nigga is—*besides* Python's cousin? That muthafucka runs the whole fuckin' show down in Atlanta. That nigga ain't nobody to be messin' with. Why in the hell are you going out with him?"

"Yo. What's up?" Kobe asks, appearing at my doorway still holding his Xbox controller.

Freddy turns toward him. "Do you know who the hell she's going out with?"

"Nah. I just know that she's been with that stalker Kalief. Why? Who is it?"

"Diesel Carver."

The color instantly drains out of Kobe's face. "What? Are you fuckin' crazy? Since when do you date niggas in the game?"

"In the game? The muthafucka writes all the rules and regulations in Georgia. Everybody is waiting and peeping on that gangster's next move. We all know we're eating off his connects from the A while boss-man is underground."

"Calm down, Freddy. It's not what you think. Kalief says it's just a business dinner—for my career. He's supposed to have a lot of connects in the industry." I repeat Kalief's line.

"Kalief put you up to this?" Freddy asks, plunging from stun to shock. "Is he going with you?"

The doorbell rings.

He's here. My heart leaps into my throat. "I gotta go." I squeeze past them, clogging my doorway.

"I don't like this," Freddy says like I didn't pick up on that.

"Don't start. I don't tell you boys who you can go out with. Do me the same courtesy." I smile at Grandma, napping in her favorite La-Z-Boy, as I head to the front door. However, when I open it, I'm greeted with another surprise: a limousine driver, dressed head-to-toe in black, holding a single rose.

"Ms. Blackmon?" he asks.

"Yes?" I glance over his shoulder at the Mercedes-Benz limousine parked out front. Not only that, but a mob thirty to forty deep is already milling around it.

The driver smiles and tips his black cap at me. "Good evening. I'm Miles and I'll be your driver this evening. Mr. Carver would like for you to have this." He hands me the rose.

"Thank you." I blush.

"Are you ready, ma'am?"

"Whoa. Hold up." Freddy grabs me by my shoulder. "Where that nigga at? He can't come to the door like a fuckin' gentleman? Tell that nigga to get out of the car and introduce himself."

"I'm sorry, but Mr. Carver is not in the vehicle. He is waiting at your next destination."

"My next destination?" My hackles rise up. "Where is that?"

"I'm sorry, ma'am, but I'm not at liberty to say. I believe Mr. Carver would like for it to be a surprise."

Kobe sucks his teeth. "Oh. This nigga is doing the most."

Miles offers me his arm. "My lady?"

My curiosity is piqued; I suck in a breath and step out on faith.

As we head to the limo and the nosy crowd, Freddy shouts, "You got your cell phone, right?"

I wave at him over my shoulder.

"I'm gonna call and check up on you. Make sure you answer your damn phone."

Miles opens my door.

"I MEAN IT, CLEO! YOU PICK UP!"

I slide into the backseat, marveling at how the leather feels like butter.

The driver shuts my door and then rushes to the driver's seat. I can only guess that everyone knows whose car this is. It's the only way to explain how he's able to cruise over into Gangster Disciple territory.

"I'll have you to your destination in a jiffy," Miles says. "If you'd like something to drink, there's a full bar there in front of you. You also have control of your air and satellite music stations."

I glance around, noting the ride was only missing a kitchen sink. "I'm good," I tell him.

"Very well, ma'am." He hits a button and the blackened partition slides up.

As we ride out of the neighborhood, I fidget around, trying to prepare myself for anything. But I've never imagined myself being in this position, so it's hard.

Twenty minutes later, we're pulling into General DeWitt Spain Airport off Whitney Avenue and North Second Street. "Why in the hell are we at the airport?" The butterflies in my stomach transform into hopping bullfrogs. *What in the hell have I let Kalief talk me into now?*

The limo rolls to a stop and I give myself a pep talk while waiting for Miles to open my door.

"Ms. Blackmon." He offers me his hand to assist me out.

When I stand, I stare up at a magnificent private Learjet that screams money. "I don't fucking believe this shit."

Diesel steps out the door of the jet, dressed to the nines in all white. He looks as if he just stepped off the pages of *GQ* magazine. My weak knees knock as he descends.

What the hell is wrong with you? Pull it together.

That shit is easier said than done. When I met Diesel at his club, I peeped that he was a good-looking dude, but light-skinned niggas never did a damn thing for me. But stripped from his muscled thugs and thot girlfriends, I'd be lying if I said that I wasn't feeling some type of way right now.

"Evening," he says, drinking me in. "That dress looks more beautiful on you than I imagined it would."

"Thanks . . . but, uh. Aren't you kind of pouring it on a little thick?"

"What do you mean?"

I laugh at his fake humbleness. "The dress, the limo . . . the plane."

"Surely you didn't think that I was just going to scoop you in a hoopty and swing you through a Taco Bell drive-thru like maybe your boy Kalief does, did you?"

My defenses shoot to high alert. "Don't presume to know me or my relationship with Kalief. I'm only here as a favor to him."

Diesel lifts one brow. "If you were my woman I'd kill a man for even suggesting you go out on a date with him."

His words are a cold slap for which I have no response. Anything I say will just justify my man pimping me to erase his debt.

"I'm sorry," Diesel says. "That was rude of me. I'm certainly grateful that you *are* here with me." He offers me his arm as well as a perfect Colgate smile. "Shall we?"

This is it. I glance at him and then the plane before taking a deep breath and sliding my hand into his. A night with the devil.

51

Cleo

Diesel keeps our destination a secret. However, thirty minutes later, I recognize the Atlanta skyline when I see it. He keeps the conversation light by peppering me with questions about my life and family. I do a fair job of keeping my defenses up, but by my third glass of champagne, my tongue loosens.

Before I know it, I'm telling him all about my sister, Essence. How she died, what she was like, and how much I miss her. Before I know it, I'm all in my feelings and the seeds of revenge start to sprout in my heart.

"I'm sorry for your loss," he says. His face softens with compassion. "I know what it's like to lose people close to you."

"Oh?"

He nods and drops his gaze. "I came into this world losing the very person who gave me life. Before that, shortly after I was conceived, I lost my father in a hail of bullets from the Atlanta police." He sighs. "After that I was sent to live with my father's legal wife. You can imagine the tension of her having to raise her husband's bastard from a streetwalker."

Damn.

"Still. She was the only mother I really knew, and I came to love her and my stepbrother and sister. But tragedy struck

again and they died in a fluke house fire. I was the sole survivor."

As he tells the story, I note that while he's making all the
customary gestures—dropping his eyes, lowering his voice—
there's real emotion on his face.

I set my champagne down. "That's horrible," I say, since
he's waiting for a response.

He sighs and flashes me the weirdest smile. "Well. What can
you do?"

"Yeah. I guess."

We fall into an uncomfortable silence before he shifts into
an awkward transition. "You really do look beautiful tonight.
But . . . I think that you're missing one thing."

"Oh?" I look down at my dress.

Diesel produces a square red velvet box. It can't possibly be
another gift. "For you."

"I don't think—"

"C'mon." His smile stretches wider. "The minute I saw it,
I thought of you."

I stare at him—and then at the box.

"C'mon . . . You know that you want to take a peek."

He's right. Drawing a deep breath, I reach for the gift.
When I pop it open, I gasp.

"I'm a man who loves to spoil beautiful women."

I can hardly breathe as I stare at the diamond and platinum
necklace. "This must have cost a fortune."

"You like it?"

"It's gorgeous." In fact I've never held anything so beautiful.

Diesel stands from his seat just when the pilot announces
that we're on our final approach for landing. "Let me help you
put it on."

Nervously, I climb to my feet.

"Turn around."

I follow his instructions. My breath thins when he moves
up behind me into my personal space. I keep it together while

he places the expensive piece around my neck. When his fingers brush against the back of my neck, my knees start knocking.

"There. Turn and let me see," he says.

Slowly, I twirl around with my best princess grin. But he doesn't step back and the space between us is a mere few inches. I can feel his warm breath caress my face. Though this man in *every* way is not my type, he is kind of leaving me breathless.

"Beautiful," he praises.

My nervous gaze melts into his and for the first time, his cool green eyes hypnotize me. Before I can blink, his lips are on mine and I'm drunk off his very taste. It starts off soft and sweet, but then a hunger takes over both of us.

The plane's wheels touch down and we're jolted off of our feet and fall onto the floor.

Diesel laughs. "Are you okay?"

Stunned and embarrassed, I glance around. "Yeah. I think so."

We look at each other again and then collapse in a fit of laughter. The ice is officially broken. We're unable to pull ourselves off the floor until the plane rolls to a stop.

Minutes later, we're whisked away in another limo to the Philips Arena and are ushered through the back door to a Prince concert. Shocked as shit, I completely lose my mind. For nearly three hours, His Purple Highness plays all his greatest hits. After the show, I get to meet the Artist as well as his latest band.

Diesel stands back and lets me enjoy the moment. When we return to the limo, I recap every detail, every set, and every song while he just smiles from ear to ear.

"How did you know that he is my favorite?"

"Oh. A little birdie told me," he says nonchalantly.

Kalief. My excitement takes a nosedive as I remember why I'm really here. *He paid for me.*

"Is something wrong?" he asks.

"No. I'm good," I lie and then start to sulk.

The next stop is to *Diesel's*, a sophisticated modern steak-house in the heart of Buckhead.

"You own a restaurant too?"

"I *own* many things," he says, grinning.

That uncomfortable feeling starts to twist in my gut.

"Ah, Mr. Carver, we've been waiting for you," a toothy hostess says as we enter the restaurant.

I stare at her because she looks more like a runway model than a hostess. When I glance around the packed house, I note that all the waitresses are gorgeous. A trickle of insecurity has me propping up my shoulders and lifting my head a tad bit higher as I fall in line behind the hostess.

Along the way, familiar faces crop up around me. I slowly start to realize that half the Atlanta music industry and a few reality television stars are in the house. And more impressively, a number of them stand up to speak with Diesel.

I'm awed by Diesel's sudden transformation, as he becomes a networking god. Within seconds, I'm shaking hands and being introduced as his next up-and-coming star. Once I get over being tongue-tied and starstruck, I'm flabbergasted when one after another expresses some interest in me.

By the time we make it to the private room he has reserved for us, I've convinced myself that somehow this is all just a dream.

"I hope you're hungry," he says. "Because I'm starving."

The hostess hands us our menus.

I can't stop staring at him. Kalief and the streets weren't lying about this man. He really is a man with solid power within the industry. Emotions war within in me while he places our wine order.

"Now what's wrong?"

"Nothing. I'm just . . . surprised. That's all." I fidget in my seat.

"Relax," he tells me. "Enjoy yourself."

"I don't know what to make of you."

He chuckles. "That's not the first time I've heard that."

"Why did you bribe me to come on this date?"

"Bribe?"

"Agree to wipe out Kalief's debt if I went out with you tonight."

Diesel doesn't hedge from the issue. "Because you would've never agreed otherwise."

True.

The waitress returns and presents the wine bottle to Diesel. I watch him as he goes through the whole routine of inspecting the label, swirling the sample, sniffing and then finally tasting the wine. After giving the waitress the approval head nod, he returns his attention to me.

"Let's get past the *how* I got you here and focus on the *why.*"

"Okay. Why?"

"Two reasons," he says nonchalantly. "One: I'm extremely attracted to you."

I tell myself not to blush, but I'm not sure that it's working.

"And two: I want to make all your dreams come true." His tone is no-nonsense. "Does any of that interest you?"

"Yes," I answer him with equal honesty.

His smile spreads. "Well. We're finally getting somewhere." He holds up his wine glass. "Let's toast to that."

I hold up my glass.

"To new beginnings," he says.

"To new beginnings."

52

Hydeya

"**A**re you sure that you want to go?" Drake, my six-foot-one Italian husband says as he serves my morning coffee. "Your father will understand if you don't."

"Spoken like someone who has never met my father. He'll say that he understands, but he won't. We're supposed to be turning over a new leaf, remember?" I accept the coffee cup and welcome its warmth between my hands. Last night the heat went out and we had to sleep in an icebox.

"Yeah, but still. If you're not up for it, you shouldn't spend your first day off in a long, long time, attending this thing." Drake sits down next to me on the bed, and pulls back his ink-black hair.

I smile because I know what he's doing. "You just want me all to yourself," I say. I place my foot against his arm and play-fully push him away.

He gives me a brief smile. "Guilty as charged. No offense, but I'm starting to feel like a bachelor again, and I'm lucky if I can get you to stop by for a booty call."

I stop the cup halfway to my lips. "Bachelor?"

"C'mon, baby. I know how important your work is to you, but you're rarely home, and when you are home, you're still working cases. Even the ones that you're not supposed to be working."

"Oh God. Not you too. It's bad enough that I have Fowler and the chief planting knives in my back."

"I'm not doing any such thing. I'm just saying that I'm feeling neglected."

"We just went out a few weeks ago."

"Yeah. And it was nice."

"Just nice?"

"No. *That* part was great." He leans over and brushes a kiss against my forehead. "But it's hardly enough. I married you because I want to have more sex with you, not less. C'mon. Did you forget that we're supposed to be starting a family this year?"

Oh God. I roll my eyes. I can't even imagine putting a baby on my plate on top of all that I have going on.

"What? Did you change the plans again without consulting me?" he asks, hurt twisting his face.

"No. It's nothing like that," I lie. However, the problem with being with someone for so long is that they learn how to read you like a book.

"Aww, Hydeya. Don't do this." He springs up from the bed.

"Don't do what?" I ask defensively. "You know how much this new promotion means to me, and now I have the chief threatening to take it away."

"Maybe that's not such a bad idea. Maybe you are in over your head."

"What?" I set my coffee aside on the nightstand and climb out of bed. "What are you saying?"

"Look, Hydeya. I know you love your job. I respect that. But what about *me*? What about *us*? I'm supposed to be getting something out of this marriage too."

"And what? I'm supposed to quit my job and let you pump me full of babies? Is that it? How the fuck is that fair?"

"Why in the hell do you think people get married? We're supposed to be creating little people that look like us. I'm not ashamed to admit that I'm looking forward to being a father. All my friends have two or three of them. Even my parents are asking me when we're going to make them grandparents, like every other day."

The more he talks, the more I feel like I've been cast in a horror movie.

"What?" He catches my expression.

"Nothing."

"Damn it, Hydeya. Don't make me feel like the bad guy. We made plans together. We had a plan."

"Plans change sometimes."

"For how long?"

"I don't know. I just know that I'm not ready to juggle all of that right now. I want to do my job, and I want to do it well. We still have plenty of time for kids."

Drake clamps his jaw and shakes his head.

Guilt rattles through me, but I can't help how I feel. Yet, at the same time, I don't want to signal that I'm bailing on the re-lationship. I draw a breath and soften my approach as I slide my hands around his neck. "I'm not saying that I'm bailing on the family plan completely. I just want to postpone it for a little while. That's all."

"For how long?" he presses.

"I don't know. Another year—or two." *Or three.*

"A year," he says, latching on to the lowest number. "You promise."

"I can't promise but—"

"Damn it, Hydeya!" He breaks away from me. "Quit jerk-ing me around."

"Then you quit being selfish and unreasonable. If the shoe was on the other foot and your career was taking off, I'd under-stand and adjust our plans."

"What the hell is that supposed to mean? What the hell is wrong with my career? The guys and I have booked that audition down at that new club. It'll be a long and *local* gig. I thought that's what you wanted after our last summer tour."

"I did. I do. That's great, but that's not what I mean. I just . . ." I sigh, frustrated. "I don't want to argue. Not today. I'm stressed out enough as it is. The job. Isaac."

"Then go," he says, equally upset. "Go to the funeral. Go babysit King Isaac. That's what you really want to do anyway."

"Don't be like that."

"Be like what? Isn't that the real reason you want to go to that funeral—to verify whether or not your father is really out of the game?"

He got me on that one. I don't believe that my father is going to walk away from so much power in the streets to take up gardening or some shit, especially now that Maybelline is dead. According to his many prison letters, she was the whole reason that he was going to turn over a new leaf and become a new man. Power has a way of digging its claws into people.

"One year," I tell him.

Drake stops pacing. "What?"

"One year from today and I promise that we can start seriously trying for a baby."

He searches for the truth in my eyes. When he sees that I'm on the up-and-up, his smile returns in full bloom. "Deal."

53

LeShelle

Python is struggling to be strong, but I know that it's fucking with him that he can't be here at Momma Peaches's funeral service. I decided to take the risk to come incognito and represent for the both of us. Rocking a fierce honey-blond blunt haircut wig, large Jackie O–style glasses, a large black church hat, and a matronly looking black dress.

It's been three weeks since the shooting, and everyone wondered if and when Isaac would send Memphis's original OG lady gangster to paradise. That's a long time to keep a body in a freezer. It comes as a surprise that the services are being held at the very church where she lost her life. The bullet holes are still visible for everyone to see. Not to mention the Power of Prayer's church-building fund needs to be used to replace the carpet instead of relying on whatever bootleg carpet cleaning service did this whack job. Everyone can still see where the old lady bled out.

The stage looks nice. Flowers teem around the entire church stage and casket. The neighborhood must've bought out an entire flower shop. During the viewing, I have to admit that Momma Peaches looks as fierce in death as she did in life. Beautiful to the end.

I'm not a sentimental bitch by any means, but even I get

choked up listening to story after story from the residents of Shotgun Row. I'll admit I get caught up in my feelings. Despite my being with Python for nearly five years, Momma Peaches never warmed to me. I don't know why. I was always nice to the old bitch. Mainly because Python acted like Momma Peaches walked on water.

The choir stands and sings a few songs that have me shouting a couple of amens along with everyone else. It's a beautiful service for a packed house.

Soon I'm wondering, *Who will miss me when I go?* Depending on Python's criminal status, he'll probably not be able to arrange or come to a service. My thoughts then wander to the only other family member I have: Ta'Shara. For the first time in about a month, my blood pressure doesn't shoot up when she pops into my head. Doesn't mean it changes shit, but . . . I don't know. My ass is tripping.

Cleo Blackmon steps in front of the choir. I shift in my seat, thinking about her sister, Essence. Cleo opens her mouth to sing, and I'm blown away again. How in the hell does this girl not have a record deal already? Jealousy crawls at my throat. The only talent God has ever given me is how to pop my pussy and hustle in the gutter-streets of Memphis.

This bitch, I have no idea what the fuck she's still doing here. I cut my gaze to Diesel in the middle of Cleo's song, and once again this muthafucka is enraptured with this girl. My jealousy spreads. By the time Cleo closes her mouth, there isn't a dry eye in this bitch.

Isaac, dressed to the nines in a black suit, sets a few tongues wagging. The man definitely has swagger. The only other man who trumps Isaac is Diesel. Mesmerizing in a rich blue Tom Ford suit, he melts every pair of panties and a few diapers in the building.

I hang back as the two men approach one another with fake smiles and stiff handshakes. No one misses them sizing each other up. I can hear the buzz from a few soldiers questioning which of the two powerhouses were running shit. The census favors King Isaac. No one trusts the brotha from the dirty A.

Not that Diesel confides in me, but he has to be feeling some kind of way about Isaac's early release. He's made quite an investment in Memphis's Gangster Disciples in Python's absence. His grand club in the heart of Beale Street is just one example. He's going to want a return for the arms, drugs, and security he's provided. Whose pocket is that shit going to hit? *Damn Python for calling that nigga up here in the first place.*

When Isaac takes the stage for the eulogy, he tells everyone how he and Momma Peaches met at Goodson Auto shortly after he'd moved here from Chicago. He swears that she stole his heart the second his eyes landed on her. He drifts into a few regrets and vows that their love will live on long after he joins her in the grave.

I want a love like that.

After the service, a smaller crowd piles into their cars to travel to the burial.

I'm stunned when Cleo climbs into a Mercedes with Diesel. *What fresh hell is this shit?*

Avonte follows close behind. My confusion deepens when Diesel's car doesn't continue on to the cemetery.

"Everything okay?" Avonte asks.

"Huh? Oh. Yeah. I'm good." I twist back around in my seat, but my mind remains on the new couple. If Diesel wins the new power struggle, Cleo could be a political threat. But the shocks keep coming when Memphis's new captain of police, Hydeya Hawkins, arrives at the burial.

54

Hydeya

Half the city of Memphis appears to have showed up for Maybelline Carver's last party. As Drake and I exit from our car and follow the line of mourners to the burial site, I note all of the old as well as the young. Not everyone is wearing their Sunday best. There are quite a number of people sporting the Gangster Disciples colors and flags.

Drake leans over and whispers, "Are you sure it's safe to attend this thing?"

His question echoes inside my head. "I'm sure that it's going to be okay," I say. "If not, I still have my piece in my purse if anything goes down."

I scan the crowd on the wild notion that Terrell Carver may make a surprise appearance. I know how close he was to his aunt. Can he really resist the temptation to say his final good-byes?

"Most of these people came to pay their respects to a woman who has been in the game for a long time," I assure him.

I spot Isaac as soon as we arrive near the site.

The second Isaac sees me, he stops shaking hands with the other guests. There's no mistaking his genuine surprise. Excusing himself from the line of mourners, he makes his way over to us.

"You came," he says, opening his large arms and sweeping me inside of them. "Thank you. This means a lot to me." Slowly, he shifts his eyes over to my husband. "And you must be Drake," he says, releasing me and assessing my husband, up and down.

Drake eagerly thrusts out his hand. "It's nice to meet you, Isaac."

My father glances down at the white hand offered to him. For a brief moment, I fear he's going to leave Drake hanging, but he flashes a quick smile and accepts the handshake. "It's a pleasure to finally meet you."

Drake relaxes. He'd feared a snub as well.

"I wish we could've met under better circumstance," Isaac adds.

"Me too."

The conversation fades and we all just stare at one another, hoping someone has something else to say.

"Oh. I brought you something," I say, handing over the Bible. "It's Maybelline's. She, uh, had it with her at the church that day."

His smile returns. "Thank you. I appreciate you returning it to me."

We share a genuine moment before he has to excuse himself.

"Well, I better get back to greeting the other guests. I hope that I can still cash in that rain check soon," he says. His gaze shifts back and forth between Drake and me, and though he is still smiling, he's trying to get the piece of the puzzle to fit.

"That will be great," Drake jumps in, completely missing my father's disapproval. The men shake hands again and Isaac strolls off.

"You know, I don't think that you have anything to worry about. He seems like a really nice guy."

I smile at Drake's ability to always see the best in people.

At promptly three o'clock, Pastor Rowlin Hayes clears his throat to gain everyone's attention. "Death has visited us once again. We are left to mingle our sorrow with thanksgiving. Thanksgiving for the life we knew her to have had; thanksgiving that for her the day of pain is over; thanksgiving that God, in his infinite wisdom called our beloved Momma Peaches home. However, our thanksgiving does not veil our mourning, for indeed the rending of our hearts at the loss of love and memory is as old as humanity itself."

"Amen," someone shouts.

"So mourning is indeed ancient, and our search for relief is equally ancient. Those of New Testament times were no exception. Paul, in writing to the Philippians, says that death is the desire to depart and to be with Christ. Taken in and of itself, there is comfort in that passage, but when we understand that to which Paul may have been referring, it brings us even more solace."

Pastor Hayes's eulogy holds everyone captivated.

I, of course, keep stealing glances at Isaac to see how he's holding up. He's the Rock of Gibraltar. His strength has always been something I've admired.

Drake whispers something.

I lean over to ask him to repeat it when the first burst of gunfire interrupts the service.

Gasps, screams, and prayers erupt from the crowd as some run and others dive for cover. Pure chaos breaks out.

"Everybody get down!" someone shouts.

Before I have a chance to think one way or the other, I'm off my feet and Drake scrambles to throw his body on top of me to shield me.

I try to twist around to see what's going on, but Drake's two-hundred-pound body makes that shit almost impossible. Gunfire rattles off for what seems like eternity. Bullets ricochet all around us. Some slam into Maybelline's mahogany casket.

My purse! Where the hell is my purse? For the first time in a long while, I am thrilled to see the Gangster Disciples rise to their feet to return fire. I finally spot my purse a good five feet away. "Honey, my purse," I shout, hoping that he can hear me and will let me grab it. But he keeps me smothered under his weight and I fight to wiggle my way out. I don't have time to argue with him. I'm a cop and I don't need him to protect me from doing my job.

Freed, I reach my purse and retrieve my weapon.

Tires squeal and then shoot off into the distance. Soldiers in the Folks Nation take off behind their attackers. When everyone understands that the coast is clear, the crying and screaming crowd clamber back onto their feet. There are more than a few bodies, bloodied and mangled, who don't get up.

"Shit." I turn around toward Drake and then stop cold at seeing his lifeless eyes. The emerald grass soaking up his brains and blood.

55

LeShelle

"What the fuck?" I straighten my wig and jump up from the grass. Women and children are screaming everywhere while I pat myself down to make sure that I'm not hurt. For a second there, I thought . . . I shake it off. These clouds of gloom and doom keep creeping up on me lately.

"C'mon," Avonte shouts. "We got to get you out of here before the police show up."

The police are already here. I shoot a glance to where I last saw Captain Hawkins. She's turned into a statue. Utter shock blankets her face. When I follow her gaze to the man a few feet from her, I recall them walking to the burial together. *Her husband?*

"LeShelle," Avonte hisses. "Let's go."

"I'm coming. I'm coming." I turn and take off back to the car. My ass doesn't even hit the backseat before we hear the wail of police sirens.

Avonte floors it out of the cemetery and gets us out of Memphis in record time.

I'm still wrapping my head around everything when I walk into the door.

"Are you all right?" Python barks. Clearly, he's heard the news.

"Yeah."

"You're sure?"

"Yeah. Yeah." I shake the shit off again. "You know damn well that I've been through worse shit than that." It's true. I've been shot and stabbed numerous times—but I've never had this bad feeling that I can't shake.

Python is enraged. "You know who's behind this shit, don't you?"

I blink because truly I haven't the foggiest idea.

"Fat Ace! That nigga is out of control, stacking violations all over the place with no remorse. We're hitting that nigga, you feel me? The foul muthafucka is about to feel the heat."

He's so amped that he's talking a mile a minute.

"I'ma pump so much lead in that piece of shit that the devil ain't gonna recognize his ass."

"When?"

"Soon. Believe that. We're moving on that nigga soon. We've been making moves since Aunt Peaches was killed. Isaac and I are amassing an army. We're going to hit them direct. Right where they live on Ruby Cove."

56

Hydeya

I'm in shock. It's odd to mentally recognize that while experiencing it at the same time. After the shooting, I'm aware of the chaos, but I remain still through it all.

Drake is dead. No reaction.

I repeat the words in my head—and still no reaction.

It's like my entire being is rejecting the information. Drake can't be dead. We'd just agreed to start a family next year. We made plans.

Why didn't you try for a baby last year, like you said—or the year before that? At least then, you'd still have some part of him. Now you have nothing. Finally, an ache penetrates my heart. In no time, it grows. Before I can adjust, the pain overwhelms me and drops me to my knees.

"Hydeya!"

Someone is calling my name, but I can barely hear over a woman's scream. Only when I run out of breath do I realize that it's me.

"It's okay. It's okay. Look at me," the voice says.

When I don't follow orders, I'm slapped so hard that the physical pain distracts me from the emotional one enough to pull me out of my trance.

It's Isaac.

"Breathe," he reminds me. His strong hands on my shoulders and his firm, commanding gaze have a calming effect. After a couple of deep breaths, I'm myself again.

"You good?"

"Yes. I think so."

He nods. "Good. Come. Let's move you over here until your colleagues get here."

I allow him to lead me away from Drake. Better not to see him lying there like that. When the first patrol car rumbles onto the scene, Isaac, clutching his wife's Bible, moves away from me to see about some of the other injured mourners. That's when dread mixes with my grief. There's going to be a lot of questions and I better come up with some answers.

57

Cleo

"What?" I press my cell phone tighter against my ear. I couldn't have heard Kobe right. "Yes. I'm fine. We just left the funeral not even an hour ago." I give Joe, the senior engineer, a signal that I need to take a brief break, even though we've just started the session. "Do you know who did the hit?" I ask.

"Word going around is it's those bumble-bee flaggin' muthafuckas. You know the shit is on now. My homies say that Python has been ready to make a move for weeks, since he saw that ugly monster gun down Momma Peaches. At first niggas were a little salty since his cousin Diesel and his team of soldiers rolled into town tryna do a hostile takeover. Big man must believe in that trickle-down bullshit because ain't nobody eating like they used to."

I glance out to the other side of the studio glass to see Diesel is also on the phone. Only he appears to be pleased about something.

"But everything is about to change now that King Isaac is back. He's going to take our asses to higher heights. Fat Ace done fucked with the wrong nigga. You hear me?"

My brother is hyped as hell, but I don't share his enthusiasm about who's up and who's down in the street wars.

But the shit about Diesel concerns me. The ink hasn't even

dried on the management contract that I signed. I certainly have no illusions that Diesel is no angel, but he can help me finally get a shot in the industry. At least I hope so.

I sigh. Doubt has now been replanted in my head. *What the fuck did I do?*

"I'm glad you're all right," Kobe says. "Nana can breathe better now."

"Yeah. Thanks for checking in on me. I'll see you when I get home. Oh. Wait. Kobe?"

"Yeah?"

"Have you heard from Kalief? I've been calling and texting him and he hasn't contacted me."

"Nah. I'm sure he's blazed up somewhere. Y'all two made up?"

I ignore the question. "I'll talk to you later."

"A'ight."

I disconnect the call and then head out of the sound booth. When I enter the engineer's room, Joe is gone and Diesel is handing over a large envelope to his boy Beast. It strikes me as odd, but I don't know why. I've seen him pay Beast a few times like that at the club.

Diesel dismisses Beast and then turns toward me, smiling. "You ready to get to work?"

Maybe he doesn't know.

"Umm. We're going to have to do this another time," I tell him. "There was a shooting at Momma Peaches's burial."

He scrubs the smile off his face. "Oh. Yes. I got a call. That shit is crazy." Diesel shakes his head. Apparently that's all he has to say on the matter.

"Anyway, my grandmother is worried. I need to get home."

Genuine disappointment surfaces. "Sure. Sure. I understand. Go home. Calm your granny down." He reaches over and picks up my signed contract and holds it up. "We got plenty of time to get this started. We'll be working together for a *long* time."

Remorse

58

Lucifer

I know that I'm supposed to take Profit with me out to the federal pen, but there's no way in hell I want him anywhere near me. I never know when the fuck his tongue will jump down my damn throat. My last few visits were hard, especially when I had to tell Smokestack about Mason's passing. We have him back, but this time I have to tell Smokestack that he's lost the love of his life, Dribbles. If ever there was a true love story between a prostitute and a pimp, it was Smokestack's and Dribbles's.

I've known for a while now that Smokestack harbored hopes that one day he and Dribbles would get back together. On her end, she'd given up on what could've been and had moved on. It didn't mean that she no longer loved him, but she had realized that they weren't good for each other.

It was a miracle that he'd gotten permission to attend the premature funeral for Mason. It was highly unlikely that he'd be able to convince the warden to let him attend the real funeral for his wife. A car horn blows and Tombstone slams on his brakes, nearly jetting me from the back to the front.

"What the fuck?"

"Sorry," Tombstone apologizes. "I . . . guess I have a lot of shit on my mind."

I pull myself together and settle back into my seat.

"Both GG and Qiana are missing," he tells me, like I'd asked.

"I'm sure that they'll turn up."

The muscles in his face flex. Clearly, he wants to tell me more of the story, but settles on, "I'm sure you're right."

When we arrive at the prison, I walk into the visiting room, all eyes turn toward me. The OGs are from various gangs in the city. For the first time, they are not only looking at me because of my status in the streets but because overnight my belly grew another four inches. There's no hiding that my ass is pregnant now.

I keep my head up and I challenge any stare that stays on me too damn long. I don't want anyone to get it twisted; this baby doesn't mean that I'm going to take any shit.

Settling into my usual seat, I wait for Smokestack to be led out. When ten minutes pass, I start to wonder whether he's coming. After another ten minutes, I give the guard a look that reads, *"What's up?"*

When I've waited a full thirty minutes, the weeping women and the crying babies around me begin whacking on my last nerve. Despite him being behind bars, everything that goes on in the streets makes it into the prison grapevine. Perhaps Smokestack can't bring himself to face me. Mason wished he could be the one to tell his stepfather the bad news, but given his own prison record, he's ineligible to visit him.

He's not coming. I climb back onto my feet with my shoulders heavier than when I entered. When I start to walk away, the door finally opens and Cousin Smokestack enters the room. Instantly, our eyes lock. It's hard to pretend not to see that his are swollen and red. It's touching to witness that much love.

I return to my chair while he forces himself to walk with his usual swagger. No matter what you're going through, you can't let niggas see you sweat. Smokestack is a very handsome man. Still has a pretty-boy face though he's close to fifty.

"Thanks for coming," he says.

"You know that you don't have to thank me. We're family."

His gaze falls to my round belly. "Definitely. You're about to make me a grandfather."

I smile. Though his blood doesn't flow through Mason, Smokestack has made it clear that Mason is, was, and will always be *his* son. For the first time, a strained and awkward silence flows between us. There's so much to say with little clue on how to say it.

"I'm sorry for your loss," I tell him.

His head drops a notch as he mumbles, "Thanks."

I give him a minute to collect himself before I get down to business.

"King Isaac is out," I say.

"Now *that* I did know."

"Diesel Carver has moved to Memphis."

He nods. "I heard about that too."

"And Python is out there. Pissed off."

Smokestack bobs his head and grows serious.

"We're going to need help."

"Then you came to the right place."

59

Shariffa

Tupelo, Mississippi

"What the fuck do you mean, I can't come home?" I blow up at Lynch. "It's been three weeks. I can't stay out here in this bitch forever!"

"It's not going to be forever." He sighs like I'm working his last nerve or something instead of the other way around.

I cross my arms and tap my foot. "Then how long?"

"I told you. SOON!"

"What fuckin' day is soon? Point that bitch out to me on a muthafuckin' calendar."

"Goddamn it, Shariffa. Get off my fuckin' ass with this shit. Don't forget that I'm doing this to protect your conspiring ass."

"Awww. Here we go again." My neck swivels around. "Miss me with that shit already," I snap back. "I'm a mutha-fuckin' big girl. I can handle my damn self out here in these streets. I ain't scared and I'm done apologizing for blasting be-fore thinking on that Bishop hit. I'm not gonna keep lickin' the crack of your ass over the shit. Only niggas who ain't ever fucked up can step up to me on this shit. It's time to move the fuck on."

SLAP!

Lynch's backhand happens so fast that my head snaps back hard. I have to check to make sure that it's still attached to my neck.

"Shut the fuck up! Damn!"

I blink and swallow some damn pride, but the shit ain't going down too easily.

Lynch looks like he really wants to go in, but instead storms away from me to collect himself.

"Feel better?" I ask, shaking off the sting of his backhand. "You feel more like a man now?"

"Shariffa," he warns.

"I wish your ass would just boss the fuck up and get our soldiers to fall in line. Are you running shit or are they running you, nigga?"

Lynch's chest swells up as he steps into my personal space. "Who the fuck is you talking to? You need to get that fuckin' bass out your voice!"

"Oh. You can check *my* ass, but those other niggas that are clowning you? You just bend the fuck over and take it like a real bitch, huh?"

BAM!

I drop to the floor and feel a tooth rattle around in my mouth. I don't give a fuck. I spit that bitch out, pick myself up, and square off with his ass again. "That's all you got? Huh, nigga? I've done fought bigger pussies than you." I take both hands and throw my weight into a hard shove. I ignore the fact that it only causes him to move back an inch.

He cracks his knuckles as if the next punch is going to send me into the middle of next week.

"Ever since I got with your ass, it's been one muthafuckin' excuse after another, while your pussy-ass crew can only lock down Mickey D corners and shit. Y'all ain't got no heart. No ambition. No direction. That's because your weak ass is sitting on a cardboard throne, thinking your ass is important. I got news for you, muthafucka. Ain't nobody scared of you. *NO-BODY!* Not even our fuckin' kids!"

"Shariffa," he warns.

I'm so heated now that I don't care what his ass does. "I'm not staying here another night. I mean that shit. Your ass don't deserve a boss bitch like me. I tried to upgrade your fuckin' gangster, get you on in some kind of way. But the minute I bring you on the field, you start shitting in your pants because some fucking VL bitch punked your ass? Get the fuck out of here. You may as well just pull down your pants and give me your dick since your ass ain't using it."

"Aaaarrrgh!"

BAM! BAM! BAM!

Lynch goes total fucking Mayweather on my ass. Despite my ass being wiped out on the floor, he lands one punch after another so that my entire world turns into pain. I hang on and refuse to black out.

"I'm so sick of your goddamn shit!" He stands up and commences to stomp the shit out of me. When he's satisfied, or remembers that I'm the mother of his kids, he finally stops. "Now look at what the fuck you made me do," Lynch says, huffing and puffing.

He steps back, cursing and swinging at anything else in the room.

My body screaming, I pull up into a sitting position, catch my breath, and then work my way up onto my feet.

Lynch doesn't hear a goddamn thing until I snatch the biggest blade out of the butcher block. He turns and looks me up and down.

"What the fuck do you think you're going to do with that?" he asks.

The muscles over my right eye spasm.

Lynch moves toward me, curious. "You're about to really overstep your fuckin' bounds again," he warns. "You know good and damn well you had that ass-whupping coming. You're fucking hardheaded as shit. That's your muthafuckin' problem."

I creep closer, my swollen and bleeding lip pulses as fast as my heartbeat. "And your fuckin' problem is that you're a goddamn pussy—just like your side bitch, Trigger. You should have heard that bitch scream before I sliced her ass up."

That puts a pause in his ass. "What?"

"You heard me. You two double-crossing muthafuckas played the wrong bitch. Better be glad that I didn't throw some damn barbecue sauce on her chopped-up ass and serve her to you."

Rage takes over Lynch as he charges toward me.

I knee those glass balls real hard and when he doubles over, plunge my blade dead in his throat. "Muthafucka."

He springs back in shock. His eyes wide, his hands lock around the handle of the knife, but before he can yank the shit out, he drops to his knees while blood sprays every damn where. Two seconds later, I charged his life to the game.

60

Lucifer

"Bed rest," Dr. Modi says, plopping down behind his desk and lacing his fingers together.

"But the baby is okay?" Mason and I ask at the same time, looking at him with eager eyes.

He hesitates. "At the moment the baby is fine. You'll—"

Mason cuts him off. "What the fuck do you mean *at the moment?*"

The doctor clears his throat. "It looks like you may have placenta previa."

My heart leaps out of my chest. "What the fuck is that?"

"It means that your placenta is lying unusually low in your uterus and it is either next to or covering your pelvis. Seeing that you've entered your last trimester, there is a good chance that we're going to have to deliver you early by cesarean—but we're not going to do that unless and until it's absolutely necessary. We want to keep him in the womb as long as we possibly can."

He's talking calmly, but it's not doing a damn thing to calm me the fuck down.

"Does that mean that there is going to be something wrong with my son?" Mason asks, sounding alarmed.

"No. Nothing is definitive, but I must stress to you how important it is for you to take it easy."

"Oh. You don't have to worry about that, Doc," Mason says, taking over again. "I'm gonna make sure that she follows orders."

Any other time, I'd probably dig in and fight back. I've never liked taking orders, but there might be something wrong with my child. I spread my hands across my round belly and at that same moment, the baby kicks.

I gasp.

Mason jumps in alarm. "What is it?"

"He kicked."

"No shit?" Mason's lips stretch wide as he leans over in his chair and stretches out his hand to feel for himself.

We wait, but the baby isn't responding to his touch. Mason's excitement nosedives.

Kick!

"I felt it." Mason lights up. We laugh and stare at each other while something wonderful courses between us. This is the moment when we've finally become a real family.

"Promise to take it easy?" he asks.

"I promise."

61

Shariffa

Pregnant. I'd heard the rumors but I didn't believe it until I saw for myself. I hardly recognize the swollen woman waddling out of a Memphis obstetrics office. I've had a devil of a time trying to locate and tag this bitch. She doesn't look so intimidating now. If I play my cards right I can use her handicap to my advantage.

I'm not proud of it, but I'll use whatever advantage I can get when it comes to dealing with this bitch. There's no way that I can get my old life back, so I don't see why the hell she should have hers. After I take care of Lucifer, I'll have to pack up and leave this city forever. Soon I'll snatch my kids back from Lynch's mother and we'll head out west to Texas, or maybe even California.

A black SUV pulls up to the curb and Lucifer and Fat Ace quickly hop into the backseat. When it peels away, I shift my ride into drive and follow two cars behind. I've hatched at least a thousand different plans on how I can get at Lucifer. So far every one of them has had one flaw or another. I have to face the fact that there's no perfect plan. Hell, there's barely a decent one. I just need time and opportunity—and right now, I have plenty of time.

62

Hydeya

It's been years since I've cried. I don't know if I even remember how. I keep playing the scene at Momma Peaches's funeral over and over in my mind. The shit happened so fast—I should've been better prepared. I should've been on alert.

I should've . . . I should've . . . I should've . . .

"We think you need to take some time off," Chief Brown says. Her usually stony expression is a soft mask of compassion. "You're suffering from an incredible loss right now. You need to take this time for yourself. And take all the time that you need. We understand."

"I think. . . . maybe it's better if I keep busy—keep working," I tell her.

Chief Brown clasps her hands and then casts a look over at the deputy mayor. "I'm sure that you *think* you feel that way, but you need to grieve properly."

I frown. "There's a *proper* grieving process?" I push back.

"It's been settled," she counters, her hard countenance slowly returning. "Lieutenant Fowler will take over your duties for the short time that you're gone. Just make sure you turn over all the files and charts that you're working on."

I seethe in my seat. "How long am I supposed to be grieving?"

"I wish that you wouldn't view it as if it's some sort of punishment. We're only trying to help you."

Sure you are. "How long?"

"I don't know. Six to twelve weeks? It depends on when the department's psychologist gives you the okay."

"I have to see a psychologist now?"

Her thinning patience shows.

"Fine. Whatever." I stand to leave, knowing that she hates when anyone else ends a meeting before being dismissed.

"Your gun and your badge."

"Am I on administrative leave or am I being fired?" I ask.

"Standard procedure," she says.

Grinding my jaw, I unholster my weapon and set it and my badge on her desk.

The chief stands and takes my whole identity and shoves it into her top drawer. "This really is for the best."

"Sure it is." I turn and walk out of the office.

Fowler wastes no time catching up to me as I march back to my office—or what *used* to be my office. "How did it go?"

I keep walking.

"Hawkins?"

"How the hell do you think it went?"

"You're on leave?"

"Yep. And congratulations. You're the new acting captain of the department now."

"Really? You're blaming me for this?"

"Yes—no." I shake out my troubled thoughts. "I don't know. Fuck it. I'm grieving—cut me some slack."

Fowler grabs my arm to slow me down. "How are you really holding up?"

I glance around to make sure that no one is paying attention to our conversation. "You want to know how I'm holding up? Barely. And the one thing that keeps me sane has just been snatched from me." I pull away and continue my march to my office.

Fowler doesn't enter, but leans his weight against the door. "I'm sorry, Hydeya. I know that you're not in the headspace to hear or believe that—but I am. I know what you and Drake had was special. This has to be completely devastating."

I find a small box and start cramming my personal belongings into it.

"Did the chief ask why you were at the funeral?"

"Told her that I was following up on the Maybelline Carver case."

"So you still didn't tell her that Isaac Goodson is your father?"

My gaze snaps up to his. "No. There's no fucking reason for her to know. So keep your damn mouth shut."

"What the fuck? I'm not going to say anything. Why the hell would you even suggest that I would?"

At his hurt look, I start to feel like shit. I have been snapping his head off a lot lately and he doesn't deserve it. "I'm sorry. At least you don't have to deal with my bitchy behavior for the next six to twelve weeks." I pick up my box and head for the door. "Keep my seat warm. I'll be back."

63

Lucifer

The streets are talking again. This time they're saying that chinky Crippette bitch, Trigger, is R.I.P. But to top the shit off, muthafuckas are spreading the word that I wiped her ass off the map. I don't mind the muthafuckin' rumor. It was probably put out in these streets as a cover for that bitch and Shariffa going M.I.A. All that extra shit those Grape bitches are doing isn't necessary.

When the time is right, I'll see those last two bitches for that dirty hit they did on Bishop. Far as I'm concerned, they're living on borrowed time. For now I'll have to put my homicidal fantasies to the side. Because right now every time I close my eyes my damn belly blows up another two to three inches. Now nothing in my closet fits. Hell. Even my damn feet are huge. My nose has bubbled and my hands are starting to look like sausages. This morning I had to slather a tub of butter on my hand to get my engagement ring off before I had to have the finger amputated.

I'm not normally vain, but this shit ain't cute. At least the doctor said that everything looked fine on the ultrasound and confirmed that we are indeed expecting a baby boy.

"How are we doing this morning, beautiful?" Mason asks, coming up behind me and kissing me on the neck.

"Beautiful? I look like a damn beached whale."

He chuckles. "That's not true. You look like you're about to have my baby. I can't think of anything more beautiful than that."

Sweet, but I don't believe a damn thing coming out of his mouth. Not after a night of awkward lovemaking when I almost peed on him. How come nobody told me that not all orgasms are real orgasms when you're pregnant? After I shut the show down and told his ass no more pussy until after the baby is born, Mason has been slathering on the compliments, hoping I'll change my mind.

Maybe I will. I can't imagine going another ten weeks without riding the perfectly good dick lying beside me.

Despite my ass feeling hot, I let him nuzzle on me and then settle his hands around my belly. I know what he's waiting for, but for some reason the baby refuses to move for him. If it weren't for Dr. Modi letting us hear the heartbeat, I'd think something was wrong. Meanwhile, the baby has found its sweet spot, sitting on my bladder.

Mason waits a little longer and then sighs. "Well. We got ten more weeks before we'll be properly introduced." He looks at me. "Excited yet?"

"I feel a lot of things, but excitement isn't one of them."

He laughs. "I hope with the next one, you'll have a better attitude." He hugs me tighter, but it just makes me feel smothered and I have to wiggle my way out of his arms.

"C'mon now. Get off me."

He releases me, but his laughter deepens.

I flash him the bird.

"All right. I'll stop teasing you."

"Thank you."

"That is, when you tell me what day you want to finally stand before a preacher. Tomorrow . . . next week?"

My neck nearly swivels all the way off. "You have lost your

damn mind if you think that I'm going to waddle my fat ass down an aisle."

"I told you that you look beautiful."

"Boy, bye." I walk back into the bedroom.

Mason follows. "How about a justice of the peace?"

"Oh God. It's hot in here. Did you turn off the air conditioner?" I plop down onto the bed, still at a loss as to what I'm going to wear, since the bedsheets are probably the only things that'll fit.

"For the millionth time, the a/c is working, Willow. Don't change the subject."

"Look. Whatever you want to do is fine with me," I say, fighting tears. I really don't know what I'm going to put on.

"Really?" He walks over and tries to pull me up from the bed.

I struggle real hard to muffle my crankiness.

"So. City hall or a church wedding? I know weddings are supposed to be a big deal with you females."

I cut him a sharp look. I can't imagine fussing over colors, patterns, dresses, and menus. "Nah. I'm good. The simpler the better, but *after* the baby is born."

"Nah. Nah. I want my boy coming into the world legit."

I feel where he's coming from. It's a new beginning for him. Time for him to be the man and put down real roots—a final push away from the Carvers. Despite my ass hating the Carvers and their Gangster Disciple affiliations, I still feel some kind of way that Dribbles failed to reunite the family. Ever since we put her into the ground, there has been no real talks about his real mother, his older brother, or the aunt that was dying in his arms. We'll probably never know what happened in that church before Python came in blasting. We just know that a storm is brewing and we gotta be prepared.

"What time is your meeting?" I ask, hating that I have to sit this one out.

Mason peeps his Rolex. "Actually, Profit and I need to head out."

"You really think Profit is ready for this?" I remember how I had to save his ass when the last arms delivery went south with those Angels of Mercy muthafuckas.

"The fastest way to teach his ass how to swim is to throw him in the water."

I hear what he's saying, but I'd feel better if I was the one that had Mason's back—always. "So you trust this dude?"

"I trust Smokestack," he says it in a way that makes it clear that I should've gone to his stepfather for a new connect from the giddy up. But there's nothing new about it. We're going back to the same people who'd always provided us with weapons: *the police.*

"C'mon. Smile for me. I'm sure that this Lieutenant Fowler cat is on the up-and-up."

64

LeShelle

After a good dicking down, a bitch can't help but pass the fuck out. But even in sleep, I still keep dreaming about that green-eyed monster, Diesel. The shit doesn't make any sense since the nigga is determined to take me down. There is just something about his fucking cockiness and swagger that's touching me on a level that Python has failed to do—and if I'm honest, other than the hot shit a few hours ago, it's been a while, since there has been a disconnect both physically *and* mentally.

Since I've been the bitch fighting to keep our asses in the game, Python's mental implosion over that brother shit has turned me all the way off. But a nigga like Diesel? I can't see that ever happening. That muthafucka keeps his eyes on the ball at all times. And now to hear his presence even gives King Isaac pause? That's the sort of nigga a bitch like me could really rock with.

But what about the bedroom? Can Diesel do a bitch the way that she needs to be done? My body screams yes despite never having tasted his ass.

An image of Cleo singing and Diesel being so enraptured resurfaces in my mind. Jealousy in its purest form grips me by the throat and thrashes me around even in my sleep. When it feels that I'm seconds from dying, I bolt up, gasping and sweating like a fucking pig. A few seconds later, I come to my senses and take a look around. The bed is empty.

Where the fuck is Python?

I throw the tangled sheets off my body and storm out of the bedroom. At the sound of hushed voices in the living room, I return to the bedroom and put on some clothes. Once dressed, I rush my nosy ass up into the living room and see at least a dozen top-level Gangster Disciples hunched over in an intense business discussion.

Python, listening and playing with his new Burmese pet, resembles the old Python, commanding the room like a boss and strategizing his return. For a moment I forget about my traitorous thoughts about Diesel.

A knock on the door pulls me out of lustful fantasies and puts all the niggas in the room on ten.

"Who the fuck is that?" Python asks, the last one to climb to his feet.

I'm just as curious as the rest of them until Shank, another Gangster Disciple on the come up, steps back and announces, "It's Avonte."

Python's gaze zooms to me. "You going somewhere?"

Fuck. Qiana. How in the world did I forget? "Yeah. I got this little thing with the Queen Gs I promised to run through. I shouldn't be gone but a couple of hours."

Shank lets Avonte in.

"What? A party?" Python lifts a dubious brow. "Do you think going to something like that is wise? The streets are still hot—for both of us."

"I know that," I say, irritated. "I know how to handle myself."

Python pauses to think the shit over before giving me his approval.

I let his ass act like he's my daddy and then tell Avonte, "Give me a minute, girl." I rush to put on my Timbs and strap up. Before I step out of the house, Python peels himself from his meeting to stop me at the door, his pet snake coiling around his arm. "You be careful out there," he says.

"I will." I give him a quick peck on the cheek, but Python's muscular arm blocks my path. "I mean it. You check in when you get to where you're going."

I frown. "Why the hell are you acting like it's the last time you're going to see me?"

His midnight gaze roams my face and then that strange feeling creeps over me again. This time, the heavy dread won't shake off.

"Just be careful," he says and then slaps me on the ass before stepping away from the door.

"Let's go," I tell Avonte and march out to the car. We pile inside with Myeisha and Erika and head to Hack's Crossing.

"Where the fuck is this bitch?" I pace back and forth under the moonlight at Hack's Crossing. I don't believe this bitch played me again. It never pays to give bitches second and third chances. But that's okay. There's not a fucking rock in this fucking city where she can hide from me. Why are bitches always trying me?

The longer I wait, the angrier I get. I'd planned on making the shit quick. None of that wet shit that Lucifer prides herself in, but the longer these bitches take, the more I rethink it.

My cell phone buzzes from my back pocket. It's a text message from Avonte. Her, Myeisha, and Erika are spread throughout the small park and casing the entrances.

HOW MUCH LONGER DO YOU WANT TO WAIT?

Annoyed, I grit my teeth, mainly because I now suspect that the bitch ain't coming again. Instead of firing off an angry text, I ignore her ass. We'll wait until I get good and damn ready to go. My pace quickens around this oak tree.

My phone buzzes again. I glance at the screen.

ARE YOU STILL THERE? HOW MUCH LONGER?

I roll my eyes and stuff the phone back into my pocket.
Maybe I should take Diesel's ass out. I stop walking and weigh
that as a possible solution. But how in the fuck do I get at that
nigga? The muthafucka is far from dumb and probably would
see my ass coming from a mile away. Still, the idea intrigues
me. Everybody fucking bleeds—and everybody's guard comes
down at some point. I need to figure out his weakness.
Pussy. Every nigga's weakness.
An image of Cleo, singing on that stage, floats to mind. I
need to use the Queen G to my advantage.
SNAP!
What the fuck was that? My head whips around—and when
I don't see anything, I strain my ears to detect another sound.
SNAP! SNAP! SNAP!
Snatching out my gun, I crouch low and look around.
Somebody is out there. The seconds tick by as my heart hammers
against my chest. Staring into the park's inky blackness is like
staring into a vat of crude oil. I can't see shit.
Where the fuck are my girls?
I reach for my phone, grateful for the small light from the
screen. Quickly, I blast out a text.

THE FUCK ARE YOU, BITCHES?

I wait and wait, but don't receive a response. I hit the call
button. The bitch doesn't pick up. *I know that these bitches didn't
leave my ass out here.* I crouch lower and then back into a nearby
bush for additional cover. The phone buzzes and a strange message
flashes on the screen.
What the fuck?

65
Ta'Shara

My heart trips inside of my chest, making it difficult to breathe *and* stay focused. Has everything that I've gone through with my sister really come down to this, my hunting her in the middle of the night with a group of Flowers? A voice in the back of my head reminds me that at the end of the day, LeShelle and I share the same blood and that should still mean something. However, a stronger, louder voice tells me to fuck all that shit.

"Psst." Mack tugs my arm. "We're going to split up. Ain't no damn way that bitch showed up here by herself."

I nod.

"Are you all right?" she asks, peering closer at me. It's dark as fuck out here. What if LeShelle and her crew pick us off before we can get them? "Ta'Shara?" she whispers. "Are you sure you're good with this? It's your call."

"I'm good," I tell her. "Stop asking me stupid-ass questions." In order to keep my head in the game, snapshots of my prom night flash in my head. The men that my *dear* sister allowed to molest me while I cried out for her help. How LeShelle stood there and watched—and then crudely carved the Gangster Disciples initials on the side of my ass like I was some damn cattle. My blood turns ice-cold. I'm more than ready to do this shit.

Mack is staring.

"Go," I snap. "We don't have all night."

A slow smile breaks across her face. "Time to go Queen G hunting." She winks and then scrambles off.

Now that the drugs have slowly left my system, my confidence wanes a bit. I've proven that I'm a good shot, but Profit once pointed out to me that shit is different when faced with an actual moving target. Swallowing a large knot of anxiety, I creep between the bushes and trees and remind myself why I'm here. LeShelle must be stopped—because much sooner than later, she's coming after me too.

But time stretches like a muthafucka in this big-ass park. The bitch could be any fucking where. Are we too late? Are we too early? Too bad we can't raise Qiana's ass from the dead and ask the bitch what time this shit was supposed to go down—or maybe LeShelle didn't think her dumb ass would show up?

"Oh. How much longer is this bitch going to keep us out here?" a voice off to my right asks.

Who the fuck is that? I crouch down and glance around.

"I know. Right?" a second voice says. "I ain't got all fucking night to be out here with this part-time gangster bitch. Her and Python ain't been running shit for a while any damn way. Why the fuck are we still taking orders from her? Those Vice Lord bitches ain't coming and she got us out here in this wet-ass shit."

The voices inside of my head split off again. One panicked and the other cold as ice. I stay in the cold side, numbing my feelings as I creep forward.

"Text the bitch back," one of the voices says. "If she doesn't answer, I say we leave her ass out here."

An image of Kookie and two other Queen G bitches that

were there the night of my rape flashes in my head. LeShelle always has a small pack of minions with her when she does her dirty work. But these two are sloppy. Through the bushes, I see the glow from a cell phone screen. I click off the safety on my weapon, take aim, and fire two muffled shots.

One wrangles out a sharp gasp between the first and second shot, but both targets fall with a soft thump into the wet grass. A smile curves my lips as the cell phone's glowing screen tumbles about a foot away from them.

Standing over the two bodies, I stare and wait for my ass to feel some sort of remorse—but none comes. If anything, there's a deadening inside—and there's a strange sort of freedom in death, a freedom that's exhilarating and consuming. Using my foot, I roll the bodies over so I can get a good look at their faces. Neither of them are Kookie or the other girls that were there the night I was raped. Still: no remorse.

I remind myself that there's no telling how many Queen Gs are out here and to stay on alert. I edge past the two dead bodies to pick up the discarded phone. As I hurry away, I don't pay the same attention to my footing.

SNAP!

I freeze and curse my sloppiness. The rain transforms from a light drizzle to a steady downpour. The phone in my hand vibrates.

WHERE THE FUCK ARE YOU, BITCHES?

A smile blankets my face as I text LeShelle back.

STAY RIGHT THERE. I'M COMING FOR YOU, BITCH.

66

LeShelle

STAY RIGHT THERE. I'M COMING FOR YOU, BITCH.

What the fuck?

I find the free flashlight app on the cell and then swing it wide around me. Before I'm able to make anything out, the muthafucka is shot out of my hand and another bullet whips by my face, burning the side of my cheek. Hand stinging, I fire back.

Poof! Poof! Poof!

Return fire comes from every direction. I hit the dirt face first and then crawl to the other side of the bush. *Shit. Shit. Shit.* My plans have crumbled all around me. *Stay calm. Stay calm.* That shit proves impossible as my adrenaline skyrockets. Another bullet clips my damaged ear. Out of reflex, I cry out, but then clamp my jaw shut.

Poof! Poof! Poof!

Did that bitch come out here with the whole Flower army? How in the fuck did I underestimate that kiddie gang-banger? And where the fuck is my backup?

More bullets whip by my head and I blindly return fire. I scramble from under the bush and make a mad dash toward another oak tree. A bullet sears into my thigh. Shocked, I stumble, and once again hit the ground face first. A tooth rattles around in my mouth. I quickly spit that fucker out, jump back onto my feet, and take off.

In no time, I make it to the lake in the heart of the park. A stone fountain is bubbling and park benches are scattered around. The alarming part is that there are very few areas to hide. I fly across the open field, certain that I hear my attackers gaining ground. Despite the script flipping on my ass, I'm calm enough to try strategizing a way out of this bitch and how to reposition for a better advantage.

Unbelievably, the thrill of the game has me on a high that gets my fucking clit thumping to the point of orgasm. "Come on, you blood clots. Come and get me."

The seconds that it takes for me to reach the park's fountain feel more like hours. That's when it strikes me that something isn't right about this. They could've put me down a while ago. *They're fucking with your ass.*

That's a real possibility, I argue with myself. I also realize that this isn't the time to try and second-guess whether I'm running into a trap. I only have a second to come up with my own chess moves.

I reach the fountain, duck behind it, and then try to pick up on any movement in the direction I came from.

There. A dark figure races to one of the thin trees dotting the perimeter.

I take aim and fire.

A scream rips through the air as the body stumbles and falls.

Gotcha. Mentally, I give myself a high five, but know that there are more bitches out there. But where? I push that thought to the side and remain on survivor mode. Once I get my breathing under control, I keep my footsteps light as I continue to move around the fountain. From the corner of my eye, I spot the entrance to a walking path off by the side of the lake. The only problem is that it's close to the body I just dropped. I scan the area for another exit option.

There isn't one.

All right, LeShelle. You can do this shit. I take a few more seconds to pump myself up and then I take off running. The burning pain in my leg has reduced to a dull ache.

More bullets zip by my head at an alarming rate, but I'm still flying. That is until my shoulder is nailed from the back. I jerk forward and, once again, lose my footing. This time when I hit the ground, my weapon bounces out of my hand and out of reach, and pain ricochets throughout my body.

GET UP! GET THE FUCK UP!

I make the attempt, but my leg is having none of it.

What the fuck is going on? A new wave of fear nearly stops my heart. This can't be how this shit ends. It can't.

Another bullet blasts through my shoulder. The explosion of pain surprises me as well as the tears that spring to my eyes.

GET UP! GET THE FUCK UP!

Miraculously, I manage to get back on my feet. I keep going, though I'm not as fast as I was a few minutes ago. It has a lot to do with the fact that I can't get enough air into my lungs. This wasn't how this shit was supposed to go. This was supposed to be a simple hit job on a damn teenager and a fucking baby. How the hell did shit go left? How the fuck could I have gotten shit this fucking wrong? Me?

The next shot drops me like a stone. A fire roars from my left side up toward my lungs. *Noooooo! Get up.*

I lift my head from the dark, wet grass and spit out a mouthful of dirt and blood. I cling to denial. I can't die out here. I'm the queen of these fucking streets. Don't these bitches know who the fuck I am?

My life, including a whole bunch of shit that I'd long forgotten about, passes before my eyes as well as all the dreams that are on the verge of happening. Python and I are moving back to Memphis. He's going to reclaim the throne of the Gangster Disciples.

The rain is falling hard now, driven sheets that feel cool against my fevered face and wash away some of the blood dripping from my mouth.

Squish. Squish. Squish.

Someone is coming. No. There's more than one. For the first time in a long while, I feel the cold fingers of fear wrap around my heart. *This is it.* Reality bangs against the door of my denial. My mental stability shrinks away. Suddenly this shit is funny as hell.

A bitch kicks my side to roll me over. I laugh until my blurry vision focuses on the face hovering over me. *Ta'Shara?*

"Hey, Sis. Long time no see."

67

Ta'Shara

An incredible amount of power surges to my head as I stare down at my piece of shit sister, wiggling around in the wet grass. The look on her face is priceless. My girls Dime, Mack, and Romil surround her too.

"What the *fuck* are you doing here?" LeShelle spits. "Where the hell is that Qiana bitch?"

"Sorry. She couldn't make it, but don't worry. You'll be joining her soon enough." I squat and place the barrel of my gun against her bleeding left side and press.

"AAAAAARRRGH!"

I snicker. Her pain amuses me. After a minute, I ease the pressure on her wound to allow her to catch her breath.

"You fucking bitch," she hisses through deep gulps of air.

"*I'm* the bitch?" I ask for clarification. "You who couldn't stand to see me happy without you? You who insisted on dragging me down into this fucking gutter to play this shit on your level? You wanna judge me?"

LeShelle hacks up a mouthful of blood and spit and then launches it right into my face.

Enraged, I take the butt of my gun and hammer it back and forth against her face until I hear something crack. When I stop her entire face is covered in blood. She's a grotesque mess. However, in true LeShelle fashion, the bitch starts laughing. It's that same maniacal laughter that she gave from outside the Douglases' burning home. That same laughter that claws at me in my dreams.

Why does she hate me so much?

It's a question that I didn't mean to ask myself, but's one that I can't just dismiss either.

"What do you want to do?" Mack asks.

"Let's take the bitch for a ride." I stand up and allow the other Flowers to snatch LeShelle to her feet.

She lets out another scream of pain before collapsing into another fit of laughter. "What the fuck is you going to do, Ta'Shara? Kill me?" She shakes her head and then locks gazes with me. "You don't have the fucking balls. You're not built for this shit like I am. You're out of your damn league."

"We'll see about that."

LeShelle's laugh deepens.

Mack, who's had enough, slams the butt of her gun on the back of LeShelle's head, knocking her out cold.

68

LeShelle

I wake up wondering why every inch of me hurts and why there is a weird, dirty, metallic taste in my mouth. I try to open my eyes, but the muthafuckas are swollen shut.

"Well, look who's decided to join the party." A familiar voice laughs.

I redouble my efforts to open my eyes. Sitting in front of me with her head cocked to the side is Ta'Shara. Next to her are two Flowers that she's befriended. Suddenly, everything comes crashing back. I laugh. What fucking fresh hell is this? And how in the fuck did a B-team gangster squad beat me?

"Hello," Ta'Shara says, smiling. "Comfortable?"

I try to move but can't. I'm tied to a chair. I don't know why, but that shit is funny too.

"Yeah. Chuckle it up," Ta'Shara says. "I guarantee you that you won't enjoy this as much as I will."

I laugh and then I notice how vacant her eyes are. No. Not vacant. Dead. My laughter dies and my interest is piqued. I've turned Ta'Shara into a fascinating creature. For the first time, I worry that she really does have the balls to kill me.

She sees that I finally understand the situation and a thin, evil grin slides across her mouth. "While you've been sleeping," Ta'Shara begins, "I've been trying to decide exactly what I want to do with you. What would be the right retaliation?"

"That's another one of your problems." I smirk. "You *lack* imagination." An emotion finally flickers in Ta'Shara's eyes, but then when I blink, it's gone.

All kinds of emotions ripple through me, but it's the anger that I cling to. We lock into an epic staring contest until I crack. "Is this your plan? To stare me to death?" I ask. "Should've known. You're still trying to get your gangster training wheels off."

"Maybe I'm waiting for you to give me a reason why I shouldn't kill you."

I'm careful to make sure my smile matches hers. "I can't think of a single thing." *She can't do it.* For all her bravado and her menacing-looking friends, Ta'Shara is stalling because deep down she's still an uptight, bougie bitch who's in way over her head.

"Why did you have me gang-raped and branded like an animal?"

I struggle to pull it back together and recalculate my position.

"I'm waiting," she says. "How the fuck was my prom date a threat to your imaginary throne?"

Shaking my head, I continue to smirk at her. "It was the betrayal, you stupid bitch. It's the fact that I stuck my neck out for you time after time to protect you, but when I ask you to do one damn thing *for me*, you wouldn't do it. I hope his ass was worth it."

Another flicker.

"What? Don't tell me there's trouble in paradise." I laugh. "Figures. What is it? Another woman?" When Ta'Shara flinches, I know I've hit the jackpot. "HA! Serves you right with your uptight, righteous ass. First thing you learn out here in the streets is ain't no nigga loyal."

"You had me raped," she hisses, tryna keep me on subject.

"Girl, bye. Don't whine to me about a couple of rusty nig-gas fucking you. How many times did I have my pussy stretched the fuck out by all those foster daddies you love so much, huh?" I swallow hard as sweat pours down my face. "You're an un-grateful bitch and you deserve everything that happened that night."

Poof! Poof!

Both of my knees explode open. "AAAAAAAARRRGH!" I scream at the top of my lungs. When I run out of air, I start hy-perventilating. Throughout my performance, Ta'Shara's expres-sion never changes.

"Why did you kill Essence? She was a loyal Queen G and didn't do anything to you."

Panting, I try to think. "I don't know. It was fucking Tues-day and I was fucking bored."

Poof! Poof!

She nailed my shoulders. "Awwwww, GODDAMNIT!" *Embrace the pain. Embrace the pain. Own it.* My life's mantra, but it's hard this time. The pain is everywhere.

Ta'Shara cocks her head the other way. "Are those tears I see?" she asks.

I shake my head, but I feel the wetness on my face.

"Awww." Ta'Shara lowers her weapon, stands, and slowly walks toward me. Against my will I recoil as if scared of my lit-tle sister. Once she is within inches of the chair, she leans down close—and then runs her tongue up the side of my bloody, wet face.

"Salty . . . and bitter."

"Fuck you."

Slap!

I grin. At least her backhand isn't as bad as another pistol-whipping.

"You know, I actually thought about lining up a team of Vice Lords so you could experience what it's like to have a train run on you, but then I thought about it and the monster you married, and I concluded that your sick ass would enjoy the shit too much."

I smirk. "You don't want your big sister to show you how it's done?"

A male's voice booms from the other side of this vacant warehouse. "What the hell are we doing all the way out here?" He and another girl enter the room.

Profit.

His gaze locks on me before shifting to Ta'Shara. "You found her." Rage transforms his face into a mountain of granite. How the hell this muthafucka is still breathing is still beyond me. I'd put enough lead in him to stop a damn elephant.

Ta'Shara keeps her attention focused on me. "C'mon in. My sister and I were just finishing a little sister-to-sister conversation."

Profit snatches out his gun.

I flinch when the safety is clicked off. I have no doubt that this nigga wouldn't waste time jaw jacking and would unload a full clip into me. My hackles rise. *Someone is walking across my grave.* The old saying causes another smile to twitch across my lips. I know beyond a shadow of a doubt that I'm not getting out of this shit alive.

"Don't shoot," Ta'Shara says. "She's all mine."

Unbelievably, a ray of hope returns, but that's quickly doused when one of her Flowers approaches and the powerful smell of gasoline singes my nose.

Ta'Shara continues with her needling questions. "Why did you kill the Douglases?"

With nothing to lose, I look her right in the eye. "Because you loved them more than me."

Another emotion flickers in her eyes and just like the two times before, it vanishes. Ta'Shara stands and walks over to her friend with the gasoline can. Like a robot, she takes it, holds it over my head, and pours. A blinding pain rips through me as the flammable liquid pours into my every wound. It burns everything. My eyes. My nose. My mouth.

"You like fire, don't you?" Ta'Shara asks. "You lit Essence on fire. Burned the Douglases and even your friend, Kookie. So my unimaginative ass figured I'll give you what you love."

Real terror seizes me. "Ta'Shara, wait."

"Mack?" Her friend hands her a box of matches.

"No. Wait," I sputter. "Shoot me. Make it quick."

Still in robot mode, Ta'Shara removes a match, strikes it. "Any last words?"

"Don't do this," I plea. "I'm your fucking sister."

"That's where you're wrong. I don't have a sister. Burn in hell, bitch." With that she flicks the match my way.

"NOOOOOOOOOOOOOO!"

WHOOOOOOSH!

69

Ta'Shara

LeShelle's bloodcurdling scream rips throughout the abandoned warehouse and seems to go on forever. I watch, fascinated, as the orange flames consume her. Within a few seconds, LeShelle rips out of her ropes and bolts to her feet. She waves her arms around and then takes a step toward me.

Fascinated yet determined, I hold my ground, not thinking what I'll do if she actually reaches me.

Profit rushes forward and plants himself between a flaming LeShelle and me. However, there is no need. LeShelle takes two steps and then crashes to the floor.

Black smoke curls above the orange flames. The putrid smell of burning flesh tickles my nose. Still, I can't take my eyes off of her. Her long hair is the first to burn away. Her clothes, second. However, her screams go on and on. It's the second body today that I've watched smoldering like this. Qiana was an accident, and therefore I didn't appreciate how the fire comes alive and consumes its victim—like it's doing with LeShelle now.

As the minutes tick by, you can see the glowing beast searching for something else to consume. When it's denied another victim, its energy wanes. Its flames shrink and its glow dulls.

It's sad.

Mack, Romil, and Dime have turned their backs to the scene. Even Profit tries to shield me from watching the horrific murder. I edge around him. I don't want to miss a thing. I don't know how much time has passed before I'm just staring at a smoldering stack of bones.

"I killed them because you loved them more than me."

What a crock of shit. She killed the Douglases to hurt me. She probably even hoped that I would've been home that night. Whatever good had been in LeShelle had died when she chose the streets over me. She started hating me when she could no longer control me. Still staring at the charcoal bones, I wait for a flood of guilt and remorse to wash over me. But it doesn't. Neither does a wave of sadness or satisfaction. The sad truth of the matter is that I still feel absolutely nothing.

Soon, I'm aware that four sets of eyes are staring at me. Are they waiting for me to break down? Or are they wondering why I'm not?

Profit wraps his arm around me. "C'mon, baby. Let's go."

I shrug off his touch but remain mindful not to say anything too revealing in front of the girls.

Profit steps back, confusion etched in his face.

I only asked Mack to bring him here because he deserved to see Ta'Shara die and to watch me put an end to the bitch. None of this shit means that we're cool again.

"We need to get rid of the body," I tell him.

He nods. "I'll take care of it. You and the girls go on ahead." He looks to Mack. "Take her to *my* place."

I don't bother telling him about the two bodies we left at Hack's Crossing. As far as I'm concerned, he may as well make himself useful.

"C'mon, girl," Mack says, swinging her arm around my shoulders. "I'll take you home."

I allow her to lead me out of the warehouse. When we pile into Mack's car, once again I feel everyone's eyes on me. Each of them seems too scared to say something. We ride back to Ruby Cove in a tomb of silence. Yet, LeShelle's screams still echo inside my head. It doesn't scare or haunt me. In fact, I find it strangely comforting to know that she's eternally burning in hell.

I laugh. "Ding-dong. The witch is dead."

The other girls muster up a couple of chuckles.

"Are you sure that you're all right?" Mack asks, her face a mask of concern.

I grin up at her through the rearview. "Never better."

Minutes later, they drop me off in front of Profit's crib. Before I head inside, Mack leans across the driver seat to call out to me. "Call me if you need anything."

I give her the thumbs-up and continue my trek to the house. "Ding-dong. The witch is dead." I can't get that out of my head now.

Once inside, I waste no time heading to the bathroom for a much-needed hot shower. I scrub myself from head to toe at least five times before I'm squeaky clean.

After I shut off the water and towel off, I dig back through my clothes until I find the box of matches. As I stare at it, I can't help but marvel at the amount of destruction contained in such a small thing. I leave the bathroom, holding the box like it's the precious from *Lord of the Rings*. I scrounge around the house until I find an ashtray, and then hurry back into the bedroom.

I pull out one match. Strike it. And then watch a beautiful amber glow magically appear. It immediately starts to gobble up the small stick of wood in order to survive. When it burns my fingers, I drop it into the ashtray and then watch the flame slowly die out. Quickly, I strike another match and watch the process all over again.

Another match.

Then another.

Five matches.

Ten matches.

Each time, the flame is more fascinating than the last. How come I've never noticed this shit before?

At long last, the bedroom door opens and Profit steps inside.

"Is it done?" I ask.

"Yeah."

I stand from the bed, still intoxicated with bloodlust.

"I—"

I slap a hand over his mouth, shutting him up. He gets the hint and nods. I remove my hand and then start jerking his jacket off of him.

Profit pulls his shirt over his head while I yank at the button on his jeans. Once undressed, I shove him over toward the bed and damn near attack him like a wild animal. I can still smell that burning-flesh scent in his hair and skin. My pussy is wet. My clit and tits are hard. If I don't get him inside of me soon, I'll go crazy.

Profit tries to start with all that kissing bullshit, but I'm not having that shit. Kissing is too intimate—too personal. I'm not interested in that shit.

"I wanna fuck. That's it. You got it?"

Hurt ripples across his face, but he understands that it's either that or he can take his ass out to the couch. Once he nods, I rip the towel off my body, steady his fat cock, and then ram him inside me.

Closing my eyes, I listen as LeShelle's screams fill my head. Suddenly I'm no longer dead inside but very much alive. I throw everything I have into each thrust and grind.

"Oh. Shit. Slow down, baby," Profit says, locking his large hands on my hips to try and control my flow.

I knock them off and then pin them high over his head. "I'm going to fuck this dick the way that I want to fuck it. You got it?"

He gives me a look that reads that he can easily overpower

me, but knowing that he wants to stay off my shit list, he's going to let me work out whatever the fuck I got to work out. Shit. It's not like there's nothing in it for him. But now staring into his intense face starts pissing me the fuck off. While still fucking him, I rear back and punch the shit out of him.

"What the fuck?" Angry, he flips me over and takes the top position. "Have you lost your damn mind?"

Tingling everywhere from his own stroke game, I still manage to snatch my hand free and slap him again. How dare this muthafucka cheat on me. SLAP! SLAP! SLAP!

Tired of my ass beating on him, Profit flips me onto my back, mushes my head down into the pillow, and pounds me from the back until we're both screaming in ecstasy.

70

Ta'Shara

I can't sleep. LeShelle's dying screams still have me smiling up at the ceiling. *I'm free. I'm finally free of that bitch.* It seems too good to be true. *But now what?* I bounce the question around in my head for a while and I slowly begin to panic when an answer doesn't come back to me. Who I once wanted to be seems so far away. A doctor.

A sad laugh tumbles from me in the darkness. I haven't even been to high school in the last year. Hell. I can't imagine even going back to Morris High School. I can't imagine doing anything I used to do.

I glance back over my shoulder to where Profit is sleeping like a baby. Can I even go back to this relationship? Sure. My body still craves his touch, but could it ever be more than that? Will I ever be able to trust him again?

The alarm clock sounds off, startling me.

Profit bolts up and looks around. He smiles when he sees me. "Hey." He reaches over and shuts the clock off.

"Are you going somewhere?"

He peels out of the sheets. "Yeah. Mason and I got a run to do—but I'll be back." He leans over the bed to kiss me. At the last second, I turn my head and his lips land against my cheek.

The smile melts off his face. "Are you going to be here when I get back?"

I hate to do it, but I look him in the eye and answer him. "No."

Hurt, he pulls up from the bed. "So nothing's changed?"

Silence.

Turning, he huffs and snatches his clothes up from the floor. "Whatever. You do what you got to do," he says.

I sit up and peel out of the sheets too.

"I don't understand you," he says, hopping into his pants. "I love you and I've apologized for that mistake. *One* mistake."

Silent, I start dressing too.

"Oh. So now you're not going to say shit?"

"What do you want me to say?"

"What the fuck do you think? I just told you that I love you."

Silence.

"Fuck this shit." He slams on his black T-shirt, snatches up his Timbs, and storms out of the bedroom. A few seconds later, I hear, "Lock up when you leave!" The front door slams.

A few tears skip down my face while I finish dressing. After that, I take another look around our bedroom with my heart squeezing out of my chest. *Get the fuck out of here before you fuck up and change your mind.* I tuck my gun in the back of my black jeans and then grab the box of matches from the nightstand.

Outside, I scoop out my cell phone and call Mack.

"Yeah?"

"Wake your ass up," I joke. "Come and get me."

"Where you at?"

"Where you think?"

There's a long pause. "You sure?"

"I called you, didn't I?" Something moves from the corner of my eyes. "What the fuck?"

"What?"

"Not you." I squint over at Mason and Lucifer's crib. "Hey, Mack. Let me call you back."

71

Hydeya

I make it through half a bottle of Jack Daniel's before I decide to risk a DUI for a pop-up visit on Shotgun Row. The look on Isaac's face is priceless when he answers the door.

"Hydeya?"

"The one and only," I sing, crossing into the house without waiting for an invitation.

"What are you doing here?" he asks, shutting the door and following me in.

"What does it look like? I'm cashing in that rain check." I reach the living room and am startled to see a room full of some rough-looking men. "Am I interrupting something?"

"Just having some friends over," Isaac says. "Maybe we can do the rain check thing another time?"

My gaze falls on what looks to be a cache of firearms. "Correct me if I'm wrong, but aren't those weapons a violation of your probation?"

The men all share conspiring looks.

Isaac pulls in a deep breath. "Go home."

I don't want to go home. The house seems so empty without Drake scurrying around, making me coffee, giving me unsolicited shoulder rubs and whispering how beautiful our future children will be. My sorrow must show because Isaac's face softens. "Are you okay?"

"Yes. I am officially attempting to grieve *properly*," I tell him, smiling like a fool. "Apparently, it's a condition to getting my job back."

"You lost your job?"

"I'm on *forced* administrative leave." I laugh. "So you can relax. I can't arrest and haul you and your *friends* into jail."

"You're drunk."

My laughter deepens. "You are correct. I think I must've gotten my brains from your side of the family."

His friends share another look. "Yep. That's right, guys. *This* asshole is my father."

"All right, enough." Isaac walks over and grabs me by the arm. "You're going to sleep off whatever the hell you've been drinking."

"Oww. You're hurting me," I whine as he drags me to a bedroom down the hall as if I weigh nothing. "And I'm not sleepy!"

"Close your eyes and count sheep," he snaps, giving me a final shove and then shutting the door.

"Hey!" I hear a click. Frowning, I reach for the doorknob and find the sucker locked. "Hey! You can't lock me in here. I'm a police officer!"

"You're on leave," he shouts back through the door.

"Isaac! Come back here and open this damn thing!" I pound on the door. "Isaac!"

He isn't coming back.

"Grrrr!" I kick the door a couple of times before giving up and slinking over to the bed. Maybe I am just a *little* tired. It won't hurt if I take a brief nap.

Walking a straight line proves to be a challenge because I walk right into the nightstand instead, knocking over every-thing on it. "Damn." I attempt to bend over and pick up everything, but end up falling over. My butt bone lands solidly on the corner of a book. "Ow." I reach under and pull it out. It's Maybelline's Bible. "Sorry about that, Lord." I move to set it back on the nightstand when it slips out of its book cover and an envelope falls out. I pick it up and turn it over. There's a name scrawled across it. *Mason.* Curious, I rip it open and begin to read. By the time I finish rustling through the pages, I've sobered up. "I have a brother?"

72

Lucifer

"Push. Push," Dr. Modi coaches from between my legs.

Déjà vu. I'm once again submerged in pain as I push and grind to get his baby out of me, but no matter how much I grunt, curse, or scream, he refuses to budge. In fact it feels like he's spinning and clawing to stay in the womb.

"It's okay, Willow. You got this."

I look over. It's Bishop again—the left side of his head still missing. I grab his hand. "No. I can't do this. If he comes out, he'll die. You gotta help me."

Bishop smiles. "Don't be silly. Everything is going to be fine. I'll take good care of your baby."

What the hell is he talking about? He's dead. I release his hand and try to shove him away. "No. No. I don't want you taking care of my baby," I pant. More pain seizes me and I wonder if I'm going to survive this nightmare. "Awwwwww. Mason! Where is Mason?" I don't understand why he isn't here.

Tears splash down my face as I fight not to push, but my body has a mind of its own and the contractions are never ending. "No. Please. I don't want this. Make it stop!"

Bishops laughs. "It's a little too late for that."

"Push. Push. Push," Dr. Modi shouts.

"Aaaaargh. Shut the fuck up, you piece of shit mutha-fucka!" I growl at the smiling doctor between my legs. I hate his fucking face.

"Here comes the head," Dr. Modi cheers. "Push!"

"Aaaaargh! I swear to God, after I deliver this baby, I'm going to fuckin' kill you!"

The doctor keeps smiling. "Push!"

Sweat pours down my face and burns my eyes. I can't see a muthafuckin' thing. And I'm alone. I'm so fuckin' alone. This isn't how this is supposed to be. Mason is sup-posed to be here. Why would he leave me all alone?

"Don't worry." Another voice joins this madness. "I'm here."

I look to my left and am stunned by the face approach-ing the bed. "Dad?"

He smiles and lights up the room. "Hello, Willow."

Seeing him somehow cuts my pain in half. It's been so long and he looks exactly the same as the last time I saw him—right down to the bloody rose on his chest where he'd been shot. "Daddy, my baby. You got to help me save my baby."

"Shhh. Calm down. I know you got a lot on your plate, but you can't worry about that right now. You need to wake up."

"Can't worry? B-but he's going to die."

"You **have** to wake up."

"What?" I can't process what he's saying.

"There's somebody in the house—and they've come to kill you."

My eyes pop open in the semidarkness and catch the gleam of a steel blade as it makes a sweeping arc down onto the bed.

Instinct kicks in. I roll to the other side of the bed instead of reaching for the gun tucked underneath the pillow.

The knife slices into the pillow-top mattress with a muted *thump*, ripping through the material.

I keep rolling and crash over the left side of the bed. The gravitational pull is cruel and I hit the hardwood floor with alarming force, belly first. Pain shoots through every limb of my body. I struggle to block it out as my hand flails for the other piece tucked into the nightstand, but my movements aren't as quick as normal.

"Grrrrrrrrrr!" My attacker leaps over the bed and grabs a fistful of my hair and tries to yank it out of my scalp.

Another bolt of pain rips through me while cartoon stars spin behind my eyes. Before I can get that shit to stop, my head is mashed into the wall. I make a big dent in that muthafucka because I taste bits of plaster. Balling my fist, I strike out and sock this bitch dead in her pussy—my first clue that my attacker is indeed a woman.

She grunts, but the punch has less effect than if my attacker had been the opposite sex. It's enough for her to release her hold on my head for a millisecond, and I'm able to sweep my arm out and hit those knees.

She drops like a stone.

I spring up on this bitch, but I lose a second when something warm rushes down my inner thigh. A punch hits me square in my jaw, knocking my ass to the left, where I trip over the foot of the bed.

More cartoon stars. *This bitch is pissing me off.*

My attacker launches toward me again. I block her first two blows, keeping my elbows together, like Bishop taught me. When I come out from behind an arm shield, I wail on this bitch like a heavyweight champion. In no time, I pin her to the floor, my fist as bloody as my thighs.

She whimpers.

While I got this bitch under the moonlight spilling through

the window, I snatch the wool mask from her head. When her hair stops tumbling out, I'm shocked. *Shariffa?*

This bitch ain't this muthafuckin' bold. But there's not a damn thing wrong with my eyes.

Enraged, I wrap my hands around Shariffa's neck and squeeze with everything I got. "You stupid bitch!" My arms tremble as my grip tightens.

"ACK. GACK." She chokes, clawing at my hands.

"That's right. Let me hear death rattle around in your chest. When you're gone, I'm going to take my fucking time peeling and slicing your ass from your head to your toes."

"ACK. GAAACK."

"There's not going to be anything left of your treacherous ass. I'm going to make damn sure of that shit."

"ACK. GAAAACK!"

This bitch is seconds away from passing from this world to the next when an ungodly pain shoots up from my abdomen and straight to my brain.

"Aaaaaargh!" The scream is out of my throat before I have a chance to stop it. Then it happens again and I pitch over and hit the floor, gripping my belly.

I'm only mildly aware of Shariffa coughing and wheezing next to me.

Pull it together. Pull it together. But I can't. *The baby!*

Shariffa scrambles for the knife.

Somehow I swing out an arm and grab her ankle. She trips with a loud *thump!*

Desperate, Shariffa kicks me with her free leg. My head. My neck—and then a firm kick straight to my belly.

"Aaaaaaargh!" *This dirty bitch.* But she's going to win this battle. The knife glistens in the moonlight before it makes its second swinging arc straight toward my baby.

BAM!

The bedroom door is kicked open.

Shariffa jumps.

POW! POW! POW!

She is lifted into the air as the bullets slam into her, and then she collapses into a bloody heap beside me.

"Lucifer!" Ta'Shara rushes into the room and drops down beside me. "Lucifer, are you all right?"

I want to answer her, but instead I tumble into darkness.

KING DIVAS

De'nesha Diamond

ABOUT THIS GUIDE

The questions that follow are included to enhance
your group's reading of this book.

Discussion Questions

1. Are you surprised that both Momma Peaches and Dribbles died trying to heal an injustice done to the Carver family? At some point is it best to allow sins of the past to remain in the past? Have you ever been in a position where you had to let sleeping dogs lie?

2. Captain Hawkins was forced to take administrative leave. Given what's going on around her, does she stand a chance of exposing the city's corruption, or will she be dragged into the Carver/Lewis family drama?

3. How do you feel about Kalief's indecent proposal to Cleo in order to pay his debts to Diesel? Was she wrong to let her ambition override her suspicion of the gangster?

4. Diesel Carver has made his first couple of chess moves, but with King Isaac's unexpected return, do you think it would be wise for the Atlanta gangster to cut his losses, or should he double down for a Memphis takeover?

5. Young lovers Profit and Ta'Shara are at a crossroads. Do you believe that Ta'Shara was right to leave the relationship, or should she have forgiven his *mistake*?

6. Ta'Shara has embraced her dark side. Given all that she's lost and been through, do you believe that there is a pathway back, or will the streets claim another diva?

7. How do you feel about Shariffa killing her husband? When she was banished from the Grape Street Crips, did you believe Lynch was ever going to bring her back home?

8. Do you believe that Mason and Python will ever be able to get to the truth about their pasts? Would it change anything?

9. How do you feel about Shariffa's attack on a pregnant Lucifer? Do you believe that she and/or her baby will survive?

10. With the last Diva book around the corner, which diva do you believe will be left standing?

Ta'Shara

Oh shit. I stare down at Lucifer and all the blood and carnage around the room. My mind draws a blank on what the fuck I'm supposed to do. "Okay. Okay." I force myself to breathe. "Lucifer, hang on. Don't you think about dying on me," I say. That's the worst possible thing that could happen. *The phone.* I jump to my feet and race to hit the bedroom's light switch so I can search around for a landline. The horrific scene is even worse under the harsh bright lights.

Don't think about that now. I can't find the phone, but I know that there's one downstairs. "Lucifer, I'll be right back," I shout, knowing she probably can't hear a damn thing I say. I race out of the room and take the stairs two at a time. At the bottom, I find a portable unit sitting in its base on an end table by the sofa. I snatch it up and punch in 9-1-1.

As soon as the operator comes onto the line, I blurt, "I need an ambulance. I have a pregnant woman unconscious and bleeding out."

"Calm down, miss. Can you please tell me your name?"

"Yes. It's Ta'Shara Murphy. Please. Hurry. Someone broke in here and tried to kill her. I shot the intruder but—"

"Miss, please. Slow down. Help is on the way. Did you say that you shot someone?"

"Yes. Damn it! Hurry! She's lost a lot of blood."

"The police and ambulance are on the way, ma'am. But I need to get a little more information from you."

"SIX POPPIN', FIVE DROPPIN" an army of voices shout from outside the house. A second later, a barrage of bullets comes flying into the house. Before I can think or move away from the window, I'm lifted off my feet and thrown back. Pain sears through me as the onslaught continues and the house turns into a war zone.

Don't miss
HER SWEETEST REVENGE
by Saundra

For seventeen-year-old Mya Bedford, life in a Detroit project is hard enough, but when her mother develops a drug habit, Mya has to take on raising her younger siblings. Too bad the only man who can teach her how to survive—her dad—is behind bars. For life. All he can tell her is that she'll have to navigate the mean streets on her own terms. Mya's not sure what that means—until her mother is seriously beaten by a notorious gang. Then it all becomes deadly clear.

Available July 2015 wherever books and ebooks are sold.

1

Sometimes I wonder how my life would've turned out if my parents had been involved in different things, like if they had regular jobs. My mother would be a social worker, and my father a lawyer or something. You know, jobs they call respectable and shit.

Supposedly these people's lives are peaches and cream. But when I think about that shit I laugh because my life is way different. My father was a dope pusher who served the whole area of Detroit. And when I say the whole area, I mean just that. My dad served some of the wealthiest politicians all the way down to the poorest people in the hood that would do anything for a fix. Needless to say, if you were on cocaine before my father went to prison, I'm sure he served you; he was heavy in the street. Lester Bedford was his birth name, and that's what he went by in the streets of Detroit. And there was no one that would fuck with him. Everybody was in check.

All the dudes on the block were jealous of him because his pockets were laced. He had the looks, money, nice cars, and the baddest chick on the block, Marisa Haywood. All the dudes wanted Marisa because she was a redbone with coal-black hair flowing down her back and a banging-ass body, but she was only interested in my dad. They had met one night at a friend's dice party and had been inseparable since then.

Life was good for them for a long time. Dad was able to make a lot of money with no hassle from the feds, and Mom was able to stay home with their three kids. Three beautiful kids, if I must say so. First, she had me, Mya, then my brother, Bobby, who we all call Li'l Bo, and last was my baby sister, Monica.

We were all happy kids about four years ago; we didn't need or want for nothing. My daddy made sure of that. The only thing my father wanted to give us next was a house with a backyard. Even though he was stacking good dough, we still lived in the Brewster-Douglass projects.

All those years he'd been trying to live by the hood code: "livin' hood rich." However, times were changing. The new and upcoming ballers were getting their dough and moving out of the hood. Around this time my dad decided to take us outta there too.

Before he could make a move, our good luck suddenly changed for the worse. Our apartment was raided by the feds and my father was taken to jail, where he received a life sentence with no possibility of parole.

My mother never told us what happened, but sometimes I would eavesdrop on her conversations when she would be crying on a friend's shoulder. That's how I overheard her saying that they had my father connected to six drug-related murders and indictments on cocaine charges. I couldn't believe my ears. My father wouldn't kill anybody. He was too nice for that. I was completely pissed off; I refused to hear any of that. It was a lie. As far as I was concerned, my father was no murderer and all that shit he was accused of was somebody's sick fantasy. He was innocent. They were just jealous of him because he was young, black, and borderline rich. True, it was drug money, but in the hood, who gave a fuck. But all that was in the past; now, my dad was on skid row. Lockdown. Three hots and a cot. And our home life reflected just that.

All of a sudden my mother started hanging out all night. She would come home just in time for us to go to school. For a while that was okay, but then her behavior started to change also. I mean, my mother looked totally different. Her once healthy skin started to look pale and dry. She started to lose weight, and her hair was never combed. She tried to comb it, but this was a woman who was used to going to the beauty shop every week. Now her hair looked like that of a stray cat.

I noticed things missing out of the house, too, like our Alpine digital stereo. I came home from school one day and it was gone. I asked my mother about it, and she said she sold it for food. But that had to be a lie because we were on the county. Mom didn't work, so we received food stamps and cash assistance. We also received government assistance that paid the rent, but Mom was responsible for the utilities, which started to get shut off.

Before long, we looked like the streets. After my father had been locked up for two years, we had nothing. We started to outgrow our clothes because Mom couldn't afford to buy us any, so whatever clothes we could get that were secondhand, we wore. I'm talking about some real stinking-looking gear. Li'l Bo got suspended from school for kicking some boy's ass for teasing him about a shirt he wore to school with someone else's name on it. We had been too wrapped up in our new home life to realize it. When the lady from the Salvation Army came over with the clothes for Li'l Bo, he just ironed the shirt and put it on. He never realized the spray paint on the back of the shirt said Alvin. That is, until this asshole at school decided to point it out to him.

Everything of value in our house was gone. Word on the streets was my mother was a crackhead and prostitute. I tried to deny it at first, but before long, it became obvious.

Now it's been four years of this mess, and I just can't take it anymore. I don't know what to do. I'm only seventeen years old. I'm sitting here on this couch, hungry, with nothing to eat, and my mom is lying up in her room with some nigga for a lousy few bucks. And when she's done, she's going to leave here and cop some more dope. I'm just sick of this.

"Li'l Bo, Monica," I shouted so they could hear me clearly. "Come on, let's go to the store so we can get something to eat."

"I don't want to go to the store, Mya. It's cold out there," Monica said, pouting as she came out of the room we shared together.

"Look, put your shoes on. I'm not leaving you here without me or Li'l Bo. Besides, ain't nothing in that kitchen to eat, so if we don't go to the store, we starve tonight."

"Well, let's go. I ain't got all night." Li'l Bo tried to rush us, shifting side to side where he stood. The only thing he cared about is that video game that he has to hide to keep Mom from selling.

On our way to the store we passed all the local wannabe dope boys on our block. As usual, they couldn't resist hitting on me. But I never pay them losers any mind because I will never mess around with any of them. Most of the grimy niggas been sleeping with my mom anyway. Especially Squeeze, with his bald-headed ass. Nasty bastard. If I had a gun I would probably shoot all them niggas.

"Hey, Mya. Girl, you know you growing up. Why don't you let me take you up to Roosters and buy you a burger or something?" Squeeze asked while rubbing his bald head and licking his nasty, hungry lips at me. "With a fat ass like that, girl, I will let you order whatever you want off the menu."

"Nigga, I don't need you to buy me jack. I'm good." I rolled my eyes and kept stepping.

"Whatever, bitch, wit' yo' high-and-mighty ass. You know you hungry."

Li'l Bo stopped dead in his tracks. "What you call my sister?" He turned around and mugged Squeeze. "Can you hear, nigga? I said, what did you call my sister?" Li'l Bo spat the words at Squeeze.

I grabbed Li'l Bo by the arm. "Come on, don't listen to him. He's just talkin'. Forget him anyway." I dismissed Squeeze with a wave of my hand.

"Yeah, little man, I'm only playing." Squeeze had an ugly scowl on his face.

Before I walked away I turned around and threw up my middle finger to Squeeze because that nigga's time is coming. He's got plenty of enemies out here on the streets while he's wasting time fooling with me.

When we made it to the store I told Li'l Bo and Monica to watch my back while I got some food. I picked up some sandwich meat, cheese, bacon, and hot dogs. I went to the counter and paid for a loaf of bread to make it look legit, and then we left the store. Once outside, we hit the store right next door. I grabbed some canned goods, a pack of Oreo cookies for dessert, and two packs of chicken wings. When we got outside, we unloaded all the food into the shopping bags we brought from home. This should get us through until next week. This is how we eat because Mom sells all the food stamps every damn month. The thought of it makes me kick a single rock that's in my path while walking back to the Brewster.

When we got back to the house, Mom was in the kitchen rambling like she's looking for something. So she must be finished doing her dirty business. I walked right past her like she ain't even standing there.

"Where the hell y'all been? Don't be leavin' this house at night without telling me," she screamed, then flicked some cigarette butts into the kitchen sink.

"We went to the store to get food. There is nothin' to eat in this damn house." I rolled my eyes, giving her much attitude.

"Mya, who the hell do you think you talking to? I don't

care where you went. Tell me before you leave this house," she said, while sucking her teeth.

"Yeah, whatever! If you cared so much, we would have food." I got smart again. "Monica, grab the skillet so I can fry some of this chicken," I ordered her, then slammed the freezer door shut.

Mom paused for a minute. She was staring at me so hard I thought she was about to slap me for real. But she just turned around and went to her room. Then she came right back out of her room and went into the bathroom with clothes in hand.

I knew she was going to leave when she got that money from her little trick. Normally, I want her to stay in the house. That way I know she's safe. But tonight, I'm ready for her to leave because I'm pissed at her right now. I still love her, but I don't understand what happened to her so fast. Things have been hard on all of us. Why does she get to take the easy way out by doing crack? I just wish Dad was here, but he's not, so I got to do something to take care of my brother and sister and get us out of this rat hole.